Too True to be Good

Also by Joseph Bauer

The Accidental Patriot
The Patriot's Angels

TOO TRUE TO BE GOOD

JOSEPH BAUER

Archway Publishing books may be ordered through booksellers or by contacting:

Archway Publishing
1663 Liberty Drive
Bloomington, IN 47403
www.archwaypublishing.com
844-669-3957

ISBN: 978-1-6657-4123-1 (sc)
ISBN: 978-1-6657-4103-3 (hc)
ISBN: 978-1-6657-4102-6 (e)

Library of Congress Control Number: 2023905564

Print information available on the last page.

Archway Publishing rev. date: 04/13/2023

In memory of Katie, dear big sister
and first writing partner.

When sorrows come, they come not
single spies, but in battalions.

—William Shakespeare

CONTENTS

PART ONE

PART TWO

PART THREE

PART ONE

1

MURDER AT THE WILLARD

Jack Renfro, the graying homicide detective from the District of Columbia Metropolitan Police, knew it from so much experience it seemed almost boring when he stepped into the room and saw the scene before him. Mob killings in hotel rooms usually involved a quickly subdued male victim who knew his executioners, with little or no signs of struggle. And yes, a pillow with a bullet hole through it.

And those were Renfro's first thoughts when he entered the room in the ever-elegant Willard Hotel on Pennsylvania Avenue and saw the body on the king-size bed. Housekeeping, delivering afternoon bathroom supplies, had discovered the body only thirty-six minutes earlier. If there had been nothing else, Renfro promptly would have sized up the murder as a probable organized crime hit, the elimination of a member who couldn't keep his mouth shut, or maybe his pants buckled around the boss's wife.

But this time something didn't rhyme.

On the body, a scribbled note was left, to which four one-thousand-dollar bills were paper clipped. To Jack Renfro, that changed everything.

Burial money for the family was all it said.

It was not entirely unheard of; Jack had seen it himself once before in an Italian mob hit thirty years ago. A sort of morbid death benefit for a mostly well-meaning minion gone astray, emblematic of the perverse magnanimity of a delusional don just human enough to require some balm for his conscience. *Oh, the painful decisions we must make in this business. May he rest in peace. A little something for his family. We aren't completely evil. We have sympathy too.*

But in this room, and from the looks of this victim, Renfro thought the five-word message struck a decidedly discordant note. He adjudged the dead man, facedown and bound at hands and ankles, to be midthirties. Wiry and fit. He was well dressed, to say the least, with polished European shoes and longish black hair, expensively coiffed. He looked nothing like a man destined for a pauper's grave.

The fact that he was bound with plastic strip ties meant there were at least two perpetrators, the detective knew. A lone assailant could never have incapacitated a strong victim like this without obvious signs of struggle.

After taking three dozen photos with his smartphone camera, he lifted the pillow lying atop the back of the murdered man's head. The blood visible on the bed all had flowed to the victim's right side, and a single burned hole appeared in the pillow. Jack surmised initially a single gunshot. Trained killers normally fired only once in a hotel. Two or more shots, even muffled, were exponentially more likely to be heard by someone than a single burst. But when he lifted the pillow, he saw clearly that *two* shots had been fired into the back of the man's head—one about even with the top of his ears and another lower, nearly at the neckline.

"Odd," Renfro said to his young partner, Audrey Sanderson. "And stupid."

"What do you mean?" she asked.

"The killer fired two shots and through the same hole in the pillow."

"Why is that stupid?"

"For one thing, the only reason to shoot through a pillow in the first place is to keep the sound down," Renfro said. "That and … well …"

"Back spatter," Sanderson filled in the blank.

"Yeah. And you lose some of that—a lot more than you'd think—when you fire again through the same place. Someone might notice it, hear it."

"Maybe he had a suppressor and wasn't worried," Audrey said.

"Possible," Renfro said. "But it's pretty foolish to put a firearm that's been discharged against a pillow, even with a suppressor. Especially with a suppressor. That weapon was hot for the second shot. He could have started a fire. He was lucky he didn't."

"What's a little fire after you've committed murder?" Audrey said.

"On the twelfth floor of the Willard? It would set off the fire alarms almost immediately. That would shut down the elevators. You'd have firefighters and security people climbing every stairwell. And this place is so close to the White House."

Indeed, the stately landmark nearly abutted the Old Executive Office Building that was literally connected to the White House, where many executive branch department chiefs were located. As such, it was a preferred hotel for government dignitaries and political events. "Police and Secret Service are always crawling around here," he said.

"What are you getting at?" asked Audrey.

"I doubt these were experienced hit men," said Jack Renfro. "At least not American style." He reached into the dead man's left hip pocket, removed his wallet, and held up the New York driver's license he found in it. He paused, squinting to read the lettering against the hologram. "And I doubt that *Mr. David Kahn* here—if that's his real name—was too experienced either. Probably a messenger or courier who knew something he couldn't keep knowing."

"Maybe he had no idea what he was involved with or that he was in danger," said Sanderson.

"Or maybe he knew exactly what he was involved in, and that's *why* he was in danger," said Renfro.

The detective placed the note and money, still clipped together, into a small evidence bag. "But this note," he said to Audrey, "this is just a sham. Amateurish. A poor attempt to make this look like a mob hit out of the movies. And so is that driver's license. This guy could be anybody."

Without moving the body, he knelt next to the bed to see as much of the man's face as he could. When he returned to his feet, he motioned to Sanderson to do the same.

"What do you think?" he asked her. "American? Or not?"

"He's a little dark for a Caucasian," she said. "Sort of looks Eastern European or Eurasian. Romanian or Turkish maybe? Or even ethnic Russian. Chechnya? But he could be American. Hard to say."

Renfro patted down the man's pockets and checked the suit coat that lay next to him.

"No cell phone," he said. "No weapon either."

He returned the driver's license back to its slot in the wallet and looked in the bills compartment. A colorful, thick ticket sprang out and fell to the floor.

"What do you know? He's a baseball fan," Renfro said, picking up the ticket and examining it. "This is for tonight's Nationals game." He handed the ticket to his partner. "This *is* an odd one."

"It's *some* seat," Audrey said. "Field level, near home plate. Right next to the owner's suite, I think."

"Right, I forgot. You're a fan too." The senior detective was pleased. "How do you look in a vendor's uniform?" he asked. Sanderson was average height with short auburn hair and tomboy looks. She looked the part, Renfro thought. "I think you're going to the ball game. Maybe Mr. Kahn here wasn't going alone. It would be interesting to find out."

"Do you really mean it about the vendor outfit?"

"Absolutely. With a wire and earpiece."

"Why don't I just use the ticket?"

"Think about it," Jack said. "They leave this drummed-up note on the body. Then they find this ticket. They know not many people go to a ball game alone. So they go themselves—thinking the same way I am—to see if somebody else is meeting him there. Learn if he's working with somebody who knew the same things he knew, the things they don't want out."

"So they're smarter detectives than they are killers?" Sanderson couldn't resist.

"Or maybe they missed this ticket altogether," Renfro said. "But we know this guy intended to go to the game. And if he was meeting somebody there, we need that person. He or she's bound to know something about what he was into. What got him *here.* There may be more to this than either of us can imagine now."

He walked to the open room door where a uniformed officer stood with two dark-suited men from hotel security. The veteran detective spoke first to the hotel men, amiably, as if he were a house guest asking where he might find lunch in the neighborhood instead of delivering instructions at the scene of a murder.

"I want to keep this under wraps for the rest of the day," he said to them. "Better that the killers not know he's been found so soon. No report to anybody. Change the lock code so no one else can get in. Electronically, without touching the lockset. It hasn't been dusted yet. Can you promise me that, or do I need to speak to the hotel manager?"

"We can handle it," the older of the two security men said. "And we'll talk to the housekeeping person who found him and tell her to keep it to herself for now. She's reliable."

Renfro turned to the police officer with them. "You too," he said to the uniform. "Nothing at the precinct. Tell them I need you outside at the street for the rest of your shift, and your replacement needs to stay there too. Anyone at the station has a problem, have them call me."

"No yellow tape here even?" the uniform asked.

"None. I'll tell the coroner to stay away until midnight."

"Got it," said the security man.

The police officer nodded.

Renfro signaled for Sanderson, and the two of them started down the hall. Then Renfro paused and walked back alone to the two security men. He handed them each his card.

"One other thing," he said. "Get the hallway camera on that door. Anybody goes to it, *anybody,* call me right away."

It was three thirty when Renfro and Sanderson reached the sidewalk outside the hotel. Jack motioned to the bellman standing next to his unmarked car at the curb that he would be to it in a moment.

"Have you ever dealt with Homeland Security?" he asked Sanderson.

"Not yet."

"Call them on the liaison line. Tell them we've got a one-eleven homicide and that I'm sending over the vic's wallet for print forensics."

"What's a one-eleven homicide?"

"Possible terrorist involvement."

2

WHERE IS EVAN REESE?

In her three years leading the bureau's financial crimes unit, Hannah Harris had never sensed what she'd been feeling lately. A break was coming, she thought. All the planning and research, all the costly resources, were paying off.

The signs, vague and confusing as they were, pointed to a growing pool of money streaming into the country from a web of small tributaries. A few of the capillaries had been ridden to ground and found innocuous. But many others remained tantalizing, a Rubik's Cube of transactions clicking and twisting through the global banking system, their ultimate intended destination and purpose still to be determined. Important dots, though, were beginning to be connected, including a steady flow of accumulating cash pulsing through a serpentine route from New York to Washington.

But as the afternoon grew late without word from her agent working deep undercover, Hannah Harris grew more nervous with each quarter hour. She sensed her anxiety but at first put it down to the importance of the day.

Her man undercover had been working, until today, only in greater New York. This was the first time the criminal syndicate had dispatched him to Washington to make a delivery, and it was the first time a single drop was for a large sum: $250,000. It was much more than could ever be directly deposited in a banking institution by the usual business without being flagged. But what was most intriguing to Harris and her unit was its delivery point. The smaller, earlier deliveries all had been made to the usual kinds of smaller, cash business depositaries. Dry cleaning shops, restaurants, side street law offices. Such establishments easily could blend small amounts—ten and fifteen thousand dollars—into their customary business banking deposits without notice. But according to yesterday's report from her agent, today's delivery was to be made at—of all places—the Washington Nationals baseball game shortly after the first pitch at 7:10 that evening.

Evan Reese, the agent she had personally selected for the assignment, had seemed at the time ideal for the circumstances, or nearly so. Born in Minnesota to Romanian immigrant parents who changed their surname to better assimilate in the upper Midwest, Evan could put on an Eastern European accent better than any other agent she knew. Even his Russian was more than passable, no small virtue in gaining the trust of the Ukrainian conclave, known simply as the Kievs, that he had infiltrated in Brooklyn, posing as a driver looking for a job as a taxi driver. But most important to the bureau, he was a certified public accountant, entirely at ease in financial vernacular and nuance. Before joining the FBI, he had worked in cyber security and fraud detection for Deutsche Bank. He could read the intricate pathways of the international banking system the way most people could read road maps.

Evan Reese did have one drawback though. A wife.

"I wish you weren't married," Hannah had said to him in their final meeting before he took the assignment.

Evan Reese blushed. The FBI unit chief was an attractive woman, unreasonably so, and unmarried. She sat across from him in an armchair, her long legs crossed, a fairly high-heeled pump hanging off her foot.

"What does that mean?" he asked.

"Oh, not *that,"* Hannah said, now blushing too. "For Pete's sake, not *that*. I mean, because this is deep undercover work. It's dangerous. About as dangerous as anything a bureau agent would ever do."

"I get that," he said.

"If you had kids, I wouldn't even consider you," she said.

"But wives are expendable?"

"I'll be honest. I looked for somebody single. Looked hard. Thought I found one too. Do you know Agent L.T. Kitt?"

"The woman from the Pittsburgh office?" he asked. "The dog trainer?"

L.T. Kitt, through no design or wish of her own, had become a kind of cause célèbre in the bureau after her fieldwork in matters of national security and involvement with the president, personally.

"Yeah. She's done a lot of undercover. Very good. But she just married Tug Birmingham, the ex–army ranger now working in the Secret Service on the president's protection detail. And she's in the DC field office now."

"I think I did hear about that," Reese said.

"That puts her too close to public view. And we could never use anyone in the president's orbit."

"I see."

"So it's down to you, Evan. But only if you want it. I don't want to force this on you. Not with all the risk. These are bad people, and you have a wife to think about."

"It's what we do," he said. "She knows that."

And so the life of Evie Rezcepko began.

His early embedding into the Ukrainian group in Brooklyn's Brighton Beach neighborhood had gone smoothly. Hannah began to relax. She saw that he relied on his training, which was comforting. He didn't rush anything or cause himself to appear prematurely interested in the group's activities or entitled to know anything about them. The keys to ingratiation and integration with criminals were silence and passive compliance. You never asked a question too soon, and you didn't ask *any* question until your acceptance was cemented. And even then, patience was critical.

Once an agent gained the trust or affection of *one* criminal member, it was tempting to begin intelligence gathering about the group's designs. That was always a mistake. Thugs are pack animals. They make allegiances in threes and fours and fives. For an undercover agent, having only a single ally inside, unless it was the boss himself, was as good as having no ally at all. You needed a *cadre* of support, the confidence of an established subset of the group, to receive the larger pack's blessing and become an insider in your own right.

His initial insertion was deftly managed. The bureau knew that the Kievs operated a ring of taxi medallions in Brooklyn and Queens. Most of the cabs roamed the boroughs legitimately. Their drivers, comprised mainly of Middle Easterners and Puerto Ricans, were unaware of the criminal ventures of the owners. But a central hub of the cabs was reserved for use solely in the Kievs' clandestine activities and for the personal transportation needs of the syndicate members. When you thought about it, it was a sensible way for a criminal to get around New York unnoticed and untrackable. Just stay in a yellow cab—your own yellow cab.

The Kievs made sure that every driver in the "spokes," as they called the special cabs, was an Eastern European and very preferably Russian speaking. It was just easier all the way around. They were culturally compatible, prone to allegiance, and could tell a take-out order of borscht from wonton. Surveillance showed that the group hired its drivers for the hub cabs nearly exclusively from a small employment agency on Carroll Street near Utica Avenue in Brooklyn, catering to Eastern European job hunters.

Rather than directly approach one of the Kievs' medallions to seek work—solicitation always risked suspicion—the bureau placed Reese in the lobby of the job agency so that the group would come to *him*. He spent hours studying surveillance photographs taken of the syndicate members making prior visits to interview and hire drivers. Many of the photos were blurry or taken from great distances. After four days of sitting and forty-four dollars in Starbucks coffee, it worked.

"You understand the driving we need is not the usual, so to say," said Yuri, the Kiev senior member, when Evan was introduced to him in the small interview room at the job agency. The tall, muscular Ukrainian was neatly dressed in a black shirt and tailored slacks. His tightly cropped full beard, a mix of grays and black, made his age difficult to assess, but Evan thought it early fifties, at most.

"No, I don't know what you mean."

"I mean you don't drive around and pick up just *anybody*."

"Then how do I make money?"

"The money is no problem," the Ukrainian said, apparently amused. "We pay you. We pay you to take us where *we* need to go. Wherever *we* need to go. And after a while, maybe make errands."

"On a schedule though? I need regular work."

"You're not even hired yet, Evie Rezcepko. Why do you talk about a schedule? Trust me, you will drive."

"I am a good driver," Reese said. "And I need the work. So okay. But if it is not enough driving, you understand, I can't stay."

It was wise of the young agent to seem tentative, not too anxious for the job. But he worried that he may have overplayed it. Yuri looked at him with serious eyes.

"I told you, you're not even hired yet! Why do you talk about quitting?"

But then the tall Ukrainian smiled. "But I like that," he said. "*Why*, I don't know." He laughed, and Evan smiled. "But I like that, Evie Rezcepko," Yuri said.

Entry was made.

Hanna Harris and her team at New York headquarters watched from afar with satisfaction as young Agent Reese progressed. *Watched* because listening was out of the question, at least until there were solid signs that he had achieved a status of trust inside the syndicate. A listening device was unacceptably dangerous in early days. Its discovery could mean swift execution.

He posted his reports at least once daily, always when alone, always on the secure cell phone used only for that purpose. He told the Kievs he was living in a ramshackle walk-up in Queens (the bureau had secured it for his cover), and to be sure the Ukrainians believed it, he brought one of them to it in his third week of service after picking up the member at LaGuardia Airport. He'd mistakenly left a bottle of premium vodka there, he said, that he'd acquired for another Kiev he knew the passenger would be seeing that night. *Could he stop for it and ask the Kiev to deliver it to his compatriot?* It would just be an extra ten minutes, he said. When he returned to the taxi after fetching the vodka, he was surprised that the passenger asked for the bottle in the back seat, where he quickly opened it and drank.

"For my inconvenience," the Kiev said, smiling. "No worries, Evie. It is very fine vodka. I will tell him it was me who drank it."

And he did, adding to the rightful owner when he and Reese walked into the Brighton Beach cellar the group considered home base, "Evie is living in a fleabag. You should pay him more. Since you can afford this vodka. It's very fine!" Any validation, however small, was valuable to a man undercover.

By his third month in their midst, it was plain the Kievs were taking him in. When he returned from his errands or passenger deliveries, they no longer motioned that he should leave and await his next call. He was savvy enough to accept their hospitality gingerly. He never tried to sit at the main table or make small talk. A lot of the art of infiltration was simple fermentation.

"What do you do in there?" asked Hannah during one of his call-ins.

"I stand by the wall like a waiter during the dinner speech."

"Listening, I assume?"

"Of course. Especially when they switch to Russian."

Finally, it happened. Midway through his fourth month of driving, Yuri awaited him in the cellar when he arrived, as directed, just before dinner.

"Tonight, you don't drive, Evie," Yuri said. "Tonight, we have dinner here together. Tonight, we talk. We need to talk."

Standing alone, the words of the Kievs' leader might have alarmed their recipient, but the large Ukrainian spoke them in a warm tone and through a smile. He motioned to a table in the corner where three other senior members sat waiting. A new driver—Reese had met him just the day before—arrived with take-out dinners from the best Russian café on the edge of the neighborhood. The new recruit placed the cartons before the five dinner mates and left.

Yuri did the talking—all of it. He said that the Kievs were impressed with Evie. He was punctual and carried himself well, Yuri said. The group's activities were growing, he said. A lot of money would be coming in to the Kievs, in many batches, for redistribution by the members.

"A single shipment means nothing," Yuri said. "Maybe eight, maybe ten thousand dollars."

"That seems like a lot to me," Reese said.

Yuri smiled broadly.

"You're such a *boy*, Evie! Such a *boy*! Such money means nothing."

Two of the other Kievs at the table laughed with Yuri. The third, a member with whom Reese's contacts had been marginal, did not.

"But there will be hundreds of these shipments, and some will be larger amounts, depending on who we take them to." Yuri leaned toward Reese and lowered his head so that his eyes were even with the young man's. "Evie, we want you to take this money around—to where we tell you. Sometimes to a place where you just leave it. Sometimes to a place where you meet a special person and give it to him. We get to keep some of the money we distribute. Our fee."

Yuri paused, as if almost waiting for Reese to ask how much. But Reese resisted. The Kiev leader went on.

"We will pay you more now. This does not make you a Kiev, you must understand. But it is a step. Others have come into us in ways like this. And when that happens ... ohhh ..." He rubbed the right thumb and first two fingers of his right hand together and grinned. "*Real* money, Evie. *Real* money."

Then Yuri opened his take-out dinner carton, and the rest followed.

"So we eat now," the Ukrainian said. "Maybe you think of questions while we eat. Then you can answer."

It was an odd way to frame it, Reese thought. *I may ask questions. I can then answer. Right. I don't dare ask where this money is coming from or where it is going once it is delivered. And I certainly cannot refuse to do the work. I couldn't be allowed to know any of this unless I am part of the enterprise. If I say no, I'm dead in three hours, if I'm lucky. But I don't need to ask anything; more will become clear later. And I would never want to say no to this anyway; this is why I'm here,* he thought.

The FBI agent and accountant could see that he was being enlisted into a classic layering scheme, a processing phase in one of the more common forms of money laundering. The idea was to prevent detection of the true original source of illegally obtained money, either when it is used later by the originating criminals for personal purposes or—equally likely—to fund a new crime.

The deception in such a scheme began when the original ill-gotten funds were physically moved, as cash, to an at least partially legitimate business, normally a small one expected to trade mainly in cash receipts. That business then moved them to still another low-profile business in a series of made-up transactions, usually phony purchases of goods or services never actually delivered. This way, the temporary custody of the money sounds no alarm. Yes, its bank records show its cash receipts and their deposit, but the funds' custody and use are explained by the nature of its cash business and further layered by the phony purchases. The continued passing on of the cash goes unobserved. Ultimately, what remains of the cash is distributed to a fake shell company as payment under a fabricated contract. Each lily pad along the way is paid a commission—say 2 percent of the bag—at each hop. When the money finally reaches the account of the waiting shell company, sometimes dignified by lawyers as a "special purpose entity," it is available there to the original criminals, or to whomever they desire, for whatever purpose the original criminals desire. And all of this virtually untraceable to them.

"So, Evie," Yuri said over after-dinner vodka, "have you questions? Have you decided? Do you want this?"

Reese looked around the table and saw eight eyes trained directly on his. Six of the eyes were smiling. Two were dark and expressionless, corpse-like.

Evan raised his shot glass and looked to Yuri. "To my new opportunity," he said.

"*Yes*!" said Yuri, lifting his own. "May you be loyal and well rewarded, Evie boy!"

All except the unsmiling Kiev rose from the table and moved toward the little bar on the other side of the cellar, the only well-lit section of the room. As he walked next to Yuri, Reese considered commenting on the unspoken reprobation he detected from the quiet member still sitting at the table. But he didn't have to. Yuri, leaning to his ear, made it unnecessary.

"Do not worry about Dirj," he said. "How do you say it? There is one in every crowd? It is just the way he is."

Now, months later, there was to be another one in a crowd, this time a crowd at Nationals Park, just down the street from the nation's Capitol Building. Only this person in the crowd was to meet Evie Rezcepko and leave with his cash-stuffed backpack. Where would the money go from there? For what was it earmarked? Who was the courier he was to meet working for? Agent Reese reported in that he had no idea, but he was taking the train to Washington the next morning and would call in again before settling into his hotel room. Which hotel? He didn't know yet; the Kievs were arranging it. Perhaps he would learn something by morning that he could pass along.

By then. By then. Hannah Harris looked nervously again at her desk clock. Four thirty. By then. But he had not called in.

Where was Evan Reese?

3

HUMAN ERROR IN HUMAN RESOURCES

Audrey Sanderson followed Renfro's instruction and called in the report to the liaison line at DHS immediately. To avoid delays resulting from multiple reports coming in at the same time, the system took the calls in an automated center equipped with voice recognition capability. You didn't want a caller with a lead on a suspected terrorist to be put on hold. The information from any law enforcement source was instantly recorded, converted to verbatim text, and launched to an email system. A DHS specialist watched the digital center around the clock. His or her role was to immediately direct the emails to the right hands in the right locations in federal law enforcement and the US intelligence community, worldwide.

Indeed, communication and cooperation between US agencies and local law enforcement had improved almost beyond description since the days leading up to 9/11, when intelligence and enforcement agencies shared little and rivaled much. The new protocols, and the technologies to implement them, were meant to ensure that useful information would never be suppressed or delayed again. And it had worked well. Hundreds of terror plots, many intended for American soil, were disrupted and prevented since that horrific attack in 2001, in large measure because of the diligent use of the new methods.

Sanderson's message was received in the DHS central repository at 3:37 in the afternoon. It was to the point:

> MALE EXECUTED TODAY PROX NOON AT WILLARD HOTEL, PENN AVE, DC. ROOM 1248. POSSIBLE ONE-ELEVEN.
>
> CAUCASIAN, LATE TWENTIES, EARLY THIRTIES, DARK COMPLEXION. LONGER BLACK HAIR. MAY BE AMERICAN BUT COULD BE EASTERN EURO OR EURO/ ASIAN. CHECHNYAN? SENDING EVIDENCE FOR CHECK AGAINST TERRORIST DATABASES. RENFRO AND SANDERSON, METRO HOMICIDE.

The voice recognition software was impressive. Even *Chechnyan* was spelled correctly.

Ordinarily, the notification would have been in the hands of the Washington and New York FBI field offices, and probably Baltimore's and Philadelphia's too, within a minute of receipt. That is, *ordinarily.* But on that afternoon, the specialist on duty at the center was called to a human resources meeting explaining changes to health benefits, and his coworker otherwise expected to cover his post was home with a sick child.

That is the thing about human resources. They're human.

The message about the body at the Willard was not seen at DHS until 5:18 in the afternoon.

In her office in New York, Hannah Harris was pacing anxiously, awaiting word from Evan Reese, when at 5:20 her cell phone and computer screen chimed in unison, the three-beep indicator for a terror-related notification. She lunged to her screen to read the message.

"Oh, God," she said.

Within minutes, she reached the bureau's agent in charge in Washington. Their conversation was brief.

"Did you see the DHS incident notice just now?" she asked him.

"Yes."

"I need you to get somebody over there to the Willard as fast as you can. We have an agent working deep cover who went dark today in the middle of a field op. His name is Evan Reese. The last we knew, he was heading to a hotel in DC. He meets that description."

"Send me his photo file?"

"Of course."

"I've got L.T. Kitt here. She can be there in ten minutes."

"God, if its Reese, I'll need you tonight too."

"Where? The hotel?"

"No, the ball game."

"The *ball game?*"

"It's a long story. Just get Kitt over there."

4

A TERRORIST SHOULD KNOW WHO HE HATES

They weren't, but the two Iranians who stepped out of the Occidental Grill atop Pennsylvania Avenue into the June air looked as though they could be father and son. It was just before six o'clock. The older man glanced up and down the avenue jammed with crawling traffic, typical for this time of day. His name was Ranni Sharimi.

In his heart, Sharimi knew it was not wise to be so close to the Willard after the execution. Indeed, the legendary Occidental was literally attached to the old hotel. But the grill's own unique place in American history was too alluring. Its high, dark-paneled walls and every one of its hallways were crammed from floor to ceiling with black-and-white photographs of nearly every figure in US political history. Some were century-old tin-type prints. It didn't matter if the person was revered or despised; hero or scoundrel; progressive or rock-ribbed conservative. The Occidental didn't discriminate or judge. They were all there. The presidents, the senators, the congressmen, the Supreme Court justices, a few photographed with celebrities of song or film or the world of sport. To the older Iranian, it was a veritable portrait museum of the very subject of his venom—the United States of America.

Every terrorist can use a little pumping up now and again, the older man knew, and it was good for his trainee to know who he was hating.

Besides, he and his protégé had slid easily out of the Willard without notice. And their ethnicity surely drew no attention. Not in this neighborhood or anywhere in Washington. There was no more cosmopolitan place in the world. The only thing anyone in the constant throng around the White House normally had in common, aside from the tourists, was good tailoring. And Ranni Sharimi and his trainee were as well attired as any.

Midway down the long steps to the avenue, Sharimi's phone vibrated. He stopped on the wide steps and took the call.

"Is it done?" the caller asked, without any greeting. His voice was deep and raspy. Sharimi could not mistake it. It was the voice of his commander in Tehran.

"Yes," Sharimi said. "It is done."

"You are certain he made contact with the Ukrainians in New York?"

"There is no doubt. It came from his own mouth. He met with them personally."

"And about the delivery, he made the arrangements with them?"

"Yes. He confirmed it. The details of the delivery. Where and when."

"That is good, Ranni. I thank you in the name of Allah."

"The money will be properly delivered," Sharimi replied. "It is on its way."

Which the raspy-voiced man in Tehran already knew. He had sent another operative to be sure that it was, of whom the two assassins on the steps of the Occidental Grill knew nothing.

"Good, good," the commander in Tehran said. "Have you disposed of the gun, Ranni?"

"Not yet, but I will soon."

"Good. Good. You have done well." And then the caller hung up.

—

By the time Sharimi reached the bottom step, the caller from Tehran had placed a second call to another man, also in Washington, also on Pennsylvania Avenue.

"Do you see them?" the raspy voice asked.

"Yes," the man said. "They are just across the street. They are still close to the hotel."

"Follow them until Sharimi gets rid of the weapon," the commander said. "Then kill them both. And leave at once. Don't forget the phones."

5

IDENTIFICATION

L.T. Kitt hurried into the car nearest the exit of the FBI garage. She saw it was wearing a Virginia license plate. It was a sure sign that it had been returned to the livery from an undercover assignment. But there was no time, she judged from the tone of the agent in charge's voice, to find a vehicle with a government plate. So when she pulled to an abrupt stop in the busses-only space seventy-five feet from the steps into the Willard Hotel, the unmarked sedan looked like any other illegally parked vehicle. That is, until she slapped the FBI sticker on the windshield before racing to the staircase, which the uniformed policeman standing guard on Detective Jack Renfro's orders immediately noticed. The policeman moved quickly to greet her.

"Are you going to the twelfth floor?" he asked Kitt, struggling to keep up with her.

"Yeah. There's a one-eleven up there."

"Homicide called it in. Renfroe and Sanderson. My orders are to keep everyone out."

"Well, get new orders," Kitt said. "We think he might be one of our own."

"The vic?"

Kitt didn't pause to answer. She rushed ahead and sprinted up the cement stairs.

By the time the elevator opened on the twelfth floor, Jack Renfro had reached the hotel security men guarding the hall. "She's FBI. Let her in," he had told them. "And tell her I'm on my way."

The hotel security man pressed his card key against the door pad, and Kitt stepped in hurriedly, unfolding the file photograph of Special Agent Evan Reese.

6

A HURRIED DEPARTURE

Just a block away, another federal agent raced up other stairs—the stairs to the presidential residence inside the White House.

The agent was Tug Birmingham, chief of the Secret Service detail guarding President Del Winters and her resident father, Henry. The short, stout agent leaped up the stairs two steps at a time, his arms driving hard, upward. As he did, a swarm of other Secret Service agents splayed out across the lower floors to every point of ingress to the White House. Dazed staffers watched them fly by. The staffers needed no instruction; all knew the protocol. They walked immediately to their offices, closed the doors, and turned off any television, radio, or other device making sound.

It was lockdown.

The fact that the one-eleven report had been delayed in its transmission by two hours disturbed Birmingham. Greatly. He knew there had never before been a one-eleven so near the White House. The possibility of terrorist activity on Pennsylvania Avenue—virtually next door at the Willard—was frightening enough. But that *two hours* had lapsed since its discovery without *any* security reaction magnified his alarm exponentially. Any number of people, secreting any number of devices, could have entered the building in that amount of time. And even if no penetration of the White House itself had been made, two hours was an eternity of time in which hostiles could have taken up positions in the neighborhood.

In a way, it was fitting that the response to the perceived threat fell to Tug Birmingham. The ex–Army Special Forces man was an extraction specialist and always had been. Built like a fireplug with gifts of great strength and speed, he had rarely fired a weapon on the battlefield. But he had personally carried, lifted, and dragged hundreds of wounded to safety under killing fire on those battlefields. And in fact, he was in his job this very day because of his work on such a mission four years earlier—the dangerous extraction of the large senior citizen from Pittsburgh, Stanley Bigelow, from the hands of domestic terrorists in Michigan, saving the old man—and with him the military secrets of the old engineer's covert work for this president. That same assignment had introduced him to the attractive FBI agent, L.T. Kitt, the brave dog trainer who also had assisted in Stanley Bigelow's rescue and who was now the love of the former ranger's life. And that mission had brought him to the attention of President Del Winters. Taken by and grateful for his service in Stanley's rescue, she had invited him to join—and eventually lead—her Secret Service protection detail in Washington.

When Tug Birmingham reached the top of the staircase in the east wing of the White House, the first person he saw was the first father, retired general Henry Winters. He was stepping out of the private library down the hall. Now eighty-four years old but still robust, the president's father was startled by the urgency of Birmingham's advance.

"Tug, what's happening?" he asked.

"Stay right there, General. Where is the president?"

"In her bedroom, I think. We were going to have a drink in the sitting room."

"Just stay where you are, General. I'll get her. We have to leave. Right now."

The unmistakable roar and whir of a helicopter filled the air outside. The general bent to see out the window to the expansive lawn beyond the rose garden. *Marine One* was descending to the ground.

"In *that*?" asked Henry Winters.

"No. That's a decoy. It will lift off after body doubles run out to it. But you and the president won't be in it. You'll go with me in a single car from the side entrance. The bird will fly above and cover us if we need it."

"What the hell is happening?" asked the first father.

"We don't know," Tug said. "But we're not going to wait here to find out."

7

EYES ARE SPECIAL

L.T. Kitt was not a homicide detective. But she wasn't stupid either. She knew you didn't just casually move a body at a murder scene. In fact, you *never* did, unless the medical examiner had said you could, and you had the paperwork to prove it.

She knelt on the carpeting next to the hotel bed, her eyes mere inches from the head of the young man planted facedown on the bloody linens. She put the file photo of Evan Reese faceup on the floor. The arch of the nose. The edge of the eyebrows. The smooth, high forehead. The thick, black, curly hair. The earlobes. Back and forth she looked, body to photo and back again. Then she repeated the ritual on the opposite side of the bed, studying the other side of the corpse's face.

If only she could see the dead man's eyes. Eyes told everything. Other facial features might be distinctive—or might not be. To Kitt's view, nothing about the other features were, in either the photo of Evan Reese or what she could see clearly of the body on the bed. Nothing seemed distinctive. Everything looked similar. Very similar. But *eyes*. *Eyes* were special. If only she could see the dead man's eyes.

Jack Renfro burst into the room, breathing heavily. Still kneeling, Kitt looked up at him.

"Renfro," he said, thrusting out his identification folio. "Metro homicide."

"L.T. Kitt. FBI." She rose to her feet. "Your one-eleven report has gotten a lot of attention."

"I can see that," said Renfro. "Is this your agent?" He gestured toward the body.

"I can't tell," Kitt said. She handed him the photo of Evan Reese. "What do you think?"

"God, it sure looks like him. Look at those cheeks, that thick hair."

"We *have* to know, Detective. Something is going down tonight. We *have* to know. I can't move the body. It's not even my jurisdiction."

"Well it is *mine*." The aging detective snapped on white latex gloves. "I'll take the responsibility."

Renfro crouched over the body. He slid his left arm under the left shoulder of the facedown body. He placed his right hand on the body's right shoulder. Kitt saw sticky blood from the bed linens stain the detective's gloves. He lifted the upper body of the corpse and turned it to a fetal position so that the face was directed to Kitt on the other side of the bed.

She didn't need to look again at the photograph of Evan Reese. The eyes *were* special.

They weren't Evan Reese's.

8

FIFTEEN MINUTES TO GAME TIME

When Evan finally rang Hannah Harris from the crowded sidewalk outside Nationals Park fifteen minutes before game time, he received the greeting he anticipated.

"Where the *fuck* have you been?"

"They screwed me up," the young agent said. "I showed up this morning to get the backpack, and they told me I wouldn't be going alone. This Middle Eastern dude was there. Dressed real sharp. I say, 'Who's this?' Yuri says, 'We don't know. He came with the money, and they want him to go with you.' So the guy was next to me the whole time. And the train from New York kept stalling. I tried to call from the bathroom on the thing, but I couldn't get cell reception. We were so late into Washington I didn't even get to my hotel. When we're only a block from the ballpark, the guy gets a call on his cell. Very short. All Farsi. He hangs up and nods to me. 'I may leave you now.' And then he walks away. I waited until he was out of sight and then called you. This was my first chance to check in."

"Do you think Yuri was on the level?" Hannah asked. "That he didn't know who the guy was?"

"I do, yeah. Yuri was surprised too. Definitely. He said it wasn't the same man who came to talk to the Kievs about the work. About the drops."

"Maybe the launderers are just being careful about the Kievs," Hannah Harris said. "Until they trust them. It *is* the first *big* drop."

"Maybe."

"They wanted to be sure you were taking the cash where they wanted it to go."

"I guess so," Evan said.

"Did you learn anything about him? About this new guy?"

"Not a goddamned thing. Silent as a stone. Never a single word until he said he was leaving. But I know he was armed. He was carrying in a calf holster. I saw it when he sat down on the train."

"What about the drop?" Hannah asked. "Do you know who you're giving the money to?"

"The Kievs don't have a name. But he's supposed to be in the next seat. It's field level, behind home plate."

"How will you know it's the right guy?"

"He's supposed to say, 'These Pirates always kill us, don't they, Evie?' If he doesn't say that, I'm supposed to leave."

"And go where?" asked Hanna Harris.

"To the Willard Hotel."

Hanna froze. Even on the other end of the line, Evan Reese sensed something upsetting. There was an inordinate pause.

"Evan, whatever you do, *don't* go to the Willard."

"Why not?"

Hanna ignored his question. "And you're not armed, are you?" she asked.

"No. I couldn't take a gun onto the train. I thought I'd have time to pick one up when I arrived here. But then this guy showed up."

"I'm sending someone to cover you inside the ballpark," Hannah said. "This is getting too screwy. It'll probably be L.T. Kitt. She just chased down a scare we had about you. She has your photo."

"Scare?"

"Somebody got executed in a room at the Willard Hotel this afternoon. Somebody who looked a hell of lot like you."

9

AUDREY SANDERSON LOOKS THE PART

Whatever else was proven by Jack Renfro's idea to place his younger detective in the ball park dressed as a concession's vendor, it proved credible. Audrey Sanderson's thick auburn hair sprung naturally and curled up from the sides of her Nationals cap, and the basket of popcorn cups hung comfortably from her athletic shoulders. She looked for all the world like a nightly regular. Her big, friendly eyes combed the rows behind home plate as the seats began to fill. Her biggest challenge was keeping her mind on her reason for being there. She followed baseball—and especially the Nationals—ardently. To be so close to the field and sense all of the pregame anticipation was distracting. She couldn't resist glancing and grinning at the players trotting by and popping in and out of the dugouts.

She checked the ticket in her pocket and confirmed its location. Field Level; Section 1; Row 2; Seat 6. At five minutes to the first pitch, it was unoccupied, as were the two seats to its right, toward first base, and all five to its left, leading to the aisle.

"Wire check." Renfro's voice came to her earpiece. "I'm outside. All good there?"

"I have you, Jack."

"Anyone there?"

"Not yet."

"Remember we don't have an arrest warrant. We don't have anything on anyone who might sit down. The ticket we found might mean nothing. So don't make a scene."

"Understood."

"Just get as close as you can to anybody that sits next to or near to him. Give me as detailed a description as you can. Look for scars, tattoos. Exactly what he's wearing."

"What *he's* wearing?"

"Good point. He *or* she," Renfro said. "I've got uniforms on the street at every exit, including into the parking garages. We'll take your description and stop him—or her—for questioning whenever they leave. Maybe we'll get a break and they'll resist or try to take off. Then we can take them in."

"I get it," Sanderson said. "Anything from DHS on the body at the Willard?"

"Turns out retinal scans aren't definitive from a dead body. They say you need live eyes. But they're doing facial recognition right now. He didn't come up on the no-fly database, but there's plenty more to run."

Sanderson looked up the row of stairs. An usher was leading down a young couple. He wiped off two seats in row 1, directly in front of the targeted seats.

"Just about game time, Jack," she said to Renfro. "Still nobody."

"Check in if anything changes. And one other thing. The FBI went crazy about the vic at the hotel. Thought it might be one of theirs who's working undercover. It wasn't, but they sure went ballistic over it. I don't know what that's about, but it seems like an odd connection."

"Thanks," Sanderson said. And then, "Hold on, Jack." The usher was back again with a new ticket holder.

"We have a customer," she told Renfro.

10

MORE KILLING NEAR THE WHITE HOUSE

President Del Winters had just left the White House under Secret Service escort to Camp David when DC Metropolitan Police officers were called to the bodies of Ranni Sharimi and his young Iranian accomplice on the edge of Lafayette Square. Both had been shot from close range—one in the back of the head, the other in his face.

Jack Renfro left his post outside Nationals Park and sped to Lafayette Square, just behind the White House. From his unmarked sedan, he alerted Audrey Sanderson.

"Two Arabs dead near the White House," he told her. "Stay where you are. I'm going there. Maybe there's a link."

He couldn't have known it when he said it, but Renfro was mistaken about the ethnicity of the dead men in Lafayette Square. They were not Arabs. Iranians are *not*—the great majority of them—Arabs at all. Unlike Saudi Arabia, Egypt, Iraq, the Emirates, and most other nations of the Middle East, Iran's heritage dates to the old Persian empire, historical competitor to the Arabians. While the bulk of Iranians share the religion of Islam with their Arab neighbors, there are deep divisions in their respective understanding of its teachings, hierarchy, and aspirations to caliphate. And plenty of political and military animosity too. Witness the brutal Iran-Iraq War of the 1980s.

Two things struck Renfro as soon as he arrived at the bodies.

First, both had been killed, he believed, by a single gunman. The man lying facedown was much younger than the other. The younger man had been shot in the back of the head and had been fired upon first, the detective surmised. That first shot caused the older victim to turn around, presenting his face for the second deadly discharge. Now he lay on his back, his mouth agape. Ballistics would have to confirm it, but Renfro was near certain both rounds had been fired from the same gun.

But it was Renfro's second intuition that was more troubling to him. He looked around the park. Daylight still abounded. Poor, homeless people crouched or lay on at least a half dozen park benches, and well-dressed office workers were still ambling along the sidewalks at the park's edge. You don't carry out an execution in daylight in a public place. And not six hundred yards from the White House. Unless, Renfro concluded, it couldn't wait. *No,* he thought, *this killer couldn't wait. He was hurried.*

Five uniformed officers stood in a circle around the two bodies, gesturing at curious passersby to keep moving.

"Was there anything next to them?" Renfro asked them.

"Just that change near the younger one," said the senior among them. He pointed to the coins on the ground.

Renfro knelt between the bodies. The pants pockets of the younger man were extracted so that their white linings hung out. "You haven't touched these bodies, have you?"

"No way," the uniform said. "The perps did that."

"Perps? Was there more than one? You have a witness?"

"Sorry, no. Nobody yet. I guess we don't know how many there were."

"No ID?"

"Nada."

Chatter came from the walkie-talkies on the shoulders of the uniformed officers. *"President on the move. Stand by for route coverage."*

The veteran detective made a judgment call. He knew the medical examiner wouldn't arrive for at least twenty minutes. He decided that since whoever killed these two men was in a hurry, he should be in one too. He sensed a connection to the murder at the Willard earlier the same day and the FBI's intense interest in Sanderson's one-eleven notification. And now the president was being taken from the White House in an unscheduled departure. He pulled out his smartphone and quickly stepped around the bodies, clicking nonstop photos. He checked the phone to see that the photos were clear, then yanked a pair of latex gloves from the breast pocket of his jacket. He knelt over the younger victim, lying prone, and patted the man's jacket pockets. Nothing. He rose and moved to the older dead man, lying on his back. His pockets had not been visibly emptied. He checked them carefully. First the front pockets, then reaching under gently to the rear ones. Nothing. But one side of the older man's loose-fitting jacket lay tucked under his upper back. Renfro slid a hand under his neck and along the fabric of his shirt and jacket.

"Oh my," Renfro said. "What have we here?"

He withdrew an iPhone, holding it gingerly by its edges as he used his other hand to pull out a plastic evidence bag.

He looked to the blank faces of the uniforms standing above him.

"This killer *was* in a hurry," Renfro said. "Get the coins into another bag and comb this whole area for anything else. Cigarette butts, candy wrappers, anything. Bag it all. I've gotta get this phone to DHS."

11

THIRD INNING PANDEMONIUM

Audrey Sanderson did not want to appear inordinately interested in the man descending toward her behind the courteous usher to row 2. Besides, it permitted her to turn to the field and watch the Nationals' starting pitcher deliver his final warm-up pitch. She always enjoyed the ritual moment—the crisp slap of the ball into the catcher's glove; the receiver's majestic, long throw to second base; the ceremonial around the horn of the infielders before the ball's return to the pitcher behind the mound.

But Sanderson had a job to do, and she knew it. She walked up the aisle to row 4 and stepped in for a vantage point of the man below. He had been taken to seat 5, immediately next to the ticket taken from the wallet of the body at the Willard. The young man was dressed casually but nicely. Dress jeans and a patterned shirt, maybe Ralph Lauren, Audrey thought. A mildly ethnic look, a little taller than average, long, wavy black hair. Handsome. And he wore a nylon backpack emblazoned with a large Nationals' logo that he slipped from his shoulders and placed on the floor beneath his seat. Sanderson noticed that he placed a foot through the loop of the backpack's strap, as if to secure it to himself.

The seats beside Evan Reese remained unoccupied as the game

moved through the first inning. He stirred occasionally and twice turned to look up the aisle stairs; Sanderson averted eye contact. Four times, he nervously brushed his right hand along his left calf and ankle, as if reminding himself that there was no weapon there. Spectators continued to arrive steadily, filling nearly all of the seats above and below him—but no one was brought to any of the four seats next to him leading to the aisle. A wide-open pathway at three hundred dollars a seat. Sanderson thought it odd that prized field-level seats would be empty. She stopped the gentlemanly usher as he passed by.

"Nobody using those primes in row 2?" she asked.

"They're season ticket holders. Some government guys, I think. They don't come a lot."

"Really?"

"Yeah, pretty crazy. For that money, you'd think they'd at least *give* them away. Tough to sell popcorn to empty seats. Sorry."

"How often do they use them?"

"Not as often as the brass from concessions."

"What do you mean?"

"You haven't met Chandler Bowes yet? I guess you're new."

"Who's he?"

"VP for concessions and sales."

Much later, in the calm, cool light of hindsight, Renfro, Sanderson, Harris, and Reese would agree that the melee that happened next was predictable. They were all good law enforcement officers. Skilled. Trained. Quick thinking. But each was acting on different information. Each had a different objective. None had time to coordinate with one another or connect the dots. And all were converging on the same target in a large, excited crowd.

Take me out to the ball game.

Chandler Bowes intentionally timed his rapid third-inning descent down the aisle and into row 2, empty all the way to Evan Reese's seat. He had waited at the top of the stairs nearly ten minutes until the very moment the Nationals' heavy-hitting right fielder launched a drive to the alley in left-center field. With two runners on base, the home crowd thundered to its feet at the crack of the bat. The roar was deafening. Audrey Sanderson saw the broad-shouldered, heavyset man in a sport coat hurrying to row 2 and scrambled down, hoping to block his pathway out. As the Pittsburgh outfielders raced for the ball dancing against the wall, the big man brought his face close to Evan.

"These Pirates always kill us, don't they, Evie?" he said, smiling.

Reese was momentarily stunned. The undercover agent was standing, like all of the fans. It seemed like the right thing to do since everyone else was. What startled him was that this man looked *nothing* like the man he expected. He looked like anyone's uncle, especially if the uncle was a paunchy accountant. Big, friendly face, baggy sport jacket straight off the ready-to-wear rack, loosened neck tie with an oversized knot.

"*Don't* they, Evie," Bowes repeated. Not smiling.

Reese nodded and bent over to reach for the backpack, his right shoe still securing its longest strap. He never reached it. Sanderson flung her vendor's basket to the floor of the aisle, the handgun on her hip in plain view beneath the flopping top of her uniform. And in view too of the FBI's L.T. Kitt pouring down from the mezzanine level, gun drawn. Kitt had no idea who Audrey Sanderson was, but two things she did know: that was fellow Agent Evan Reese in the second row, and there was a woman dressed as a vendor striding toward him with a gun.

No one ever said that L.T. Kitt wasn't strong. Evan Reese was about to sorely wish they had. Kitt saw the large man in the sport coat standing in row 2 and the old usher who had come down the aisle behind him. She vaulted rows 4 and 3, shoving aside the screaming spectators watching the action on the field. "Get down!" she shouted, pouncing onto Sanderson's shoulders just as the DC policewoman reached Reese. Kitt's dive drove Sanderson to the concrete, taking the stunned Evan Reese down violently with her. His face slammed against the first-row seatback in front of him, opening a gash above his right eye. *My God, this is blowing up!* he thought. *What the hell is happening?* The weight of the two women struggling atop his body jammed his face at an angle to the concrete. Blood flowed into both of his eyes, and his legs splayed, skidding the nylon backpack down the concrete beneath the chairs.

"FBI! FBI!" Kitt screamed. "Stop resisting!"

Audrey Sanderson went limp at the command. "What the *fuck*?" she said. "Get the fuck off me. I'm metro police!"

Evan wrestled free and spun on hands and knees, looking for the backpack. It was nowhere. He glared down the row in both directions. Through blurry eyes, he saw the big, stocky man in the sport coat hurrying out the opposite side of the row. Without a backpack.

12

TOO TRUE TO BE GOOD

Ten miles south of Altoona, Pennsylvania, the corn in the next field had sprouted shin high. Spring had been typical. The stalks would reach the knee by early July. Late this June afternoon, the sun was still too high to give the feeling of dusk. But the two men working out of the Nissan pickup truck parked at the culvert knew it would be arriving soon. The road was classic for the Keystone State's central valley. It rolled with the farmland and moderate hills above the banks of Spruce Creek. The state could have saved its money on the fifty-miles-per-hour speed limit signs. Nobody paid them any attention.

Even at this hour, though, when you would think drivers would be heading home to the nearby towns, traffic was light. To the men on hands and knees far out in the field, it seemed a car—or just as often—another pickup truck whizzed by every few minutes. This suited them. They were not anxious for company or notice.

They had expected to be questioned about what they were doing but hardly were. Only when they checked into the motel on the edge of town were they asked anything.

"Found work around here?" asked the matronly desk manager.

Andruzal answered. Of the two, only he managed English well.

"Some," he said. "We hope for more."

"What kind of work? Who's hiring?"

"Testing for fracking," Andruzal said. He looked the woman

directly in the eye, as he had been trained, and smiled as warmly as he could, as he would to his grandmother. "Our company is from out of state. Far away. We are just running tests to see if the equipment will work."

How true that statement was. As President Del Winters and her national security team would eventually come to know, too true to be good.

It was their third day working in the field adjacent to the shuttered manufacturing plant. Altoona Plastics had once employed hundreds there, forming trim parts for auto interiors. But like many others, its business had steadily declined, victim to labor and technology costs that rose as a drowning wave over its slim profit margins. Eventually, nothing could be done but board it up. Welcome to the plastic rust belt.

To the neighboring communities, the abandoned plant and its surrounding land were just tired reminders of bygone days, useful for nothing. But to the two men in the field and the others who had sent them there, it was serving a vital purpose.

On the first day, they had dug a straight, narrow trench out in the field. They made the trench twenty-four inches deep and one hundred feet long, more or less parallel to the road. On the second day, they dug a second one, much shorter in length, about fifteen feet to the side of the first. Then they connected the two trenches with a third excavation dug on a radius of about thirty degrees, like an elbow.

On this third day, they had arrived before dawn so that all of the parts could be taken from the truck and out to the trenches before daylight. They carried the lengths of tubing first. From the field, they saw a car pass. For an instant, it seemed to slow down, as if it might stop, or the driver was diverting his attention to his rearview or side mirrors. "Don't look his way," Andruzal said to the other man. "Ignore him." As they bent to place the pipes on the ground next to the trenches, they could see that the headlights were moving away.

They walked swiftly back to their truck, and Andruzal stood at the rear, looking intently down the dark road in both directions. No sign of more lights. He knew the road curved in each direction about a third of a mile from their position at the truck.

"Okay," Andruzal said in Farsi. He reached into the bed of the pickup, removing two metal cases, each about the size of a carry-on suitcase. They were black with a large leather handle on top and smaller ones on the sides. "We must get these out there before light comes."

All day, they knelt over the trenches, working. They placed the two metal cases into the trenches so that they could not be seen from the road. Andruzal understood all of the parts and small devices in the metal cases and did most of the assembly down in the trenches. Often, he extended his arm and asked his companion for a part or a tool, like a surgeon calling for an instrument. On the simpler connections, the companion helped.

Evening was setting in when Andruzal walked from one end of the curved trench line to the other. At one end, he turned a valve. At the other end, he knelt and studied a gauge. Andruzal reached down into the trench and adjusted the valves. Then he turned them again. His companion worried that Andruzal was taking too long. Maybe the gauge was showing a poor reading. Maybe the air was not flowing. The companion hoped there were not problems. He was tired, and he remembered working that morning before sunrise and how anxious he had felt in the dark. But his fears were founded. Andruzal rose to his feet unsmiling, shaking his head. He trod back to his helper.

"We must gather the pumps and valves and leave for now," Andruzal said. "We will have to come back soon. We need help with these things. Something is not right."

And help they would receive. It would come from a gifted, if unexpected, expert. With his own helper.

13
ENTER ADMIRAL BREW

Midnight approached as the five law enforcement officers gathered in the FBI conference room in Washington. Three of them were federal officers. Two were officers of the DC Metropolitan Police. Their impromptu joint task force was formed by accident, not design.

Hannah Harris, the financial crimes chief from the New York office, had flown down on an FBI jet as soon as she heard of the mix-up at the baseball game. She arrived at bureau headquarters just as her undercover agent Evan Reese was delivered from the emergency room by field agent L.T. Kitt. Reese was sporting twelve stitches above his right eye. It could have been worse, she knew. But to Hannah Harris, architect of the painstaking infiltration of young Reese into the Ukrainian mob, not much worse.

How to explain that night's mayhem at Nationals Park to the Kievs? Was there *any* way to save Evie Rezcepko's cover, or should she move *now* on the Brooklyn money launderers, before the full extent and—even more important—the *purpose* of the scheme could be learned? These were the questions on the minds of the FBI's Hannah Harris and Evan Reese.

Different questions were bouncing in the heads of the Washington detectives Jack Renfro and Audrey Sanderson. Why were three Middle Eastern men murdered near the White House within hours of each other? And was the ticket found in the wallet of the first victim *connected*—or a mere coincidence—to the FBI's investigation of financial crimes?

The five had barely taken seats in the room when there was a knock at the door. A tall navy captain in dress blues opened it and stood in the doorway. To the surprised law enforcement officers, he said only, "Admiral Tyler Brew is joining you." The admiral stepped in, and the captain stepped out, closing the door.

All five of the officers knew *of* Admiral Brew, but only Agent Kitt *knew* him. And she knew him very well. There was never romance between them, or the hint of it. Their bond had been forged in danger, stress, honor, and duty. And in their deep mutual affection for the aging engineer from Pittsburg, Stanley Bigelow, the unlikely private citizen whose willingness to apply his unusual technical skills in two secret military projects in the first term of President Del Winters—without hope or desire for recognition or reward—had caused Brew and Kitt to meet each other years earlier and risk their own lives in common purpose.

Now Admiral Brew held a seat among the Joint Chiefs. His sole focus was counterterrorism.

The African American military man, now forty-seven, was only the ninth Navy SEAL ever to rise to the rank of admiral. It was not that SEALs weren't qualified for the most esteemed posts. It was that most were not around after age forty. At that age, they were ineligible for new "adversarial" missions. SEALs were specialist warriors of the highest order. Most did not resent their removal from field operations; they had known the rules when they first qualified. And they knew also that the "age out" regulation was intended—and needed—to be certain that physical skills were never compromised on a mission. The life of each SEAL on mission literally depended on the unhindered capacity of every other SEAL.

But continued service jobs for aged-out SEALs, usually in training roles on domestic bases, were just not the same for most of them. For one thing, most felt deeply lucky to still be alive after hundreds of harrowing missions. Many had wives and loved ones who felt even luckier. It was a good time to step away and get on with family life. The other factor leading many SEALs to call it a day was the abundance of higher-paying—*much* higher-paying—jobs in the private sector. Billionaires, and others heading to that status, were multiplying like rabbits all around the world. Physical safety and security was top of mind for these people and their families and companies. For good reason. And you could not do much better than a Navy SEAL to protect you when the chips were really down.

But Tyler Brew never seriously considered leaving the navy. He had been raised by hardworking Alabama parents amid deep racial tension in American society. He was taught to resist prejudice by believing in himself and achieving his goals notwithstanding society's unfairness. He excelled in the navy from day one. He qualified for the elite SEAL corps with the highest obtainable ratings and by 9/11 was already an officer and SEAL team leader. His heroics in stealth missions to eradicate terrorist encampments and rescue hostages were legendary within military ranks, if unknown to the public.

President Del Winters had known Brew even before she entered public life. She was an army lawyer herself who briefed presidents on counterterrorism issues, rising to the rank of lieutenant general herself before entering public life suddenly and unexpectedly. When a popular vice president fell dead of a stroke, the incumbent president plucked her from near obscurity as the replacement. The rest was history.

She'd held the office of vice president for five years before winning the presidency in her own right. Now in her second term, Tyler Brew had featured prominently—though usually secretly—in critical events in her presidency. He had aged out of field service in her first year in office. She asked him to stay to command planning and intelligence activities. The then captain agreed. His only condition was that he remain a SEAL. Some in the military command were uncomfortable with the new president's agreement.

President Winters had designed a counterterrorism command unit and penciled in Brew as chief.

"How does a Navy SEAL lead a headquarters group with special ops from all of the branches?" one adviser asked.

"By giving orders," she said.

The admiral looked from person to person with serious eyes as he walked to the conference room table. Everyone rose. L.T. Kitt stepped up to him and extended her hand. He took it and reached his left arm around her in an embrace. He said nothing. He didn't return her warm smile. She was not surprised.

"You look tired," Kitt said.

"I am," Brew said. "I just flew in from Riyadh."

"Is something happening there?"

"You know better than to ask. How's Stanley?"

"Mr. Bigelow is fine. He's still in Pittsburgh, and I'm in Washington now. But we talk a lot, and I see him when he comes here to be with Henry Winters." The old Pittsburgh engineer and the first father had become close friends, seemingly closer all the time.

For the first time, a small smile came to Brew's face.

"And Tug?" he asked. "How is Tug?" Tug Birmingham was the former ranger, now Kitt's husband, whom Brew had brought into the mission to save Stanley Bigelow four years earlier.

"Tug is *very* fine."

Brew's smile grew a fraction. "Tug is a good man. I am happy for you."

"I am happy for both of us," Kitt said.

"Please, let's all sit down," the admiral said, "and talk about this mess. I know who each of you are. But I don't know how you fit together. Start by filling me in."

Hannah Harris looked across the table at Jack Renfro with a *you go first* expression. The senior Washington Metropolitan Police detective accepted.

"This afternoon, we were called to the Willard Hotel. A man was found dead in a room there. Executed on a bed." Renfro detailed the scene: the contrived note, the money left on the body, and his conclusion that at least two men had been involved in the killing. "The whole thing didn't seem right to me," he said. "And the victim—we couldn't tell for sure—looked like he could be Middle Eastern. That's why I had Audrey call in the one-eleven. When we found the ticket for the ball game, I thought we should follow up on it. Somebody might show up to connect the guy. But the lead had a short shelf life. The ticket was for tonight's game."

Brew listened intently to the veteran policeman. He didn't interrupt. Renfro explained that he had dispatched Audrey Sanderson to pose as a vendor in the seating area behind home plate in case anyone came to the seats adjoining the ticket found at the Willard. The admiral penned a note.

Renfro went on. "I'm waiting outside Nationals Park, and just about game time, I get a call from uniforms in Lafayette Square. There's two more men shot, and they are definitely Middle Eastern. I call in another one-eleven. Just about then, all hell breaks loose at the game, and we have this mash-up. Hannah's man here got hurt." Evan Reese, seated next to his boss, made a hand gesture, as if waving off the injury as trifling. Renfro gestured to Hannah Harris, inviting her to take it from there.

"There's a Ukrainian-Russian syndicate based in Brooklyn," Harris said. "They call themselves the Kievs. We've been looking at them for three years. Originally, we thought they might be trafficking women. But no, they're clean on that. We're sure of it. Also, not moving drugs, which is interesting. But other stuff, not so clean. Old school rackets, like shaking down businesses for protection. Betting. Loansharking. Then about a year ago, we see a lot of banking transfers in and out of the businesses their shaking and lending to. We start thinking money laundering, but we wonder who for? Just for themselves, or maybe for some larger organization?" She patted Reese's shoulder. "Five months ago, we infiltrated them with Evan under deep cover. Sure enough, they're passing money. But always in small amounts—five, ten, twenty thousand. Until today. They sent Evan down to Nationals Park with a ticket and a quarter million dollars in a backpack."

"So how did all of this go south at the game?" It was Admiral Brew's first question.

"Well, we were very worried about Agent Reese," Hannah answered. "We knew he was coming to Washington for the game tonight to make a handoff. He told us that last night. But he didn't have any details to share. Said he'd call in again this morning, but he didn't. By late afternoon, we're *really* worried. Then we see the local police's first one-eleven, and the description of the body resembles Reese. Kitt hustles over to the hotel with a photo of him. At first, she thinks it could be him, so damn similar. But it's not. When the body is turned over, the eyes are wrong. Then Evan finally calls in. He'd been tagged all day long by a Middle Eastern guy who showed up when he picked up the backpack from the Ukrainians in Brooklyn. Rides the train with Reese, stays on his shoulder all the way to the ballpark. Then the guy gets a phone call and just walks away. It gave me the creeps, especially when Evan told me his instructions from the Kievs were to go to *the Willard* if his handoff at the game was a no-show. So I sent L.T. to the game to cover Evan."

"Well, *that* she did!" said Renfro. Everyone laughed. Except Admiral Brew.

"I'm just kidding, Agent Kitt," Renfro said. "You did the right thing. You couldn't have known who Audrey was or what she was doing there." Kitt knew he was right but still appreciated the acknowledgment.

Admiral Brew turned in his chair and rubbed his chin, thinking. The others, in seeming deference, went silent. Finally, the admiral turned and put stern eyes on Hannah Harris.

"You don't really know whether Reese's cover in Brooklyn is blown, correct?"

"No, but it may be impossible to know without sending him back there," the FBI chief said. "Which would be damn dangerous."

"I can't tell you how to do your job, and I wouldn't if I could," Brew said. "Right now, we don't know if the moving money is related to these dead men. We don't know if the Kievs are working with terrorists or just being used by them, or if there is terrorism involved here at all. But until we understand whether there's a link in this confusion, we need to stay inside the Kievs if there is any way."

Hannah turned to Agent Reese. "Has there been any word from Brooklyn yet?"

"Nothing," said Reese. "But they'll expect me there tomorrow." He looked at his watch. Midnight had passed. "I should say this morning."

The captain waiting outside knocked once and opened the door, holding a satellite phone.

"Admiral, you have a call from Camp David. The Secret Service." Brew rose and moved to the door. The captain handed him the phone. The admiral listened. "No," he said. "Not yet. We have loose ends, questions. Keep the president there. I'll call you when I know more."

My, thought Renfro. *Maybe this* is *a big deal.*

The admiral returned to his seat and summed up their discussion.

"So. We've got three dead one-elevens and at least two others unaccounted for—the man that was sent with Reese today and whoever killed the three men from the Middle East. Along with a quarter million dollars that's who knows where? And a Ukrainian gang that may or may not be involved." He looked down at his note and looked at Jack Renfro.

"How did you place Detective Sanderson into the vendor's uniform so quickly?"

"Through the head of concessions at the ballpark." Renfro referred to his own notes. "Chandler Bowes."

14
CHAMELEON

In the mind of Admiral Tyler Brew, there was no such thing as coincidence. There were stimulus and response. Cause and effect. Action and reaction. Choice and consequence. Always a link. Always. A link to something, perhaps many things. So thought the career Navy SEAL, now the nation's chief of counterterrorism planning and response. To Brew, anyone who concluded that events happening in near time and place were *purely* coincidental—utterly unconnected—was not looking closely enough, deeply enough, or widely enough.

Which was not to say he believed reality was obvious or its course easily discernible. Hardly. "The truth can be a chameleon," a SEAL training instructor had told him decades earlier. "It changes colors. It changes textures. To get to what is really happening, what's really there, you need to *think* chameleon. Sometimes you have to *be* chameleon."

Now, he pondered the first reports and data in his Pentagon office. He had set them out in a single row on the twelve-foot credenza against the longest wall of his paneled office. It was his habit. When he was alone thinking, he didn't like to sit down. He preferred to stand, pace, and lean over the pieces of evidence, which he always arranged, at first, in a single row. But the placement of the items in the row changed often. He shuffled them, examining different sequences. He studied the assortment, then restudied it. Sometimes he moved the first piece to the last; an item in the middle to the beginning. And when he was satisfied finally that a connection *did* lay between one piece and another, he would pluck them both from the line and place them together, one above the other, forming a new vertical row.

After the late-night meeting with Hannah Harris, Jack Renfro, and their teams, he'd been driven directly to the Pentagon. On the way, he'd made two calls. The first was to his assistant. He asked him to come in early in the morning; he needed him to get out messages cancelling a slew of previously scheduled appointments. It was best to alert each person involved before he or she left their homes. He wanted his calendar cleared entirely, he told him, except for a four o'clock call with the president. The second call from the car was to Wilson Bryce, the technology chief at the National Security Agency.

"Wilson," he said when the civilian picked up his phone, drowsily. "Sorry to be calling this late."

"Never bothered you before, Admiral," Bryce said, glancing at the clock at his bedside. Two in the morning. "Or me either, I guess," he said. Bryce couldn't readily recall the number of times one of them had awoken the other. It wasn't the rule, but it was hard to call it the exception either. "What do you need?"

"There were two one-elevens in DC yesterday," the admiral said. "Three murders."

"Yeah, I saw them."

"I don't like them," Brew said.

Wilson Bryce knew that fewer than one in a thousand reports of suspected terrorist involvement proved to be actionable. All were looked at, but only about one-third were found credible enough to run to ground thoroughly. And of those, only about 2 percent resulted in a tactical action, usually surveillance or questioning. But what struck the NSA technology guru was that Admiral Tyler Brew himself was interested in these particular notifications. Bryce had worked many times with the admiral on terrorist responses but never this early in the process. Something was special.

"What do you want me to do?" Bryce asked.

"Your people have already run the three dead men through facial recognition." Bryce was not aware of this, which was not unusual. Specific traces were rarely kicked to his level. "There was a hit on one of them," Brew said. "An Iranian named Shamiri. Ranni Shamiri. Nothing on the other two yet. We know of Shamiri. He worked for years in Iran's intelligence service. There were reports recently that he'd gone extreme. He hasn't been seen in the usual intelligence channels in three years."

Brew was referring to the international intelligence circuits that remained above the fray of terrorism per se—back channels of communication, typically connected to diplomatic staff. Friends and foes alike used these informal channels regularly. It was an oddity of geopolitical spy craft. Even foes usually had *worse* foes in common. It was useful to keep intelligence about them flowing. Accommodation had its place, even in espionage. And certainly so in the effort of nearly every nation state to control—or at least understand—terrorist intentions.

"So, if Sharimi had turned terrorist, why was he killed here?" asked Bryce.

"I need your help to find out."

"I'll do anything I can."

"Can you work from his facial and crank everything you've got to do a reconstruct on his movements?" Brew asked. The admiral knew the general arteries of the NSA's expansive surveillance apparatus. He knew that Wilson Bryce knew every capillary.

"You mean since he entered the country?" the NSA technology chief asked.

"No, since *before* he entered the country, if you can."

"We can reconstruct every step he took once he approached Washington. There will be film for every inch. But whether we can retrace where he came from will depend on where he entered. There may be gaps."

"Well, as few as possible," Brew said.

"And the other two murder victims? You want the same?"

"I told you we didn't get a match on them."

"Admiral, we aren't the only data collector in the world. If you let me, I can use others."

"Who would you trust?"

"Interpol."

"Do it."

'What else?"

"Lafayette Square. Sharimi was killed there, with one of the others a little before or after six last night. Can you get me images of what happened?"

"Satellite, for sure," Bryce said. "Maybe ground level too, that near the White House."

"Good."

"And?" Bryce knew that if something was important enough to Tyler Brew to call him in the wee hours, he wouldn't have a wee list.

"Metropolitan police found a cell phone on Shamiri's body," the admiral said.

"You're kidding."

"We may have gotten a break. It was sent over to DHS by the police, but I've sent a navy man over to get it and bring it to you."

"You mean to my office?"

"No, I mean to *you*. He should be at your house in five minutes. I'm going straight to the Pentagon. We're keeping the president and her father at Camp David for the time being. I can't be sure something isn't still going down, at least until you've taken everything from that phone."

"Understood," said Wilson Bryce. "Give me a few hours. I'll call you sooner if I see anything big on it."

Now, standing at the credenza hours later, the older Navy SEAL glared at Bryce's first set of data. It was probably a good thing that it had taken three hours to arrive. Had he seen it before, he wouldn't have been able to sleep on his office couch even that much. Interpol's database had turned up hits on yesterday's other two bodies. The man in the Willard was a Saudi named Mustafa Al-Misham, freed from a German prison three years earlier. He'd been jailed for moving terrorist cash through western Europe. The man killed with Shamiri in Lafayette Square was also Iranian, last seen with militants in Lebanon, according to the CIA's Beirut station. His name was Davoud Dafur.

But it was the information from the cell phone Jack Renfro had retrieved from Shamiri's jacket in Lafayette Square that bothered Tyler Brew the most. It didn't seem to connect to any of the other information on the credenza. Wilson Bryce's report on the phone was brief and puzzling. The device had hardly been used. It had received only seven incoming calls, all from the same blocked number in Tehran. It held not a single text message and had been used to make only one web search and just one outgoing phone call. That call was clicked from a link produced by the lone web search: to the *Trucks and Transportation Department* of the *Potomac Power and Energy Company.*

What a random bunch of information, considered the SEAL admiral. And he thought one other thing. It was time to think like a chameleon.

15

BODY DOUBLES

The public might not appreciate it, but the public itself—and what to tell it—was always a decision point in any terrorism investigation. And it was a decision point that was revisited continually as additional information was obtained. Sometimes special influences came to bear.

A large special influence came to bear in this instance. President Del Winters wanted to go back to the White House.

The media knew she was at Camp David with her father, though all of the reports about how she had been taken there—thanks to Tug Birmingham's well-executed deception—were incorrect. Two body doubles, flanked by military escorts, had waved to the reporters assembled at a distance as they climbed aboard *Marine One* just before the supper hour the day before. Out of view inside the helicopter were five heavily armed Army Rangers, including three snipers. *Off to Camp David*, said the terse White House statement released to the press pool moments earlier. The president had decided to take advantage of the good weather for an unscheduled working break at the presidential retreat, the statement said. The news reports repeated it.

First Father Henry Winters didn't know he even *had* a body double.

"How long has *that* been going on?" he asked Birmingham in the lone armored SUV that tooled away from the side entrance as the helicopter lifted off the lawn.

"I don't know," Tug said. "He was here before I came into the security detail."

"It was really Stanley Bigelow's idea," the president interjected.

Her father turned to her in the seat beside him, his expression quizzical. "Stanley's?"

"Yes. And I thought it was very considerate of him. Since you started inviting him here and going to ball games together, he was concerned about you being out in public so much more. 'You guys are always so worried about me,' he said. 'And nobody even knows who I am. But they know who Henry is. I don't want something to happen to him on my account,' he said. I thought he was right, so I had the detail find a double for you."

"My God," said her father. "And you've used him before?"

"Whenever you and Mr. Bigelow leave the White House," Tug said. "We have one for him too. If anybody *did* follow you guys, they didn't see much baseball."

"Oh my God. Does Stanley know this?"

"No," said the president. "And don't tell him, Dad. Knowing Stanley, he'll feel like he's a burden. Which is nonsense. In fact, we owe it to him."

Since taking office, Del Winters had worked more with the old engineer from Pittsburgh than any other private citizen. His secret work had protected the nation, without public credit or reward. It was she who had introduced Stanley to her father, knowing they both shared an intense interest in baseball and its statistics. She had not initially imagined the deep friendship that would ensue. But she surely welcomed the value she witnessed it bringing to her father, the retired air force general who had raised her as a single father after her mother's early death. The two old gentlemen's backgrounds could not have been more different. But now in the twilight of their years, they shared much, including keen wit, modest temperament, and deep knowledge of their favorite game and bourbons. And, central to their own relationship, Henry saw that Stanley, not a political man, respected his daughter Delores as deeply as he himself loved her.

The four o'clock call between Admiral Brew and the president had been scheduled in advance of the events of the day before. Early that morning, Brew had sent her a secure text: "Multiple killings of middle eastern men near the White House between 1200 and 1800 hours yesterday. No active movements discerned since, but questions remain. Talk at 4 as scheduled."

"I'd like to come back," were the first words of Del Winters when the admiral picked up on the secure line.

"I don't think that would be wise," he said.

"Why? Have you learned something more?"

"It's what we *haven't* learned."

"Tell me more."

Brew told the president about the Ukrainian group in Brooklyn and the mix-up at Nationals Park. All just minutes after the slayings in Lafayette Square.

"I don't see the connection," she said. "Money is moving from Brooklyn to Washington. I'll bet Hannah Harris will tell you she's working three dozen laundering operations right now. And three shootings on a single day in DC? Unfortunately, we've had worse days. Many."

"We don't have three *Middle Eastern men* killed within a thousand yards of the White House every day," Brew said. "With at least *some* terrorism intel on each of them. And we know from the bureau's undercover agent Evan Reese that he had a surprise escort on the train to Washington—also Middle Eastern."

"So you think the money is connected to these killings?"

"I do. So does Jack Renfro." The president knew of the Washington homicide detective from local news stories over the years. "And Renfro's good."

"I've heard that."

"What the end game is, we can't see. Yet. But I think the money is needed for a plan of some kind."

The president and Brew both knew well that terrorist cell groups operated on a cash basis. Sophisticated plots could take months—even years—to arrange and execute. Even for terrorists, there is no such thing as a free lunch. Large sums of cash were needed and had to be easily accessible by cell members to pay for everything from lodging and food to travel, weapons, and bomb-making supplies. The president recalled a briefing in the White House situation room with her national defense and counterterrorism leadership. "What is the deadliest asset the terrorists have?" she had asked.

Tyler Brew answered for the group. "The ATM machine," he said.

"There *is* one advantage to your going back to the White House," he now told the president. "If you do, we don't have to tell the public anything. You could stay tonight and go back tomorrow, and all we have to say is that your break is over, and so you're returning. If you stay for any length of time, we'll have to say something to the press. And I know you won't lie to them."

"You're right, I won't."

"And if there's any hint out there that we're looking at these murders as possibly related to terrorism, the actors will know we are on to them," the admiral said. "Wilson Bryce and his people are great, but they can't get us intel *instantly.* We have at least two actors—the man who traveled to Washington with Reese and whoever killed the two men in Lafayette Square—who are still alive as far as we know. Wilson's people will be trying to find them and reconstruct their movements. It'll be days, at least."

"So it looks like I get my wish," the president said. "I can go home tomorrow."

"I need to say, again, Madame President. In terms of your own safety, it is not the best thing to do. You are safer there."

"I understand that," she said. "Keep me advised."

"Of course."

She hung up with the admiral and dialed Tug Birmingham.

"I'm going back to the White House tomorrow morning, Tug," she said. "But tell my father he is staying here."

"He won't like that."

"It's not negotiable."

But it turned out to be. As soon as Tug told Henry the next morning that his daughter wanted him to stay behind at Camp David, the first father found her in the living room and protested.

"Delores," he said, "I don't want to be stuck out here by myself. If you're safe in Washington, so am I."

The younger general stared into the eyes of the older one. His logic was compelling. She did not want to disappoint him.

Twenty minutes later, they returned to the White House together on *Marine One.*

16

THE DAYS OF BRICK AND MORTAR

The CIA would have preferred normalized diplomatic relations with Iran. Not so much because it would reduce antagonism with the powerhouse of the Middle East. No, the CIA's reasoning was more practical, more parochial. Diplomatic relations would afford the agency with the most valuable physical asset in spy craft and intelligence gathering—an embassy.

It may be that so-called brick-and-mortar is no longer as important in retailing as it once was, what with the growth of internet commerce. But in espionage, you still could not surpass it. An embassy complex provided not only cover for an intelligence workforce but the means to *cover the cover.* Naturally, there were the usual diplomatic attachés in business suits and women's wear, presumed by the host country and other intelligence observers to be thinly veiled espionage operatives. Which of course they were. Only the mildest attempt was made to claim otherwise, as it would be pointless. Since such personnel were routinely monitored and followed, they were essentially confined to the embassy itself for their substantive work, largely analysis of human intelligence gathered by others who could operate more freely, and the large volume of information electronically intercepted by the sophisticated technology housed in the seemingly staid and boring embassy structures.

But the status of the diplomatic attachés as *known ones*, as they were called, paid less obvious dividends. The fact that they were constantly surveilled when outside the embassy grounds was oddly useful. They could be sent—and often were—as decoys for any number of valuable reasons: to make *wooden drops,* for example, usually of envelopes or tubes containing disinformation, deposited in some trash receptacle after a circuitous journey from the embassy. That receptacle, sometimes halfway across the country, was itself being surveilled by other *truly* covert CIA assets from a distance. There was hardly anything more useful than knowing who retrieved such a drop for the other side. Or, in this day and age, other side*s*. "My God," one CIA agent recording such a scene reported, "there are *three* of them almost fighting for it!"

Once identified, these foreign operatives could be monitored too. And who knew? If observed in a compromising situation, perhaps even turned. Over the years, dozens of double agents had been recruited in this way.

But without an embassy, such spy craft was handcuffed. Intelligence gathering was severely limited. The CIA still conducted operations, to be sure, but they were, by necessity, far more complicated and dangerous. Usually they required collaboration with allies on better terms with the Islamic Republic, and often more than one. These operations could not avoid the sharing of US intelligence—at least to some degree. And sharing the CIA was loath to do, even with the closest allies. "Let's face it," said one senior leader in the community. "In the end, we really don't trust *anybody*."

At the moment, the agency's assets in-country in the Islamic Republic of Iran were lean indeed. Only one was classified as a level 1 asset, meaning he or she was trained for active field assignments and had the resources to initiate contact with CIA station chiefs in the region.

The only others—just five in total—were so-called level 2 sources. These were Iranian citizens carefully cultivated over the years to "listen and line" information they came across in their everyday lives. They were enlisted because their occupations placed them in locations where Iranian political, military, and intelligence officers were known to frequent. Hotels. Restaurants. One in a dry-cleaning shop near the Parliament building. If they overheard a military officer say he was meeting with a Syrian or found a ballpoint pen from an Istanbul hotel in a suit brought in for cleaning, they were to pass the information through a secure cell phone line on a special device each kept hidden and used for no other purpose. They were never to solicit information actively; all gathering was to be passive. Just hear what was said, pick up what was left. Don't ask for more. Don't look for more.

In places where large American populations lived, sources at this level could harvest surprising volumes of important information. The CIA had hundreds of them spread across Moscow and China. Their *kernels*, as the station staff called their tip reports, were collated daily. Often the kernels influenced planning and sometimes even triggered specific action. But in a city as expansive as Tehran, the likelihood of important information landing at the feet of one of just five *listen and line* sources was slim indeed.

Call it dumb luck. Call it carelessness. Call it providence. Admiral Tyler Brew didn't care how it came to pass. But when he saw the secure cable from CIA Director Jack Watson, he knew the significance of what it reported:

> Level 2 line in Tehran café reports mention today of Ranni Shamiri by two men. Café near Institute of Advanced Technology and Mechanics. Do you request follow-up and ID of speakers by our field agent there? Watson.

Brew did not make many snap judgments anymore. It was probably the largest difference from his years as a SEAL in the field. On missions, it seemed everything happened at breakneck speed. There, nothing could be held up to the light and studied from all angles.

There was no luxury of a long credenza and lines of data, maps, and reports. But on this message from his friend Jack Watson, his decision was instantaneous.

He called Watson and asked him to move on the men in Tehran as quickly as possible.

"How long will it take you to find out who they are and what they know about Shamiri?" the admiral asked.

"Tyler, those are two very different questions."

"I know."

"Our asset there will be able to identify them and get some detail on what they do and for who. But what they know about Shamiri? We'd need to take them to find that out."

"Exfiltrate them?"

"Yes. And that we'd need help on," the CIA chief said. "Maybe the Turks or the Egyptians, maybe both. And the president would need to authorize it."

"How long to put a mission plan in front of her?"

"It's not easy. I am afraid five days for a plan with preconfirmed resources, ready to execute."

"Please do it, Jack. Just as fast as you can. I'll let her know we'll be coming in."

The admiral hung up and looked down again at the items spread across the credenza. *A hell of a lot can happen in five days,* he thought.

17

ENCOUNTER AT GRAND CENTRAL

When Evan "Evie Rezcepko" Reese stepped off the train at Grand Central Station, he was wearing one thing he had not worn on his trip to Washington and *not* wearing one thing that he had. He wasn't wearing a backpack containing $250,000. He was wearing a wire.

Hannah Harris decided the matter. It was a reversal in assessment. Before this, she had adjudged that a wire on her young agent could kill him. Now, she believed it was needed to keep him alive.

After Admiral Tyler Brew left the midnight meeting at the FBI building on Pennsylvania Avenue, the bureau's financial crimes chief stayed on with Reese and L.T. Kitt to discuss next steps in Brooklyn with the Kievs. Hannah Harris's first impulse was to shut down the undercover operation immediately and move on the syndicate at dawn. She had the justification to do it. She had the resources to do it. But after learning from Admiral Brew about the murders near the White House and the possibility that her money laundering investigation might be intersecting with terrorism, she took a different view. So did Evan Reese.

"I think maybe we can have it both ways," he said to his boss.

"What do you mean?"

"I could go back to Brooklyn with backup," Reese said. "If I'm blown, we should know right away—or damn soon. If I am, we take them then and there. But if I'm not, we keep it going and see what's happening."

"You might be dead before we can get to you."

"That's been true since I first went in there."

She couldn't argue with his statement. It *was* true. And she, Reese, and Kitt all knew that if there was any chance the Kievs' activities were intended to fund a terrorist operation, this was a poor time for caution.

"I'm happy to be part of his backup," L.T. offered.

"Well, I know you can tackle," Reese said.

Hannah Harris was not as humored. But she did appreciate the agents' courage. "All right," she said. "L.T., take the train to New York with Evan. I'll put together teams in the city. One to move with you from Grand Central to Brooklyn. Another one in place at the Kievs' diner in Brighton Beach. At the first sign of trouble, Evan, the *first* sign, they're coming in. Your charge code is *rush.*" She meant the verbal signal Reese should send if he needed rescue.

"So I'll be wired?"

"Absolutely. Kitt, too, and everybody else."

When the Amtrak from Washington was two minutes out from Grand Central the next morning, Kitt left her seat beside Reese and waited near the door. Hannah Harris had already sent the names and photos of the five New York bureau agents who would join her as the security team to protect their undercover—they hoped *still* undercover—colleague. As the train rolled in slowly, she recognized two of the agents, leaning at posts thirty feet apart on the platform. She presumed the others were positioned in the main station lobby or on the street at the agreed exit to East Forty-Second Street.

Reese had texted Yuri in Russian at seven that morning. He said he would be back in New York by noon and would go directly to the Brooklyn cellar. In his text, he said only that the drop at Nationals Park had been "difficult."

Yuri had not answered.

Reese stepped off the train, L.T. Kitt following just a few paces behind. She purposely carried two backpacks stuffed with newspaper, one slung over each shoulder. It widened her path and allowed her to keep other passengers from moving too close. She glanced at the two agents straddling the path up to the main floor, and they joined in laterally on either flank. By arrangement, they all took the stairs. Escalators were always to be avoided in an escort. They were slow, and personal movement was far too restricted in the event of attack. At the top of the stairs, Reese paused, and Kitt stepped in front of him. It was planned. The flanking agents took three steps forward and stopped too. Reese panned the half of the lobby nearest to them to see if any Kiev, or the Middle Easterner who had tagged him on the train the day before, was advancing. He saw no one. "Green," he said quietly into his wire. The group began moving again, and Kitt resumed her position behind him.

In an unmarked sedan parked on the street outside, Hannah Harris listened anxiously. Across the dashboard and on the passenger seat lay photos of the known Kiev members—the same grainy shots that Reese had used in the Brooklyn employment agency to recognize his new employer five months earlier. A yellow cab slanted in from the street and parked directly in front of her. The driver and two other men climbed out. She immediately recognized the tallest man, known only as "Yuri." She glanced at the photo array. One of the others appeared in the lineup. Yuri extended his arms to stretch, raising them high above his head. Hanna saw the Glock semiautomatic pistol strapped to his belt beneath his light windbreaker.

"Kievs coming in," she said into the wire. "Three in all. One is Yuri. He's got a Glock."

The two agents flanking Reese moved quickly forward to opposite sides inside the main entrance from East Forty-Second. They drew their weapons but concealed them in their jackets. Hannah Harris, who hadn't taken firearms practice in over a year, hurriedly grabbed a gun from the glovebox of her sedan and followed the three men into the terminal.

Grand Central was quintessential Grand Central at lunchtime.

In addition to the usual throng of passengers and families milling around schedule boards and ticket kiosks, hundreds of Manhattan office workers were striding through in all directions, taking shortcuts to favorite eateries, all to the sound of constant arrival and departure announcements blaring from the loudspeakers. Reese saw Yuri across the floor, moving directly toward him with his usual long, muscular gait. He tried to make eye contact with the Ukrainian, but Yuri had not seen him yet. *Should I stop?* Evan asked himself. *Should I stand my ground? No,* he thought. *Standing still and waiting for him would seem defensive, unnatural. No, just keep walking to him. If he says nothing when he reaches you,* he told himself, *greet him as if it's just another day at the office. Unless there is rage in his eyes. If there is rage in his eyes, send the charge code.*

Evan forced a smile to his face and trained his eyes on Yuri's as the two strode toward each other. It was maddening to Reese that the syndicate leader still had not recognized him. At fifty feet, there was still no eye contact. A family with a double stroller crossed between them. They would be upon each other in ten seconds, perhaps less. *Maybe he is avoiding my eyes on purpose,* Evan thought. *Maybe he knows damn well he's walking right to me.*

"Can you tell anything?" Hannah Harris asked through the wire. "Should we just take them now?"

"Not yet. Hold," Reese said.

Only an instant later, Yuri's eyes met Reese's. But before Reese could take their measure, another young family crossed in front of the Ukrainians. The father was holding a young boy in a canvas pouch hung over his chest. The child looked to be only a year old or so. Yuri's eyes diverted to the young boy's. The big Ukrainian raised one arm in Reese's direction, as if in simple acknowledgment, and leaned his face down toward the child. He was smiling broadly. "Oh, what a beautiful boy!" he exclaimed. "You must be proud daddy," he said to the father, who seemed neither alarmed nor surprised. It had probably happened three times already merely crossing the terminal. "Thank you," was all the father said as the family moved on.

The tension left Reese instantly. Whatever else Yuri might be, he was not an actor. He had been sincerely taken by the handsome child. He was *not* in a livid mood. And even more telling, Reese knew Yuri was far too intelligent a criminal to engage any citizen, much less a family, moments before a fracas. No, Reese now knew, his own cover was *somehow* intact.

"Evie, my Evie!" Yuri greeted him. He embraced Reese so firmly that the agent feared his wire might be sensed or even disabled. "You are safe! You did well!"

"I am not even sure of everything that happened," Evan said. Oddly, it was the truth.

"*No one* knows everything, but you succeeded in making the delivery! Even when attacked by the police!"

"How do you know this, Yuri?" Evan asked. "You didn't know the police were coming for me, did you?"

Hannah Harris had stepped a safe distance to the side and listened. Her agent was clever and cool in a situation that could not be practiced in advance. She was pleased but still uncertain that he could leave safely with the three Kievs.

"*No,* Evie, of course not!" Yuri said. "It was not *our* fault the police came. It was not your fault either. The customer must have been careless. Someone from the customer must have done something that tipped the Washington police. They were watching the seats. They called the baseball team—what do they call them?"

"The Nationals."

"The Nationals. The police called them before the game and asked to put a detective in the stands. Somehow the customer learned this. He didn't say why, but the customer's messenger said it was to arrest you with the money. He said two policewomen jumped on you. Hurt you. Look how they hurt you!" The tall Ukrainian touched Reese's forehead tenderly, avoiding his stitched wound. "But you managed to hand off the money anyway! He said the police took you away. That is why he called me. He asked if you would talk—could we trust you? I told him, 'Evie? Evie is good boy and loyal.' But I was afraid, Evie.

Afraid we'd lost you. How *did* you get them to release you?" Yuri looked Evan right in the eye.

"They didn't have anything on me," Reese said. "At first, I didn't know what was happening. I thought maybe some fans had gotten in a fight and fallen on me. But then they showed me badges. But by then, the money was gone. I told them I didn't know anything about any money. Eventually, they let me go."

"The customer has its money, Evie. *That* is what matters. You succeeded. And you are safe."

Reese decided to take a chance.

"This customer," he said. "Who *is* this customer?"

The question removed the smile from Yuri's face.

"Evie, why ask that question?" He wore the expression of a disapproving uncle. Reese had the sense not to repeat the question or even try to justify it.

"I am sorry, Yuri. I know my place." Supplication can have unexpected benefits; sometimes it prompts new information.

"Besides," Yuri said, "we never get to really talk to this customer. Only messengers. A different messenger each time, Middle Eastern guys. Like the guy who showed up and went with you on the train. We never saw him before. And the guy who called to tell me you were attacked by police at the stadium. I don't know who *he* was. Except he didn't sound Middle Eastern like the others. He just sounded like an old man." The Ukrainian patted Evan's shoulder twice, the second touch coming inches from the wire running down from his clavicle. "But we have our share of the money. And we have our Evie! So it matters nothing to me."

The three Kievs and Evie Rezcepko walked toward the main exit to East Forty-Second Street. "We brought over your cab, Evie. You drive us back."

The FBI backup team watched from the entrance as the four men climbed into the taxi, Reese into the driver's seat. Yuri sat in the back seat behind him. The agents saw the big man rustle in his seat and reach up over Reese's right shoulder.

"Evie," the team heard Yuri say through the wire. "After this, you should carry a gun. Here. This is for you." He handed up another Glock with a belt holster.

"Thank you, Yuri," Evan said into the wire. "Thanks to all of you."

In the driver-side mirror, he saw L.T. Kitt nod.

PART TWO

18

COVER INTACT

Hannah Harris waited to call Admiral Brew until Reese checked in that evening. She wanted to be sure he was safe—that the welcoming party at Grand Central was not a ruse. But when her undercover agent phoned on schedule from his dingy flat in Queens, exhausted but healthy, she knew she had to let the counterterrorism chief know.

"The lid is still on," she told the admiral.

"Amazing."

"I had my doubts at Grand Central," Hannah said, recounting the tension in the train station encounter. "But he spent the whole afternoon with them. They didn't search him or find the wire. Instead, they gave him a gun to protect himself!"

"Did you record what was said on the wire?"

"Of course."

"I'd like it."

"Of course. I'll send you the audio file right now."

"Good. Maybe we can make something out of what the Kiev said. At least get his voice over to the NSA. They may find it on intercepted overseas calls. They pull down hundreds every day."

"I didn't think of that. I guess I didn't even know that."

"Keep it to yourself. There are still people who don't like that to happen. Even the bureau restricts it to the counterterrorism unit unless they have to let it out to field agents. Only in an emergency."

"Of course."

"Did your man keep his wire?" Brew asked. He thought it likely Reese had ditched it. No one could blame him if he had. He was a dead man if found wearing it.

"He put it in a post office box near his apartment in Queens," Hannah Harris said. "Said he thought it might come in handy again."

"Smart young man you have there. I like him."

"Me too. Let's keep him alive."

19

SPLICING TIME

While Jack Watson scrambled his operatives at Langley for an immediate rendition plan for the loose-lipped tea drinker in Tehran, Wilson Bryce at the NSA was doing everything he could to reconstruct the prior movements of the three men slain near the White House and the movements before and after of whoever had slain them. It was reverse engineering of the cyber kind. There was footage from a dozen closed-circuit surveillance cameras. There were feeds from the military satellites that kept the heart of US government real estate under 24/7 review. Even commercial satellite imagery, whether its owners knew it or not, was available to the NSA.

The problem was not too little data; the problem was too much. A major complication was the fact that the cameras and recording electronics in the devices and satellites were not uniform. Far from it. Security electronics were no different from other high-tech devices: they were being upgraded and changed almost before the last model could be installed. Image definition, color, and shading of the same six-foot square of ground—and perhaps the individuals standing on it—could appear strikingly dissimilar on different devices.

"We're still working through a lot more imagery," Bryce said as he set up his equipment in the Pentagon conference room. "We don't have anything for you yet on the Willard Hotel murder or Agent Reese's mystery escort to Washington. But we *do* have this. The killings in Lafayette Square."

"How long for the rest?" the admiral asked.

"I wish I could tell you. At least a couple of days. It hasn't been easy."

"I understand, Wilson."

"The hardest part is the time splicing," Bryce said.

"*Time splicing*?" Brew asked. He had never heard the term. It was always this way when the Navy SEAL admiral met with his go-to technology adviser. About one in five words out of Wilson Bryce's mouth flew over Brew's head like a cruise missile.

"Yeah," said Bryce. "You know how if you're in a room and everybody's got an iPhone, everyone will have the *exact same time* if they hit the home button?"

"Yeah?"

"Well, these aren't iPhones. They're all over the frickin' place on timing and sequence. So every stream is broken up, like cut wires. We have to splice them together to make sense of them and get the best clarity. No single feed will give you as complete an image as a consolidation of all feeds, so we always combine them. But with the timing differences, it's easy to make an error. And if you do, it gets compounded by the next splice. Before long, the whole reconstruction is *way* off. Understand?"

"I guess so," Brew lied. Time was of the essence, and he trusted completely the knowledge and skill of Wilson Bryce. After all, Bryce was the brainiac who needed to understand the science; Brew didn't. He judged it best to just nod and move on. Or, in this case, look up at the screen.

Bryce stood beside the large monitor with a remote and a laser pointer.

"Here's Shamiri and Dafur walking in the square just before they were killed," Bryce narrated. "Jack Renfro was right. There it is … one shooter, and Dafur is shot first, from behind at close range. We calculated it from triangulated images. Fifty-three inches."

"Why is the film so jumpy?" Brew asked.

"I just told you."

"Oh yeah. *Time splicing*."

The NSA scientist sent the admiral a dubious expression—half smile, half exasperation—and then continued. His fondness and respect for Brew far outweighed the irritation that working with the sailor sometimes occasioned. He knew acutely how the Navy SEAL had repeatedly risked his life in the service of the president and the country. Bryce knew also that two of those missions had saved the life of the old civilian engineer Stanley Bigelow and how Brew had relied in those dangerous rescues in large part on surveillance information he himself had developed for him. Not that he had any choice, but Wilson Bryce had all the time in the world for Tyler Brew.

"Like Renfro thought," Bryce went on as the video rolled, "Shamiri turns and stops after the first shot. The killer takes one more step toward him. Shoots him in the face."

The reconstructed film zoomed in as the shooter stepped first to the accomplice lying facedown, all of his pants pockets exposed. But then the assassin erred. Brew and his team would later believe that the assassin's simple mistake at that moment may have made all the difference in the events to come. As the killer stood over Dafur, the edge of an object was plainly visible, even in the grainy images, extending slightly from the right-side front pocket of the victim. But the assailant stooped to the *left-side* pockets and searched them first. Ten seconds elapsed as he yanked out their contents: a folded Metro train schedule in the rear pocket and two coins from the front one. He dropped it all to the ground. Then he stepped over the body, knelt, and retrieved the device protruding from the *right front* pocket. The film zoomed yet closer. Clearly a cell phone.

The assailant started toward the body of Shamiri. Suddenly, he turned and stood straight up. An alarmed look came over his face.

"Look at what happens now," Bryce said. "We configured a different line of sight so you can see it better. Even without audio, it's pretty obvious."

The new stream came on the monitor, showing the view from behind the assailant and into the public square. A man in a business suit was carrying a briefcase on a sidewalk running through the small park. He was shouting toward the assassin.

"He's forty-six feet away," Bryce said.

The man dropped his briefcase and ran across the grass toward the killer.

"Brave man," said Admiral Brew.

The killer turned and began to race away. Then he stopped, as if to return to Shamiri's body. The well-dressed civilian continued to shout and waved his arms to draw the attention of others. The killer looked at him with searing eyes, then ran into the twilight.

"*That's* how Renfro found the phone on Shamiri," Brew said. "The shooter intended to get both of their phones, but the witness ran him off."

"Because the killer took too long finding the first phone."

"Do we know who this witness is?" Brew asked.

"Renfro and Sanderson are looking for him. We've got his face here, but I'm thinking he won't show up in any criminal databases. The only face recognition we can do on government employees are all law enforcement. And he's not that or he would have come forward already."

Brew knew from his long military experience that witnesses to violence were often reluctant to report it. There were many reasons. In the field, he had seen cases where witnesses to torture or intimidation were so traumatized or fearful that they could not bring themselves to revisit it. Sometimes forever. And he knew more than a few brave soldiers who, after acting heroically themselves, wanted nothing to do with the after-action report, even where it would mean commendation.

"Well, I don't know what more he could tell us than we can see anyway right here," the admiral said. "The only thing I'd say to him if we did find him is thank you."

"If you want," the NSA expert said, "I could probably do a reconstruct on *him*. Maybe follow him to a car or an apartment."

"On a citizen who just wants to be left alone?" Brew's tone was not pejorative, and Wilson Bryce did not take it as such. "No, he did his duty. God love 'em. Leave him be, Wilson."

20

EVEN A RICH TERRORIST CAN'T BUY HAPPINESS

Raspy-voiced Balish Behzani sat on the patio of his tall apartment building in the affluent northern district of Tehran known as Elahieh. He was not a happy terrorist.

Just a day earlier, his mood was much better. Still hateful but much better. His carefully orchestrated plan was coming together pleasingly. It had been long in the making, nearly two years, in fact. It had many moving parts, as such plots do, and many opportunities for failure. But he had so skillfully managed every step, so wisely chosen every human asset, that the plan was executing flawlessly.

Until last night.

Of course, he had always known that something would not go just right. But he had assumed it would be something minor, even trifling. An asset in the US would misplace his ATM card, delaying a purchase by a day or two. Or one of the money launderers would get greedy. Perhaps he would demand a larger percentage of the moving money and threaten to notify the authorities if his demand was not met. In such case, an extra murder might have to be added to the plan. More likely, the construction and field testing of the nerve agent apparatus would prove more difficult than hoped. Parts might fail, designs might require adaptation and retesting. There was already one report of this from the American field. After all, the original designs were Russian, and everyone knew about Russian engineering.

But all of those things were easily correctable. Time, money, or murder would solve any of them. What had happened last night, though, was a different kind of problem.

Behzani's agent had called from Washington Dulles at the designated hour. As soon as the Tehran mastermind heard his voice, he knew something had gone awry.

"Is it done?" Behzani asked.

"Yes, they are done," the agent said. "They are dead."

"Good. But is *everything* done?"

"Not everything."

"What is *not* done?"

"I have only one of the cell phones."

Silence fell. Long silence.

"Balish!" the agent said. "Are you still there?"

"I am still here, my brother," Behzani said finally. He was burning with anger, but his low voice and slow, raspy monotone did not show it. "But I am not happy, my brother. Allah is not happy. How do you not have both phones?"

"I have Davoud's. But there were people in the park. Before I could take Shamiri's, I was seen. An American was running to me. He was near. Others would be coming. He was shouting. I saw police around too."

Silence fell again.

Finally, the agent spoke. "What are my orders now, Balish?"

"Return through Istanbul. Then come to me here."

"To your home?"

"Yes. Call from the airport and again from the lobby of the building. Bring Davoud's phone."

"I am sorry, Balish."

"Just come to me, my brother. We will have tea."

21

WHITE HOUSE MANNERS

First Father General Henry Winters (USAF Ret.) was leaving his daughter in the Oval Office as Admiral Tyler Brew entered at seven thirty in the morning. The president and Henry ate breakfast together more or less daily in the residence above the east wing of the White House. But this day, she had risen early to prepare for the urgent meeting Admiral Brew had requested, to include the CIA director Jack Watson and—curiously to her—two members of the Metropolitan Police Department. She had left a note for her father on the kitchen table upstairs.

"Come on down, if you're up before 7:30."

Henry was, but barely. He would have only fifteen minutes with his daughter. He probably couldn't get past the front page of the *New York Times*, his daily morning read. He was slightly irritated by the rush. He knew he shouldn't be. He was conscious of the inner conflicts subtly advancing as he aged. On the one hand, he could not help but feel gratitude for all of the good that had come to him in his eighty-three years: a long and satisfying military career; travel to every part of the world, in war and in peace; and especially the kindness and attention of the successful daughter he had raised alone. But on the other, he could not help resenting sometimes the frequent impingements on his time with her. It wasn't that he worried about dying and losing all time with her. He was in perfect health, and he knew it; his continued vibrancy in late age may even have added to his conflictual feelings. He felt he had so much more to say to her. He had the desire and the capacity to continue to be a father, even now, maybe more so now. *Give me time with her!* he silently urged.

"General!" Admiral Brew greeted him in the doorway. "How are you this morning?"

"Happy that you deigned I could come back." He was, after all, feeling a little irritated.

"You know, Henry, that was not my decision. Your daughter was not comfortable with your safety just then."

"And three days later, all is well in the world?"

Tyler Brew smiled. "We both know that is something we can never say."

Henry softened.

"I know you are doing well for the country and my daughter."

"L.T. Kitt tells me she sees Stanley Bigelow here in Washington with you," Brew said. "How is Stanley doing?"

"Oh, Stanley," Henry said. "That man is the best thing you ever did for me. If you hadn't brought him into that secret weapons building project years ago, I would never have met him! Though, I understand you were reluctant about him back then."

"Well, in the beginning, yes. He was very big and overweight. And I guess I thought a little too old. But I love him now. You know that. He's done remarkable work so quickly, never wanting any credit. Frankly, General, I think his friendship with you is what he considers his reward."

"Well, you might be understating his rewards with Helen. She is a remarkable woman." Helen Ames was the reserves colonel introduced to the widower Stanley by Brew himself in the course of the old engineer's first covert project.

"They are happy in their marriage?" Brew asked.

"Excessively."

The general moved away from the door, carrying his folded newspaper and his china coffee cup, still half-full. He hadn't had time to finish it with his daughter inside. Tyler Brew saluted him and walked into the Oval Office.

The CIA chief was already seated on one of the couches in front of the president's desk. Del Winters brought her coffee from the desk, greeted the admiral, and sat next to the spy master. "The others you invited are out there waiting, but I wanted a word with you two first," she said. "Coffee?"

"When the others come in. Thanks," said Brew.

"I was wondering why we are involving the local police in this," she said. "A bit unusual, isn't it?"

"Yes, but in this case, I think they are useful. And needed."

"I do too," offered Jack Watson.

"Instead of the FBI?"

"In addition to the FBI," Brew said.

"Agreed," Watson said.

"Why? Doesn't it risk leaks? We can't really supervise them. There are limits to DHS authority over them as local law enforcement. Their cooperation is voluntary."

"We can trust this man Jack Renfro and his detective Sanderson," Brew said. "They've agreed to keep the work walled off from everyone else in the department. I believe them. And there are things they can look at easier than we can. Without drawing notice."

"From the media?" the president asked.

"From the players in this thing as we learn about them. Plus, Renfro's instincts are keen. Everything he's theorized so far has turned out to be right as the video reconstructions come in. Dead on."

"Poor choice of words, Tyler," the president said, more relaxed. "Fine, then." She nodded to the navy officer standing at the open door. "Bring them in, Lieutenant."

As the three waited for the DC homicide detectives, the president asked about Wilson Bryce, the NSA technology guru. She knew he was masterminding the surveillance data.

"Did you invite Wilson?" she asked Brew.

"Yes, but you know Wilson," the admiral replied. "No ego, all dedication. Says he's up to his ears working on the rest of the reconstructions. Of course, he sends his regards." All three of them nodded in appreciation, as if they hoped Bryce could hear and see them. They knew how coveted invitations to the Oval Office were. It was almost unheard of to turn one down.

Jack Renfro entered first, Audrey Sanderson behind him. It didn't occur to Renfro that protocol urged an immediate greeting to the president. He was taken aback and nervous to be there. He stopped just inside the room and looked around it slowly. The aging detective was not trim. The button on his sport coat was strained, the lapels pushed up and out. His collar wings protruded for want of stays around his loosely knotted tie. Audrey Sanderson, thirty years his junior, was relaxed, smiling, gently excited. And she seemed to understand protocol.

"Madame President," she said. "I'm Audrey Sanderson of Metropolitan Homicide. Thank you for having us."

"Oh, oh, yes," Renfro recovered, unbuttoning his jacket and improving his posture. "Madame President, Jack Renfro. Same," he said.

"The honor is mine," Del Winters said. She remained standing and did not motion them to the sofas. "I like to be as open as I can. I just discussed your involvement with Admiral Brew and Director Watson. They assured me you are talented and needed. And trustworthy with the secrecy of this investigation."

"Of course," said Renfro. "We want to be helpful, and we understand our role."

Tyler Brew began. He said the meeting with the president was intended to provide her with all that was known to date and for one tactical decision involving great risk.

"You already know the basic concerns," Brew said.

"Assume I don't," she replied. It was characteristic of Del Winters. She never presented herself as omniscient or superior. She gave respect in the same measure as she expected it. She and Brew were similar in that way, and it was one of the reasons they worked so well together. They wanted to *hear* everything, *listen* to everything, without presumption or premature judgment.

The admiral explained that the continuing assessments developed by his counterterrorism analysts studying Wison Bryce's data were leaning more each day to a finding that some kind of organized attack was in late-stage preparation. It probably was intended for a Washington target, but that was not yet clear. Year-old phone intercepts from overseas had indicated that future attacks in the US might involve decoy operations to throw off discovery.

"But if these men last week were preparing an attack, and they're already here to carry it out, why are they murdered before they can do it?" the president asked.

"Because they were never the ones intended to carry it out," Brew said. "They were all just enablers. Place setters. In the end, martyrs."

"Though they probably didn't know that part," Jack Watson said. "And probably knew only a small part of the plot itself. Their specific assignment, nothing more."

Brew asked Jack Renfro what he thought.

"I think these people watch the movies. I really do. This thing is a throwback to old mob takeover wars. We called them 'sweep ups.' Everything is designed to be sure that no one can get caught who can lead to a better understanding of what is going down. And they can't get caught if you murder them first. Watch. When we get the images on the first killing at the Willard, we'll see it was Shamiri and Dafur who did it. I'd bet on it. Then *they're* exterminated a few hours later in Lafayette Square. The guy who was sent with the FBI undercover agent on the train. He may have been sent over to kill them in the park. If he is, I wouldn't sell him any life insurance either."

"What's the end game of these *sweep ups*?" asked the president.

"To kill a person at the top."

Jack Renfro liked to be open too. Even if it wasn't protocol.

"Like you," he said.

The president was neither startled nor displeased.

"We live with that threat every day," she said flatly. "But thank you anyway, Detective." She turned to Watson. "What is this tactical decision you have?"

"One of the men killed in the square is an Iranian national." *Is.* It seemed that dead suspects had a certain shelf life before reaching *was.* "Former Iranian intelligence, maybe halfway up. Ranni Shamiri. Last couple of years, he fell out of the normal channels. Our stations over there stopped seeing him. They think he radicalized, and it cost him his job. The truth is that leadership in Tehran doesn't want extremists on its streets any more than we do. We think they booted him, and he got involved in this thing here somehow."

"You're positive on the ID?" Del Winters asked. "You're *sure* it was Shamiri that was killed?" Ah. The president moved the terrorist to *was.*

"Positive," said the CIA chief. "But we've got no intelligence on what he was doing here. How was he connected to the man killed with him, or the first one in the hotel? Then we picked up a lead from a ground source in Tehran. Purely fortuitous. We hadn't yet put out an order to listen for Shamiri. But an asset we have in a café there reports in that she heard a well-to-do tea drinker mention a man named Shamiri and Washington in the same sentence."

"When?"

"Twelve hours after the murders. The next morning, in Tehran."

"And you know who this man is?"

"Yes. He's a regular at the café. Our informant got a name from a coworker. Balish Behzani. We know where he lives."

"And what do you know about him? I don't recognize the name," the president said.

"I didn't either," Brew said. "He's new to us. So far, all we know is he's wealthy." Those facts alone were cause for concern, the president knew. The intelligence nets of Tyler Brew, Jack Watson, and the NSA were so wide that it had been rare in recent years that emerging terrorists were totally unknown even when first encountered. Cell signals, voices, and names used in intercepted calls—even when logged years earlier—were constantly cross-referenced and matched. A new player like this, especially a wealthy one, was worrisome, to say the least. "We're trying to learn about him now. We've put a dozen analysts on it."

"So what do you want to do with the information you do have?" the president asked.

But Del Winters thought she probably knew. In years past, the CIA was only loosely supervised on tactical decisions relating to covert field operations. Senior leaders in the agency—or *the company* as insiders called it—were authorized to approve even high-risk actions, such as physical renditions or forced infiltrations into buildings. The decision tree was much different now. Since the global furor over the brutal 2018 murder in Turkey of the dissident Saudi journalist Jamal Khashoggi by intelligence agents sent by his own country, the reigns were tightened, even in the US. Presidential sign-off was now required for the exfiltration of any foreigner unless that foreigner was acting in the service of the company.

"We want to take him and find out what he knows," Watson said.

"In the middle of Tehran?"

"Actually, not in the middle. Which helps. He lives up in the rich northern part of the city, Elahieh. It's like Dubai with a mountain view. Luxury retail and high-rise residences. High rollers."

"How does that make it easier?" the president asked.

"Not the red tape of the government district. It's a civilian area without a military presence. We can take a team in as maintenance men. Foul his air-conditioning remotely so his security isn't surprised when they show up. We have only one capable operative in-country, but we can slide in help from Jordan and Egypt. We take him just after dark and move him in a stealth chopper from the roof. Up to the mountains."

Del Winters listened dispassionately, then leaned back on the sofa. "Tyler," she said. "Your view?" She trusted the Navy SEAL commander implicitly. He combined bravery with temperance like no one she had ever known.

"I'm not keen on it."

"Why?" asked Watson, surprised. After all, it was Brew who had asked him to prepare a take-out plan.

"How do we keep it from blowing this up into an international incident?" Brew asked. "If we had more to go on, some proof that a plot is actually underway and this guy in Tehran is behind it, we could defend it. Even coordinate with Iranian intelligence and military before we grab him, or when we are, so they're not totally blindsided. But we're not there yet. Not even close."

Jack Renfro leaned toward the president. "Madame President, may I?" His protocol was improving.

"Of course."

"There is more we and the FBI are going to learn right here. The money laundering is connected somehow. What's with this Chandler Bowes guy at Nationals Park? We'll find out. And so far, the Kievs are not getting killed. That means something. Probably that they don't know enough to need killing. But that could be an opportunity. We can learn what they're learning from these messengers. Who knows? Maybe they will even help us. These Ukrainians are more and more Americanized. Most of them have green cards. They like it here. They're thugs, but they're not terrorists."

"Interesting," said Watson.

"I agree," said Brew.

"Well," said the president, "how you investigate *here* is your business. Do what you think is best. But I don't want to go into Tehran. At least not yet."

The navy lieutenant knocked at the door.

"Madame President, the admiral has a call," he said. "It's Wilson Bryce from the NSA."

"Put him through on the speaker," Del said. "Tell him who's on the line."

Everyone rose and moved to the president's desk to listen.

"We have something from the phone found on Shamiri," Bryce said.

"The calls?" Brew asked.

"Yes, the incoming."

"I thought you said they were all from a blocked number."

"To us, Admiral, there's no such thing as a blocked number."

The president gave a silent *heaven help us* look. "So, what have you found?" she asked.

"There were seven calls to that phone over a three-day period. The last one was made at 5:54 PM local time the day of the hotel murder and received not far from the hotel."

"How close?" Brew asked.

"Damn near it. Maybe just next door."

"The Occidental?"

"Maybe."

"And where did the call come from?"

"Tehran. No doubt about it."

"What about content?"

"We're working on it."

22

A DEAD END. LITERALLY

Not even Jack Renfro saw this one coming.

He was sure that Chandler Bowes, the concessions head at Nationals Park, would lead the investigation somewhere. He had taken Renfro's call on the first day, helping to place Audrey Sanderson in a vendor's uniform at the game that night. He was cooperative and polite and clearly in contact—one way or another—with the Brooklyn Kievs. He had to be a player in the money moves. Hannah Harris and her undercover agent, Reese, were on the same page.

"Stadium concessions and money laundering?" Harris had told Renfro. "Perfect fit. Even with credit cards these days, there's more cash at sporting events than anyplace else. And they make multiple cash deposits to banks—large deposits—even *during* the event to keep the cash from growing too big."

There was no way to know how it all came in at the game or in what denominations. The deposits used to be comprised mostly of five- and ten-dollar bills. But with prices today and merchandise sales, the deposits were commonly stuffed with hundreds too.

"We don't make money on the players," one baseball owner once quipped. "We make money on the fans wanting to *look* like the players."

Reese was sure that it was Chandler Bowes, in the middle of the chaos in row 2, who had uttered the confirming message as the intended recipient of the drop. Even though he knew too that Bowes had run from the row without the backpack, he believed, like Renfro and Hannah Harris, that the concessions manager had to be a part of the laundering scheme. Surely Chandler Bowes would lead them forward.

But it turned out to be a dead end. For Chandler Bowes, literally.

His body was found in a storage room of the parking garage attached to Nationals Park. He'd been strangled with a ligature. He had not been seen at the stadium offices since the Pirates game five nights earlier, but his absence had not triggered concern; he was not expected to be in anyway. He was supposed to attend a tradeshow in San Diego, his assistant told Renfro and Sanderson. It was the largest purchasing event of the year; he never missed it, she said. She'd booked him on a red-eye to California, leaving after the Pirates game. This year, his show itinerary was particularly hectic; more supplier meetings than usual, as the Nationals were contemplating a small modification of the team logo and new products. Even his wife was not alarmed when she couldn't reach him by his third day away. He had warned her he would be frantically busy. If the windbreaker manufacturer from Taiwan had not called Bowes's assistant yesterday to say he had not showed for an important meeting, he might still be missing.

"What do you make of this?" asked Sanderson. She and Renfro stood with the medical examiner in the parking garage. Renfro was turning in a slow circle, looking up and around the concrete columns and steel beams, hoping for cameras.

"I've always thought these guys were sweeping," he said. "But I didn't think they'd use such a wide broom."

It was plainly an execution. Bowes's wrist still carried an expensive watch, and his wallet was untouched. Only his cell phone was taken.

"Why are you surprised?" asked Audrey. "The other players are all getting killed to keep them silent. Why wouldn't they kill him?"

"The others were killed because their jobs were finished. No other roles. They were just liabilities anymore."

"You think Chandler Bowes was different?"

"I do. At least he was meant to be."

"How so?"

"He was supposed to be a regular money drop. Probably the big money drop, from what Reese says. Whoever is running this thing sends a messenger to make the arrangement with the Kievs. 'Take it here, take it there, here's the code word.' The Kievs follow the instruction. But the masterminds have to break the connection between the instruction and the delivery. So they kill the messenger. And messengers are cheap. They can find them anyplace. The next delivery gets a new one. And on and on." The stocky detective crouched to see an exit sign illuminating a stairwell down the aisle. Good. *At least one camera*, he thought. "But a good money drop—a guy like Chandler Bowes here—is reusable. Valuable. He could take out a fortune through the concessions in this place."

A pained look came over Renfro's face, contrition-like.

"No," he said, "you don't kill an asset like Chandler Bowes. Unless you *have* to."

"So why did they have to?"

"Because I called him."

23
THE ALTOONA CURVE

Stanley Bigelow and Helen Ames took their drinks to the balcony of their residence overlooking the wide Allegheny River in downtown Pittsburgh. The view was breathtaking. The hills across the river were carpeted in lush green. Recreational boats cruised below them, sending swirling wakes. Five o'clock. Seventy-three degrees. The hint of a breeze. Good bourbon. Two people in love.

"Are you still going to Washington this weekend?" asked Helen. "I'll be at Wright-Patterson anyway." Helen was still enjoying her reserve service in the Army Corps of Engineers. She had brought to the balcony a folder of drawings the base had sent for her to review at the Dayton air base with the younger engineers.

"That's the plan," Stanley said. "As long as Henry is back from Camp David."

"What are they doing there anyway? They don't usually go there during the week, do they? Did you ask him?"

"I did. He couldn't say."

"Couldn't or *wouldn't*?"

"Couldn't. But he didn't seem pleased about it."

Stanley's cell phone tinged.

"Yeah," he answered. "Yeah … yeah …" Helen knew from his manner that the call must be from his office. CSB Engineering was still thriving under his part-time guidance. His team knew he enjoyed limited assignments and consulting projects that could be completed rapidly. They called with a few each month. "All right, text me the address. I'll go out and look at it tomorrow," Stanley said. He ended the call.

"Something new?" asked Helen.

"Nothing major. Somebody called in looking for help on an underground propulsion system for fracking. It's not working. 'Out in the field,' as they say. Sounds like fun. I can take Augie along." The German shepherd was lying on his front paws in the main room, six feet from the closed sliding door to the balcony. He heard Stanley and immediately raised his head.

"Where?"

"Exciting Altoona! Altoona, Pennsylvania!"

"Oh, brother," moaned Helen. She knew there was Minor League Baseball in Altoona. It was a two-hour drive from Pittsburgh, due east into the Pennsylvania heartland. She hoped he wouldn't stay late for a night game and take the country roads home.

"Don't worry." Stanley smiled. "I know what you're thinking. I won't stay for a ball game. I need to get back anyway. I'm going to see Henry the next day. At least, I hope I am."

24

HOPE OFTEN MAKES A FOOL

Balish Behzani's operative—the one he called "my brother"—followed his instruction and returned without delay to Tehran, via Istanbul. The trip was long, and the asset was traveling on little sleep. He had been in Washington at Behzani's bidding just three days, hardly enough to shake the jet lag from the journey over, much less this double dose.

Tea in Balish's opulent apartment sounded soothing.

Of course, he never had it.

When he arrived by taxi at the luxury building in Elahieh, Behzani's security chief was waiting for him with a kind smile outside the entrance.

"Magid!" the brother called to him. "Thank you for greeting me!"

"Welcome, my brother," Magid said. "Balish is waiting for you! To welcome you too."

But Balish Behzani had a demented notion of hospitality. His security man Magid escorted the operative to the elevator.

"Davoud's phone? You have it?" he asked.

"Oh, yes." The tired traveler fished it from his jacket and handed it over.

The elevator door opened, and the two men stepped in. At the guard's demand on the close button, the door quickly shut. Things went south from there for the returning brother. Directly south, to the basement.

Somewhere in his mind, the doomed operative must have known. He had hoped that his loyalty would protect him; hoped his departure from America without detection would save him from martyrdom; hoped that Balish's low, slow, kind voice on the phone meant forgiveness for his error. But somewhere in his mind, he must have known too that hope, while a great virtue, often makes a fool.

When the elevator door opened in the basement garage, a black Mercedes sedan awaited immediately outside it, trunk lid up. The traveler did not resist. His body went slack as two unsmiling men hurled him, with unnecessary force, into the trunk. Magid spoke to one of the men.

"No blood in the car."

The sedan sped off.

25

A PATRIOT'S INSTINCT

Stanley drove the Pennsylvania country highway carefully. Augie had the broad back seat to himself but hardly used it. He preferred to look out over Stanley's shoulder, perched on his hind legs above the center console. The dog was so tall that when he raised himself like this, his large head rose well above his old master's shoulder and even with his master's own big face. They made quite a visual pair cruising along in the morning sunshine.

Stanley was always surprised how the German shepherd, now approaching ten years, could maintain his stout posture for so long. The fullness of his years seemed not to affect him much at all. His ears stood high and still displayed their rich brown and deep black tones. Only the gray setting in on the underside of his muzzle betrayed his age.

Altoona, Pennsylvania, lies ninety miles east of Pittsburgh along US Highway 22. Stanley knew the road well enough. In past years, he and Helen had traveled it five times to see Minor League Baseball games there. The home team's name, if unconventional, was a favorite of Stanley's: *The Altoona Curve*, the double-A affiliate of his beloved Pirates, playing in the Eastern League. But Stanley had never traveled farther than the ballfield or, that he could remember, south of the small city. He watched his GPS map intently and slowed as he drove south out of town. It was one of those country roads that ran in alternating stretches of straightaway and long, severe bends marked with dramatic speed reduction signs. Finally, he spotted the abandoned Altoona Plastics plant on the left. Just past its rusty, locked entrance gate, he saw the late-model pickup truck facing him, two men in work clothes standing next to it. He pulled over slowly, crossing the center lane to the road shoulder behind the truck. Augie turned in the car and fixed his gaze on the two men as Stanley inched to a stop.

The lettering on the truck read, *Potomac Power & Energy Company.*

"Mr. Biglow?" the taller man said as Stanley approached with Augie leashed at his side.

"Big-*e*-low" Stanley answered. "Three syllables. But no big deal." Stanley smiled and extended his hand. "Stanley Bigelow," he said. He pointed to Augie. "This is Augie. He answers to August too. And you are Andy?" The text had said to meet "Andy."

"Yes, I am called Andy." It struck Stanley a little odd, the way he said it. Quite formal, not very natural. Stanley could see he was ethnic, as was the other man, but he couldn't tell further than that. Both men wore caps of heavy fabric, pulled down so that their foreheads were nearly covered. It was not unusual to find immigrants in construction work, and Stanley knew more than a few big league infielders that wore their caps that way. He registered it as insignificant. Augie may not have. The dog remained standing, taking a position between Stanley and the two workers, staring up at them.

"May we take you out to look at our problem, Mr. Bigelow?" Stanley noticed that he got the name right this time.

"Sure."

They started into the field, the two workers walking ahead. Stanley made an effort to catch up with them, but Augie resisted by stopping until the leash was taut, requiring him to stop too, keeping Stanley behind the two men. The dog looked up at Stanley with serious eyes, as if to say, *Just listen to me.*

When they reached the trenches, Stanley squatted for a look into them. He saw the central pumping device and the tubing, just three inches and a half in diameter, extending from it.

"This is a propulsion rig for fracking?" he asked. "It's too small."

"A prototype," said the taller man.

"Oh."

"If we get it to work, we scale it up."

"Oh."

"But it doesn't work."

Stanley and Augie walked to the end of the trench, the two men leading. Stanley looked down at the apparatus there. "This is the penetration bit and the entry valve?" he asked.

"Yes. The pump is supposed to send the fluid under pressure to the bit and valve. But it does not reach the bit with pressure. The valve says no pressure, no matter how I set it."

Stanley was not an expert in oil or natural gas fracking, but he understood the essentials of it. He knew it involved driving water and chemicals down into the earth with fierce pressure, enough to break up rock deep underground, releasing the oil and gas deposits held in them, then venting and collecting them at the surface.

"You said the pump is to send *fluid* through the line," Stanley said.

"Yes."

"What kind of fluid?" Fluids can be liquids *or* gases. Stanley knew that made a difference when it came to propelling them under pressure. "Just liquids?"

"Mixtures," the taller man said. "Some gas." Then he added, "Mostly gas."

Augie rustled. He would not sit. Stanley was more relaxed. "Let me see the pump again," he said. They returned to the beginning of the trench. In the sunlight, Stanley didn't need even a flashlight to examine the pumping device installed in the trench. He saw the issue immediately. "There's no blowback baffle behind the pump," he said. "You can't propel gas under real pressure without stopping the blowback. You need a baffle. It needs to sit vertically behind the propulsion mechanism, blocking off the pipe completely, so that the force of the push forward can't come backward. If it can go backward, you're getting as much pressure in the *wrong* direction as you are in the right one. And only a little in either." Stanley stood up. "Who designed this?"

The taller man went to the cab of the truck and returned with a fitting in a box, about the size of a shoebox.

"Is *this* a baffle?" he asked Stanley. "I didn't know where it should go."

Stanley opened the carton and looked at the part. It had strange symbols etched on its outermost edge. He had seen similar markings before. He thought they might be Russian. A hazard warning, a sort of Russian skull and crossbones.

"Yes," Stanley said. "This is it, your blowback baffle." The taller man nodded, appearing embarrassed. "It's probably more rigid than you need. See *here*?" Stanley said. He ran his thumb over the edge of the fitting. "This is *overflanged.* Specially reinforced. It clamps off the backflow with extra strength. You wouldn't need it, really, unless you were sending something toxic down the pipe. Overkill for what you're doing, I'd think. But it won't hurt. Better safe than sorry."

Stanley opened the back door of his car, pleased that the consultation had been so quickly completed. He and Augie would be back in Pittsburgh in time for cocktail hour with Helen. But the dog did not seem as pleased. The animal paused at the open rear door of the car and turned. He looked first into Stanley's face, then to the two men standing at their truck, then back to Stanley's eyes. *I don't like this*, the shepherd's eyes said.

Then he rumbled a low growl, just loud enough to reach Stanley's ear, and hopped into the back seat.

26
CONTRITION

The surveillance tape from the parking garage at Nationals Park did nothing to ease Jack Renfro's conscience, but at least it confirmed that his contrition was not misplaced. The killer of Chandler Bowes had stepped almost casually from the storage room and directly beneath the stairwell camera. The dim light from the exit sign was more than adequate to produce a definitive view of his build and face. The time stamp on the film was 8:40.

In his flat in Queens, Agent Evan Reese looked at the image on his secure laptop. He recognized the killer instantly.

"It's the man who came with me to Washington on the train," he said to Renfro, Brew, and Hannah Harris, gathered at Renfro's police department office. "Absolutely. It's him."

At least one piece of last week's events was coming together. As Reese and his Middle Eastern escort had approached the gate to Nationals Park that night, the mystery tagalong had received a cell call. He had then departed, telling Reese only, "I may leave you now."

"He must have received an instruction to kill Chandler Bowes once Bowes took the drop," Renfro said. "Bowes was compromised because I called him and asked him to help us place an undercover officer in the stands. He reported that in to somebody. They decided they couldn't use him anymore. But they wanted that cash drop to happen first."

"So the guy tagging Reese is redirected to kill him," Hannah Harris said.

"That's sure how I see it," said Renfro.

"They didn't waste any time about it," said Tyler Brew.

Renfro put another video sequence on the monitor. "But they *did* make sure he moved the money before they killed him," he said. "Look."

The film showed Chandler Bowes standing in the garage. He raised his arm, as if signaling. A Brinks truck wheeled into view. An armed guard came out from the passenger seat and walked with Bowes to a locked hallway. Bowes opened the door and waited in the garage as the guard entered the hallway. Paperwork was exchanged. Forty seconds later, the guard reemerged with a steel case on a hand truck. The rear door of the Brinks truck opened, and a loading shelf dropped electronically. In went the steel case. Bowes stepped to the guard, took the hand truck from him, and disappeared into the hallway. The time stamp on the film was 8:19.

"The storage room where Bowes was murdered is on this same level," Renfro said. "It's also the level where Bowes's car was parked. Management parking is all on that floor. The killer probably watched the money leaving, then waited for the guy to come out to his car. He didn't have to wait long."

"What does his wife say?" asked Hannah Harris. "Does she know anything?"

Renfro said that Audrey Sanderson had interviewed the wife of Chandler Bowes for three hours that afternoon. She felt the woman was open, honest, and destroyed. Her husband had seemed his usual self, she said. Their marriage was typical for its duration. They didn't have children. Nothing out of the ordinary ever seemed to happen. They were comfortable with their own lives and with each other. She was busy, he was busy, neither monitored the other's daily minutia. She did say that a little more money seemed to be around lately. Chandler had mentioned a raise from the ball club.

"Now, that part wasn't true," said Renfro. "He lied to her." The team owner said the concession chief's salary had not changed, and no bonuses had been paid recently. "And the owner asked if we could keep his murder out of the papers. Said it would upset everybody, including the fans."

"What did you tell him?" asked Brew.

"I said we could. There's nothing in it for us—this getting out."

"Good call," said Brew. "The quieter the better until we can sort this out. The whole city will get on edge."

Brew tried silently to assemble the new information. Middle Easterners and Ukrainians. Murdered messengers, and messengers murdering. Baseball and Tehran. It couldn't be random, but where was the fit?

"One thing is driving me nuts," said Jack Renfro. Everyone looked at him. "That night in the second row, Reese saw Chandler Bowes hightailing it out *without* the backpack. Reese was on his belly, and he was hurt, but he saw him clearly enough. *Without* the backpack. But we know the Kievs say the delivery was made—they told that to Reese—and now we know the money moved out of the ballpark an hour later." The detective leaned back and paused before asking his question.

"So *who* picked it up in row 2?"

27

ENDS AND MEANS

Navy SEAL Admiral Tyler Brew had more firsthand experience tracking terrorists abroad than anyone else in the government. As a SEAL in the field, he had participated and fought in over a hundred missions across nine countries to find and kill them or to destroy their assets and equipment. He had personally commanded the last sixty of those missions. Over time, he came to know that unlike the so-called lone wolf domestic attacks, no large international terror plot ever relied on a single evil mind. There were always *two* of them. One to devise the *end*, the other to manage the *means* to it.

The *end* was the destructive force to be used. The killing mechanism. The bomb, the booby trap, the explosives-laden vehicle. In short, the *things* of death. What were the traits of the *ends* mastermind? A technical brain. Engineering knowledge and scientific acumen were key. Access to specialized materials and instruments. Perverse brilliance wrapped in radicalized hatred. It was not important that this half of the planning duo have skills—or even interest—in tactical planning or people management. He needn't be magnetic, persuasive, or gifted in the art of deception. He just had to make something that would, in the end, kill. Really kill.

But the other evil mind? The master of the *means* to the end? That was a wholly different kind of person. A complex personality. Demented but not seen as demented. Manipulation skills so perfected as to pass for gentle grace and likeability. Unfailingly deceptive, brutally decisive. A head for logistics and the sequencing of events. Utterly without empathy and incapable of forgiveness but facile in the face of unforeseen events. An embodiment of the Hippocratic oath in twisted reverse: do *only* harm.

The clues arranged on Brew's credenza were multiplying. He had organized all of the pieces relating to the Brooklyn Kievs in a column, now including the Nationals employee Chandler Bowes and the surveillance photo of his assassin, at that moment the subject of whirling disk drives at the NSA looking for a match. In another column, he arranged the images of the murdered Middle Easterners and Wilson Bryce's partial report on the contents of Ranni Shamiri's cell phone. To the side, standing alone, he placed the photo of Balish Behzani, the wealthy man in Tehran known to have uttered Shamiri's name in the teahouse.

It struck him—and worried him—that every piece of information, and every person, seemed possibly related to only *one* side of the terrorist equation: the *means* to the end side. Nothing pointed toward the *end* side.

Then it occurred to him that one single fact stood apart from all the others. It didn't connect to the Kievs, or to the movement of money, or to murder. He walked to his desk and picked up a blank note card. He took it to the credenza and copied onto the card the notation in Wilson Bryce's report of the solitary web search made from Shamiri's smartphone: *Potomac Power & Energy.*

He placed the card at the front of the line.

28
THE TEMPERAMENT OF TERRORISTS

Balish Behzani sat at the window table of the teahouse in the central district of Tehran. He was not accustomed to waiting and didn't like it, even if the tea was excellent, which it was. But he knew that for a very few, delay was to be allowed. He looked at his phone to check the time. His collaborator was ten minutes late. Through the glass, he saw his security team flanking the entry and manning the curb. Two of them were in business apparel, Iranian style. Sleek-fitting black suits, open-collared white shirts. The man at the curb was garbed in merchant dress—a flowing wrap that concealed the semiautomatic rifle beneath it.

It was another trait of the *means* mind behind a terrorist plot—paranoia. Never be unguarded.

One of the guards near the door tapped once on the glass. Behzani looked out and saw the scientist coming across the street. The man appeared distracted, looking down, an expression of concentration on his face, even as he walked within feet of passing taxis. Then he looked up blankly at the dark-suited guard who opened the café door for him.

Behzani did not rise to greet the entrant. But he raised his cup and lowered it with a clang on its saucer to draw his attention. Successfully.

The man turned inside the door and stepped to the table, still looking preoccupied.

"Behzani," the man said. It was customary among Iranian equals to avoid first names unless they were related by blood or enjoyed close affection.

"Brother, Jameel!" said Behzani. It also was customary for a *means* mastermind to ingratiate himself. "I am pleased to see you, Jameel. I am pleased to be with you."

It was true. Behzani *was* pleased to be with his collaborator. But for purely utilitarian reasons. He wanted to know—needed to know—the status of the weapon and its delivery system. In truth, he personally did not particularly like the scientist, Jameel Daash. To Behzani, the Nigerian-educated Daash was unfocused, scattered. He was difficult to talk to, with a tendency—maddening to Behzani—of pausing interminably when asked a question, then answering in short, poorly structured machine gun–like bursts, as if making up for his long pause. He caused Balish to remind himself of another valued trait in a *means* master like himself: patience with a prized mind.

"Daash," he said, "how are we coming on the weapon?"

The scientist was younger than Behzani, handsome, and muscular, enough so to spark envy in the means-master on all three counts. The scientist sat across from him, looking straight at him, expressionlessly, silently. *Oh, come on!* thought Behzani. *Just an update, not a dissertation! It's a simple question!* It was all that Balish could do to keep a kind look stretched across his face as he waited. He sensed his own fatigue setting in and wondered if his eyes belied his impatience. He hoped not. Jameel Daash was, as geniuses can be, temperamental. Temperamental to the point of explosive. It was a joke among the other assets. *"Daash is a bomb maker with a short fuse!"*

And many bombs Daash had made, to be sure. But those were earlier days. His specialty had changed since coming to teach at the Institute of Advanced Technology and Mechanics across the avenue from where the two sat in the central district. His position gave him access to chemicals and chemical processing research. Even experimental devices built by former students for use in the Iranian oil fields and chemical plants where most of them now worked, many in Russia.

Finally, Daash answered in his usual diction.

"Propulsion … the system … the pump … for propulsion … Russian parts … fucking Russians," he said. It made Balish smile, and he was in need of comic relief. The two- and three-word bursts continued, separated by intervals of unexplained silence, through all of which Balish kept his eyes locked on his own teacup, never interrupting. If you interrupted Jameel Daash or injected any comment of your own, it was back to the beginning with the machine gun bursts. No, the way to listen to Daash, Balish knew, was the same way you react to machine gun fire. You keep your head down and wait until it stops.

And by the time Jameel Daash *had* stopped, Behzani understood the picture. It was good and bad, he judged. Good in that the scientist had successfully contained the nerve agent precursors in a pressurized cannister in which they could be transported, without leakage or instability, under a broad range of temperature environments. This was hardly a minor point. Behzani's logistical plan required the agent's components to be transferred through many latitudes by mostly innocent carriers in a circuitous route to the US. The cannister containing them would begin its journey in evil hands in Syria and end in evil ones awaiting in the US. But in between, it would travel the globe with unwitting escorts and innocent transferees, until it first entered US territory crossing the Bering Strait in—of all things—a US Navy plane delivering medical supplies to a submarine base off the coast of southwest Alaska.

The bad part was that the pump and piping system to propel the nerve gas in the final attack was so far unreliable. Jameel Daash blamed the team in America that was testing the apparatus and the Russians, from whom the pump design had been stolen.

"Your idiot over there … the idiot … baffle … no baffle … he doesn't put in baffle … *where* are they doing this?" The means-master had not told Daash where he had dispatched Andruzal and his helper for the field testing. It was means-mastering 101. No implement in the scheme—even the ends-master—knew the details of any other implement unless absolutely necessary.

"It is not important where it is," Balish said.

"It must be a place where your idiot can get help," the scientist said. Balish was surprised, a bit soothed even, by his fluency. "And no fucking Russian!"

"Do not be concerned, Jameel," said means-master Behzani. "He has already received professional assistance. The man was very good. The baffle problem is solved."

29

REMEMBER THE WIFE

Due at the Kievs' cellar in an hour, Evan "Evie" Reese was about to step onto the subway in Queens when Hannah Harris called his secure cell phone. He knew it must be her; only she had the number. He carried the phone in a zippered pocket below the knee of his canvas cargo pants. It was set always to vibrate only. He was not pleased to carry it at all, but Hannah had insisted. She continued to worry that he would be found out. She wanted him to be able to reach out for help in an emergency, and he had begun using it for his daily call-ins. But this was the first time *she* had ever called *him*. He stepped back from the subway car and down the platform to take the call.

"I am surprised you called," he said. "I could have been in the cellar with them."

"Well, you keep the thing on silent, don't you?"

"But you never know. I'd prefer you didn't call me."

"Anyway, I knew where you were."

You're kidding me, Reese thought. *She really is something.* "You've got eyes on me now?" he asked.

"Yes, and that's *my* call, Evan. You can see how big this thing is getting. I'm not taking any chances. And you've got a wife, remember."

"I do remember."

"I'd like to meet her someday. But not at your funeral."

"Okay, okay, okay."

"Besides, when you hear what I am about to tell you, you may feel better about our staying close to you."

She was right; he did. She told him that the bureau had met with the owner of the Nationals and brought him in on the cash-handling activities of Chandler Bowes. The businessman was a civic leader in Washington with an unblemished reputation. He was shocked at the evidence of his manager's involvement in money laundering and anxious to know if anyone else at the stadium would be implicated. The owner could be trusted, Hannah said, and it was the quickest way to get access to the team's banking records without fueling the rumor mill. The owner himself had a useful suggestion.

"No one in the office even knows that Chandler is dead," he had told Hannah Harris.

"We don't really know if anyone does," Hannah had replied. "That assumes he was working alone in your organization. But for now, let's make that a working assumption."

"If FBI agents show up to see things and ask questions ... well ..."

"I understand," said Hannah.

"But if you sent someone in as an outside auditor, no one would find that unusual. I have them look at things all the time."

And so the investigation began at the Washington Nationals.

"Who'd you send in?" asked Reese.

"Sophie Sikes from Boston."

"She's great." Reese knew her well. She was the agent who had worked the midterm election fraud case that drew national attention a few years earlier. Since then, she had joined the bureau's financial crimes division, often working undercover. Reese had met her at a cyber training course in Philadelphia. Sharp, confident, forties, comfortable in her own skin. No nonsense but not hard-edged either.

Hannah briefed Reese on what Sophie Sikes had learned so far. Chandler Bowes had left a money trail. During the Pirates game the night of "Evie's" drop, an order was made to Brinks for a cash pickup. Bowes personally signed the deposit form. When he did, he crossed out the amount his team in the cash room had entered on the form.

They had prepared a deposit of $100,000 dollars, about two-thirds of the cash taken in by the third inning. But Bowes changed the deposit amount on the Brinks form to $345,000.

"He added two hundred and forty-five thousand dollars," Hannah reported.

"After taking his 2 percent from the backpack," Reese computed.

"And then he walked out the deposit himself."

"So it looks like he was working alone."

"At least in the cash room."

Of itself, that information said nothing about the ultimate destination of the money, other than to the daily operating account of the Washington Nationals at Third Seaboard Bank. But Sophie Sikes had learned more. Before leaving his office and walking to his death that night in the stadium garage, Chandler Bowes had left three printed invoices on the desk of the assistant manager of the accounts payable group. Each invoice bore his approval stamp and signature. In a handwritten Post-it Note, Bowes asked her to make the payments the next day. One invoice was for payment to a concessions recruiting and placement agency, Cherry Blossom Servers, with a PO box address in Tysons Corners. The amount due was $26,000. Another was from a merchandise supplier from Peachtree, Georgia, called DVS Specialties. Amount due: $194,560. The third was payable to a provisions supplier identified as GoodStuff Meats and Condiments. Amount due: $24,440.

"Exactly $245,000 in all," Reese said. After all, he was a CPA.

"Right," said Hannah. "Sophie talked to the assistant payables manager. She didn't think any of them were suspicious. She told Sophie they were all companies that the Nationals occasionally dealt with. 'Occasionally?' Sophie asked. The manager said they are not the principal suppliers for the goods and services but that Chandler never relied on so-called single-source suppliers. Once in a while, he bought from these."

"I can see what's coming," Reese said.

"None of them appear to be legitimate companies. Purely paper entities registered in Delaware. No physical places of business, no websites. Just air. Except, of course, for checking accounts at Standard National Bank. Into which all three payments were deposited the same day."

"Is Chandler Bowes tied to these shell companies?" Reese asked. "Part of their formation in Delaware? Signatory on their checking account at Standard National?"

"No. Nothing implicates him there. He drops off the money tree once he pays these phony invoices. But he knew something, he must have known something." *Have* being the operative word. He was dead.

"Well, whatever he knew, we aren't going to learn it from him," Reese said.

Hannah paused at the obviousness of his conclusion.

"That's not up there with your better insights, Evan," Hannah said. She could almost see his embarrassment through the ether space. "But maybe you can come up with something more insightful from the Kievs. When the drop was ordered in the first place, maybe they were told something about Bowes. At least they knew the money would be laundered through the Nationals. And after the foul-up during the drop, they were told the delivery had succeeded anyway. Maybe they knew more than they told you. Or maybe they know more now."

"Including that Chandler Bowes is dead," said Reese.

"And that we're inside the Nationals now, investigating."

Reese sensed where his chief was going. Once you started to turn over rocks, you never knew what might jump out from under one. If Chandler Bowes was not working alone at the stadium, it was somewhere between likely and certain that the Kievs would eventually be tipped that the feds were combing the place. Feds made thugs anxious. And feds made thug *bosses* paranoid. And paranoid thug bosses were—well—unpleasant.

"We can't control what the Ukrainians might learn or when they might learn it," Hannah Harris said. "So we're going to keep eyes on you twenty-four seven."

"I understand now."

"Now zip up that phone."

30

AUGIE IS UNSETTLED

"Will you *settle down*, Augie?"

Helen stooped and looked sternly into the dog's eyes. He looked sternly back into hers. He raised his head and barked once, deeply. Then he trotted over to Stanley, standing at his humidor, and barked once again, the same piercing baritone. "I've never seen him like this!" Helen said. "Ever since you got home from your little road trip to Altoona, he's been agitated."

"I see it too," Stanley said. "Is there food in his bowl?"

"Of course, there is."

"Well, I don't know what to think," Stanley said. "He's sure not sick or listless."

"The opposite," Helen said. "He just won't sit still."

"Very unlike him."

"Do you remember that time we heard something out in the hall?"

How could either of them forget it? He and Helen never did learn the whole of it, but one evening there were angry, loud voices outside the apartment door. An object was thrown, striking the elevator door. Stanley rose and approached the door to investigate. The dog sprang from Helen's side and bounded in front of Stanley, then turned around in front of the door, blocking him. Stanley reached for doorknob, but the dog raised his head forcefully and pushed his arm away from it. Then they heard the voices move down the hallway and the sound of a door closing aggressively. After a full minute, Augie turned in front of Stanley, facing the door. When Stanley opened it gingerly, the dog took a single step out and planted himself on all fours, looking to the left, then to the right. Then he turned around to face Stanley and started back into the apartment, literally nudging the large man's legs, forcing him to backpedal.

The German shepherd still seemed unsatisfied. When Stanley closed the door and locked it, he looked up at Stanley and let out a single, resonant bark. Then he looked across the room at Helen. Another single deep bark. *Stay right there,* he seemed to be saying. Then he loped around the circumference of the apartment, stopping in the kitchen to smell under the auxiliary hallway door before returning to the main entrance and sitting. Every ten or fifteen minutes all that evening, he repeated the ritual, except for the barking. That night, he slept at the door instead of his usual place, inside their bedroom in front of its door.

Stanley called L.T. Kitt the next day to ask her about it. After all, she had trained Augie from puppydom in the FBI's canine program at Quantico and had handled him for six years in the field in witness protection.

"What was that about?" he asked after describing the dog's behavior. "He seemed very agitated."

"I'm proud as hell of him," said Kitt. "Perfect protocol. It's amazing he would do that now, without practice in years! He didn't let you go into the hallway, just like he wouldn't let a witness under guard respond to a noise like that. Actually, Stanley, I'm glad you didn't try to overrule him and go out there. *Then* you would have seen *agitated*."

In the many months since, he had not behaved that way again, or in any other way that seemed puzzling. Until this night.

"It's like he thinks something is the matter," Helen said.

"Well, nothing *is* the matter."

"Maybe he knows something we don't," Helen said.

"Well, I know I'd like a cigar and a bourbon with my wife," said Stanley. He looked down at Augie. "Is that permitted, August?"

They all moved to the balcony. Augie, grudgingly.

31

MUTUAL INTUITION

L.T. Kitt and Audrey Sanderson worked together chasing the connection—whatever it might be—to Potomac Power and Energy. Admiral Brew had asked them to focus on it. The Navy SEAL was troubled by it; he wanted it ruled *in* as relevant—or *out*. But early work was discouraging.

The phone retrieved from the body of Ranni Shamiri in Lafayette Square had been used to place only one outgoing call. And the number had been click-dialed from a link on the utility company's website, which in turn was the only internet search launched from the device. Potomac Power's website was arranged much like any other corporation's, describing the company's departments and activities. As a utility company, there were sections for billing questions and for reporting service problems. The last in a long list of *Contact Us* entries was *Transportation Department. 212.777.2025.* That number had been clicked at 10:16 a.m. one day before the Pirates game at Nationals Park and Shamiri's killing about gametime.

To Kitt and Sanderson, the fact that the call had been made through the website link was significant. Wilson Bryce and the NSA had verified that the call *was not answered.* Had it been dialed manually from the phone's numeric keypad, it could easily be judged an inadvertent wrong number. A simple blind alley. No relevance. There were always bushel baskets of such chaff in any complex investigation. The trick for investigators was to avoid treating it like wheat. The wasted time and resources; every hour spent slogging down a blind alley was an hour *not* spent on a lead that might break the case. But something about this phone call didn't feel to Kitt and Sanderson, as it didn't to Tyler Brew, like a blind alley.

Kitt won the coin flip, so she drove the two of them in an FBI sedan to the Potomac Power and Energy trucking yard in the southwest corner of DC. Kitt, only two years now in the bureau's Washington field office, was not familiar with the neighborhood in older times. Sanderson was.

"Should have seen this area fifteen years ago," Sanderson said. "They say it was so dangerous then the joke in the precincts was that you should never patrol on foot with a partner or a team; you were better off *alone*." Kitt turned to her with an incredulous look, waiting for the punchline. "Because the muggers down here were so tough they preferred a *challenge*."

But the neighborhood had changed much and for the better. They drove past numerous small merchants, blended with national name retailers and smart-looking, diverse restaurants.

"Coffee?" asked Kitt, as a Starbucks with a drive-through appeared ahead.

"Sure."

As they pulled back onto the avenue, they exchanged observations about the call to the power company.

"Odd that there's no answer and still only one call," Audrey Sanderson said. "If they don't answer, why wouldn't you call again?"

"Especially when you think you clicked on the right link," Kitt said. "As Shamiri must have thought—assuming it was him that clicked," Kitt said. "If you thought you might have touched the *wrong* link—you know how skinny they are sometimes—you'd peck at it again. But this caller didn't. He didn't think he needed to try again. He knew he had it right the first time."

"Even though he didn't get an answer," Audrey said.

"Even though he didn't get an answer," L.T. repeated.

"Or even an answering machine, apparently," Audrey said. Wilson Bryce had told them that the NSA would have picked up *any* answer, personal or automated. In this case, there were four rings, and then the caller hung up, he reported.

Of course, there *was* a recorded message device on the line at the transportation department. Sanderson had verified that immediately. But the machine was programmed to pick up after seven rings. The customer relations manager at corporate headquarters had told her that was true for phone lines all over the utility, and Wilson had confirmed it too with NSA resources. Automated pickups used to occur after only three rings, but many customers—and even employees calling between departments—complained. They wanted a live person to answer. It was aggravating to talk into a machine all the time when, with just a few more rings, someone could get to the phone.

"I think the call to Potomac Power was one of two things," L.T. said. "It was either a decoy sent to move us away from actual participants in a plot. Or it was a signal. A signal to a person hearing it ring to do or not do something."

Both of the officers were surprised when they arrived at the truck-yard. It really was pretty much a *yard.* A big, gravel-surfaced, fairly weedy yard festooned with nearly a hundred high-intensity light poles towering above. There were only three structures, and two of them were hardly larger than a residential garage. Tool and supply storage, the officers guessed. The third building was large but not as expansive as they had assumed it would be. They knew the power company had scores of vehicles, including many massive ones. They assumed some cavernous hangar-like structure must house them. But they found that nearly all of the trucks and equipment were lined up outside, in uneven rows across the wide yard. The vehicles did not even appear well organized by group, type, or size. You could almost call their positioning across the yard random. It was hard to see any deliberate order. In one row, two mammoth cherry pickers were parked next to a box truck and three pickups. A few late-model SUVs were mixed in too. There were more pickup trucks than any other kind of vehicle, but they were scattered pervasively through all of the rows, instead of lined up together.

As they walked to the entrance of the main building, a thin, studious-looking man in his fifties came out to greet them. He was wearing a light blue cardigan sweater, which Kitt and Sanderson noticed immediately. The weather was warm, approaching seventy-five degrees before 9:00 a.m.

"Harrison James," the man said, extending his hand to each of them. L.T. and Audrey presented their credentials. "I've been expecting you," he said. "Corporate called."

They stepped into the big building. It looked like a huge factory floor—all smooth concrete—but without the machinery. Two large vehicles were parked behind one another in the center of the floor. A girded ceiling hovered at least thirty feet above. Across the floor was a glass wall. Through the glass, Kitt and Sanderson saw a brightly lit cafeteria. A few workers were visible, cleaning tables; otherwise it looked empty. Above the cafeteria were small offices, also with glass walls facing the work floor. And, at least where they stood, the temperature seemed nearly freezing. Kitt and Sanderson each rubbed their bare arms.

"Apologies," Harrison James said. "We have the air-conditioning set to the highest temperature it permits. But it still does this. We *have* to keep it on. There's hardly any ventilation in the building. When we try turning it off, we smolder." Kitt and Sanderson may have had the thought simultaneously. *At least his sweater* is *a blind alley. The guy isn't weird.* "So how can I help? What is this about?" he asked.

"A call was made to your department nine days ago from a phone that was found the next day on a man who was murdered," Kitt told him. He seemed to be surprised.

"To what number exactly?" he asked.

She recited it.

"That's the general number to the department," he said. He pointed to a desk phone covered with extension buttons. "It's on there somewhere. But we hardly ever use it. We all have our own cell extensions. Every dispatcher, every mechanic, every driver."

"Where does this general number ring? All over the building?" Kitt asked.

"Oh, no. Just here in the main office. On three or four desks in here."

"So who uses it? Who calls the general number?"

"Just the public, really. Which is why we never pick it up. It's always somebody wanting a cherry picker to get a squirrel out of their chimney or some crazy thing. One time, a woman calls, says her kid is having a birthday party, could we send out a big truck with flashing lights for the kids to play in. I've been telling corporate for years to get that phone number off the website."

"*Nobody* picks up when that line rings?"

"*I* never have. I doubt if anybody else has either. It takes messages anyway. My assistant runs through them every couple of days. Most of them get referred to community relations or just erased. Maybe the guy left a message. You want to check?"

"He didn't," L.T. said.

"How do you know without checking?"

L.T. ignored his question, and Audrey looked away, as if distracted.

"He ended the call after four rings," L.T. said.

"How do you know *that*?" Harrison James asked, his brows raised.

"It doesn't matter," L.T. said. "Let's just say your taxpayer dollars go a long way. Were you here that day?"

"Yeah, but I don't remember that call."

"I didn't ask if you remembered it," L.T. said. It was standard technique. A little discomfort never hurt. It often produced a desire to be more cooperative. Sometimes more information. But this time it didn't.

"I'm sorry I can't be more help," Harrison James said.

Kitt and Sanderson looked to each other and held their gaze. *Mutual intuition.* Audrey spoke for the first time to him.

"Well, maybe you still can. If you hear anything, or any calls come in that you think might interest us, will you call us?" She handed her plastic-coated business card to him. He took it, but Sanderson reached and grabbed it back from him. "Oh, that's not the right one," she said. "Sorry, it's got the old number." She fished into her credentials folio, withdrew a second card, in truth identical, and handed it to him. "If you think of anything else."

"Sure," said Harrison James.

"And could we have your card? In case we need to reach you."

He went to his desk drawer and gave one of his business cards to each of them.

When they climbed into Kitt's FBI sedan outside the building, the two officers turned and looked at each other as they had near the end of the interview inside. It was as if each had an assessment but was deferring to the other to speak first.

"Nice move on getting his prints," Kitt finally said.

"Yeah, I love those plasticized cards they give us now." Sanderson placed the card delicately into an evidence pouch.

"Yeah, we have them too," Kitt said.

"So what do you think we do next?" Audrey Sanderson asked.

"I think we ask Wilson Bryce to find out whether calls were made from"—Kitt lifted Harrison James's card to her eyes—"two one two, seven seven seven, two zero eight eight after the link-click call that morning."

Audrey Sanderson was thinking the same thing.

32

A DOG'S HEAVEN

"Just come here to Camp David, Stanley," First Father Henry Winters said. "Bring Augie. It's no problem at all. Del made a point of it."

Henry had lost the second argument with his daughter and was back at the presidential retreat in Maryland. He'd won the first two days before; she had agreed then that he could come back to the White House after the rushed evacuation to the safety of Camp David. But when Del Winters received her latest briefing from Tyler Brew, she changed her mind. Over drinks in the residence library, she broke the news to him: he was heading back to the presidential retreat and staying put there until Tyler Brew and his multiagency team could understand what was afoot around the White House. But she spared her father the details of what the admiral had told her. There was no need to add alarm to his aggravation. And it *was* alarming.

Brew told her that his counterterrorism analysts believed that the murders of Ranni Sharimi and Davoud Dafur in Lafayette Square and Mustafa Al-Misham at the Willard Hotel likely meant not the end of a threat but the progress of an ongoing plot. The NSA had doubled its man and womanpower monitoring phone traffic going in and out of the country. Flagged and recorded calls were being listened to by an actual intelligence officer twice as quickly, usually within three hours of interception. And what they were picking up was concerning.

"There is chatter in volume we haven't seen in years," the Navy

SEAL admiral told the president. "They're talking in code, which itself is troubling, but what we're piecing together makes it worse. The analysts say they're using a lot of deception, teasers to hide what's really happening. What they're really instructing."

"Instructing?" the president asked.

"What they're telling their assets here to do."

"And what do we think they're telling them to do?"

"For sure, we know Shamiri's killing of Al-Misham at the Willard was ordered. And then Shamiri's and Dafur's in Lafayette Square were too."

"*Sweeping up*, like Renfro said," Del said.

"Yes. The killer in the square got out of the country before we could put anything together. We know he flew out of Dulles later that night."

"To where?"

"London, then Istanbul. On separate tickets, with different passports. But it's where he went from Turkey that worries me more."

"Tehran?"

"Tehran."

The president grimaced. *My God, when will this relationship get better?* she thought. The journey since the revolution in Iran in the late 1970s and the taking of the US embassy not long thereafter—the infamous hostage crisis—seemed never to be ending. Fits and starts, mostly fits. She believed she had made inroads with the Iranians. She had striven to cool down the rhetoric between Tehran and Washington. President Obama's nuclear deal with Iran had been revoked by his successor, but the global ramifications had been muted by the adherence of other signatories. Del Winters had sought to lessen the tensions but carefully. She had authorized cooperation with the Iranian intelligence service on matters of common interest, especially pertaining to Russia, of whom both countries were regularly suspicious. But Iran's virulent antagonism toward Israel—even in the face of softened relations between Israel and many of its other neighbors in the Middle East—obstructed more dramatic overtures.

"The common link is Balish Behzani. He is one of the wealthiest men in Tehran," Brew said. "Most of his money came from his father. His father was close but—fortunate for him—not *too* close to the Shah before the revolution. Many of the Shah's friends were hunted down. Some of them imprisoned."

"The lucky ones," the president said. She knew that many of them had been executed as irredeemable infidels.

"A few were luckier still. Like Behzani's father," the admiral said. "His father disappeared with his family and his money. But he never left Iran. Before the revolution, he moved a lot of his cash out of Iran to European banks, keeping enough in his own country to live on. Live very well. And after his death, his son continues to live very well. But still, not like the old days."

"How did they avoid detection after the revolution?" the president asked.

"The way most of the wealthy in the Elahieh district did. By blending in with an affluent community that pledges its loyalty to the reigning clerics. It's a kind of truce."

"So, these wealthy families say, 'We'll let you have your power, and you'll leave us alone with our money,'" the president said.

"That's pretty much the deal."

The president turned in her chair and reflected for a moment.

"Sometimes I think we have people *here* who think they have the same deal," she said. Another pause. "But I know that's beside the point, for now. What do you think this Behzani is doing, and why is he doing it?"

"Those are two different questions," Brew said. "The *what* is harder to know than the *why*. We think the why is that his father never forgave the US for not saving the Shah and his grip—and his grip too—on Iranian oil resources. The riches that flowed to them were obscene. The son inherited not only his father's money but his resentment too. Especially the way the US turned to Saudi Arabia as its principal friend after the Shah's fall."

"Well, the Iranians never liked the Arab nations anyway. Arabs and Persians were warring all the time," the president said.

"And now the Saudi elite are rich beyond compare, while the Iranian elite live under the thumb of the Islamic clerics."

"So Behzani is motived by hate and jealousy? That's why he's doing this?"

"We think so."

"And the what? *What* is he trying to do here?"

"We think he's trying to kill you. And maybe right here in the White House. You should leave."

"Out of the question. The British and Indian prime ministers are coming in just a few days. There's a lot of work to do on the new military alliance."

Brew knew that the alliance was a signature achievement of the president. She was moving the US away from its practical reliance on countries run by authoritarian regimes, like Saudi Arabia, Turkey, and the Philippines. The presence of so many US military assets and air bases in those countries was too compromising, in her view. When these regimes misbehaved, America could not always "be America," as she put it. These countries were too important strategically. US hands were tied. It grated her. There were solid democracies with whom the US could partner instead, with the right diplomacy and leadership from the White House. India was key. Her plan was to make it a new central player in the international deployment of US forces. The British PM enjoyed the trust of the Indian government. He was facilitating the agreement.

"Well," said the admiral, "at least you will not object to our doubling up on security here."

"Of course not. That's fine. Work with Tug. And I *will* get Dad out."

"He'll blame me," Brew said, smiling. "But I guess I can take it."

"He was having Stanley to the White House this weekend," Del said. "I'll tell him to invite Stanley out to Camp David instead. Stanley's never been there. He can bring Augie along. It's a dog's heaven out there."

And so it was. As soon as the first father had settled into his cabin, he called Stanley in Pittsburgh to discuss the change in travel plans. He knew Stanley loved staying in the White House and thought he would be disappointed. But Henry was surprised.

"Why, that sounds wonderful!" his friend said.

"Now, of course, you can't just pull up to this place, Stanley," Henry Winters said. "Tug Birmingham will send you instructions and credentials."

"Besides Augie, do I bring anything?"

"I never turn down Stanley Bigelow's bourbon."

"How about a good cigar too?"

The first father paused. "You know, out here we could get away with that, even indoors."

There would not be the beverage selection of the White House bar; there would be no going to the Nationals game as they had planned. But even inconvenience had its rewards.

33
THE CENTER FIELD CAMERA

They say in football replay challenges that sometimes the film just doesn't make clear what actually happened on the field. Jack Renfro knew it was true in crime scene footage too.

The only video of the maelstrom behind home plate a week earlier was recorded by the centerfield television camera at Nationals Park. Renfro studied it again and again. The lens was focused on the pitcher and the batter for the entire sequence, except for a four-second segment when the camerawoman zeroed in on home plate itself to record a sliding play in the raucous third inning. Everything in the seats behind the action was blurred throughout. Renfro asked Brew if Wilson Bryce could do anything to sharpen the images in the crowd, and the admiral passed on the request. But the enhancements that even Wilson Bryce's team could produce were little help. L.T. Kitt's dramatic leap onto the back of Audrey Sanderson, and Evan Reese crumpling beneath the two of them, were vaguely discernable. But only vaguely. A blurry, large figure, presumably Chandler Bowes, could be seen rambling out of the row away from them. The most vivid image on the screen before Renfro was the irritating black netting in front of the faces he wanted to see. No matter how slowly he rolled the footage, there was nothing showing the cash-stuffed backpack or anyone retrieving it from beneath the seats in row 2.

Renfro wished he could just walk into the concessions department at the ball club and ask questions of everyone. Obviously, Chandler Bowes had inside help. *Somebody* had picked up that money and knew where to take it so that Bowes could complete the deposit during the game. But at least for now, Hannah Harris and Admiral Brew wanted to work undercover in Bowes's department. Especially to Brew, trying to sniff out a terrorist plot, it was more important to know *where* the money was going ultimately than how it got from row 2 to the Brinks truck that night, and even more important than rounding up any accessories to the murder of Chandler Bowes. Besides, Bowes's coworkers didn't know yet that their boss was even dead. Renfro knew he couldn't make that known by openly questioning the employees. But it turned out Renfro didn't have to ask any questions to identify the accomplice.

The accomplice uncovered himself by asking his own.

34

IT COULD HAVE BEEN WORSE

It was Sophie Sikes, the undercover auditor, who noticed him. He had come into the concessions office once before, the afternoon before a Nationals game. Hannah Harris later commended her for her keen eye, but Sophie knew she didn't deserve that much credit. The man stood out in his usher's uniform. He looked old. Slender, pale complexion, white hair. She saw the name sewn into his shirt: Hiram. He talked to Chandler Bowes's assistant briefly, shook his head, and left. Sophie didn't make anything of it, at first. But when the old usher returned the next day, approaching the assistant again, she knew she should inquire.

"Who's that?" Sophie asked Bowes's assistant.

"That's Hiram. Hiram Fowler. He's been an usher here for years."

"What did he want?"

"He asked if Chandler had sent him anything in the mail." The assistant, like all the others, was still unaware of their manager's murder. "I told him he hadn't."

"He was here yesterday too," Sophie said.

"Yes, he did come in."

"What did he want then?"

"He asked if Chandler had left him an envelope after the Pirates game last week. I told him no."

"Did he say what he expected in the envelope?"

"No, but I know Chandler left him envelopes sometimes. He told me they were tickets for Hiram. He liked Hiram."

Hiram Fowler was one of a hundred regular ushers at Nationals Park. His seniority earned him prime sections to work in the stadium. He liked the field boxes near home plate the best. He could arrive early and chat with players near the dugouts. But he enjoyed the umpires the most. He was even on a first-name basis with a few. The crew usually gathered at the screen behind home plate before the game. He would come to the screen and engage them.

"Now, give us a break tonight, fellas," he would say.

"We'll make you a deal, Hiram," one umpire once said. "We'll call 'em like we see 'em, and you keep the fans from yelling at us."

He had been raised in Cleveland. His father, a reporter for the *Plain Dealer*, was a bipartisan enthusiast of Civil War history. His idea of a local family outing was to take his children to the Soldiers and Sailors Monument in the Cleveland's downtown public square. He had even named Hiram after the little known, but true, given name of Ulysses Grant. Hiram knew it could have been worse. His brother was named Stonewall.

As soon as Renfro heard from Sophie Sikes about the usher's inquiries, he called the team owner. The homicide detective asked for a personnel photo of the usher.

"What's Hiram got to do with anything?" the surprised owner asked.

"Maybe nothing," Renfro said. "But he's been asking if Chandler Bowes left him something after the game that night. An envelope. I want to see if our people who were there recognize him."

L.T. Kitt did not, but she had been laser focused on protecting Reese when she catapulted down to row 2. Audrey Sanderson and Evan Reese, though, remembered Hiram Fowler immediately when Renfro presented them with the photo.

"The usher," they both said.

"He took me to my seat," Reese said. "But I never noticed him after that."

"I talked to him before Evan showed up," Sanderson said. "I asked him why so many good seats were empty. He mentioned Chandler Bowes. He said Bowes came down and used them a lot."

"When it went down, was the usher there?" Renfro asked.

"Maybe. I'm not sure," Sanderson said. "But he couldn't have been far away."

"He had access to the concessions office. He could have taken the backpack there," Renfro said.

"And Yuri told me the guy who called him to tell him the delivery was made *wasn't* Middle Eastern," Reese said. "Said he was 'just an old man.' Can we find out if it was Hiram that made that call?"

Audrey Sanderson was skeptical. "We don't know his cell carrier, and we don't have a warrant," she said.

Jack Renfro was practical. "Somehow," he said, "I don't think those will be problems for Wilson Bryce."

35

EVEN A PARANOIAC IS SOMETIMES OPTIMISTIC

Balish Behzani sat in his luxury residence in Elahieh, in better spirits this evening. His undependable asset who had failed to recover Shamiri's cell phone was now not only undependable but permanently indisposed. As far as the *means* mastermind knew, nothing had come of that mistake thus far. Perhaps nothing ever would, he thought.

Even a paranoiac is sometimes optimistic.

Besides, the rest of his intricate plan was coming together nicely. His operatives around the world were reporting in on schedule. Transit of the nerve gas in its disguised medical cannister, mixed with other containers of surgical anesthetics, was proceeding without hitch. Even the weather was cooperating. A gathering storm off the coast of Greenland had dissipated; a civilian cargo flight carrying sundries and medical supplies intended for the US Navy's northern fleet and the Red Cross had been able to land at a NATO base on the island country. The six crates of anesthetics—one of them holding Jameel Daash's lethal cannister—had been transferred with the other medical items to a US Navy supply plane for transport to navy surgeons awaiting them at an Alaskan submarine base. Behzani would know by tomorrow evening if the handoff at the submarine base had gone as planned.

The report from the field team in Washington was also encouraging.

Andruzal said the piping and propulsion system was now operating correctly. *Thank heaven,* Behzani thought, *for that old engineer from Pittsburgh! Such a blessing! In thirty minutes in the testing field in Pennsylvania, his knowledge saved a mission for years in the making.*

Yes, Behzani considered, this was an evening worthy of wine. He walked to his rack and selected a French Bordeaux from St. Emillion. But before he could uncork it, his cell phone tinged. He tensed. No call was scheduled. He pressed the answer key but said nothing in greeting, his practice when surprised.

"Balish?" the caller said. "Balish, are you there?" Behzani recognized the voice at once. It was Andruzal.

"Yes, my brother," he said. "I was not expecting this call."

"I am sorry, Balish. I didn't think I should mention money in my report. Because I knew Daash would see the report. And he is not about money."

"*Money*? What about money?"

"I need some more."

"More?" Behzani prided himself on financial acuity. Every step was carefully calculated, every contingency considered. He had thought all funding was in place.

"Yes, because the ATM balance is nearly zero. I thought there would still be four thousand dollars. But it is nearly zero. Because of the problem with the pump and the baffle, we had to stay longer in Pennsylvania. Another payment must be made for the trucks. And I need to buy my plane ticket to leave after the attack."

Four thousand dollars! Behzani thought. The money he'd told Shamiri to leave on the body at the Willard! He raised his hand to his forehead—he'd forgotten that in his calculation for the last drop.

"It is not your error, my brother," the means mastermind said. "It is mine. The last deposit should have been sufficient. It was meant to be, but I made a small mistake." But even as he said it, Behzani knew it was *not* a small error. Every additional movement of money brought risk. And the miscue at the American baseball stadium worried him. It had already resulted in one unplanned adjustment to the plan, the murder of Chandler Bowes to prevent the concessions manager from being questioned. "Stay on the line, Andruzal. I must think for a moment."

What happened in the brain of Balish Behzani in the next forty-five seconds would prove decisive in all that happened after. He lay down the phone and looked out at the lighted mountainside of northern Tehran. The options bounced between the neurons. Should he choose the safest? The assassin who had eliminated Bowes was still in the US, awaiting further instructions. He could be dispatched to kill Andruzal and his helper and the entire operation aborted for the time being. But what of the nerve gas already in transit? And how could the piping and propulsion system be secured so that it could be retrieved at a later time? No, Behzani concluded, the plan should go forward. There was ample cash in safekeeping in New York. His assassin could get it to the Kievs for transfer and disguised deposit. The unwitting Ukrainians had not failed him. They had managed to complete the large drop literally under the noses of the Washington police. Chandler Bowes had done well to enlist the old man who worked for him; the old man had delivered the money after the fracas. Now he could be used again. And since neither the old man nor the Kievs knew anything of what the money was truly for, there was nothing they could tell even if another cash drop was disrupted. He returned to the cell phone.

"The money will be in the machines in three days," he said. "Nothing is changed."

36

ANOTHER FIFTY-SEVEN MINUTES

Audrey Sanderson's pride was showing—maybe a bit too much—when she took the business card of Harrison James to Wilson Bryce at the Pentagon. *Good police work*, she thought. She'd produced the cell number of a person of interest without a warrant, and done so legally. She'd avoided, she assumed, a lengthy technology search.

"How about *this*?" she announced with a broad smile, slapping the card onto the NSA man's desk. Her smugness was short-lived.

"Oh, good," Bryce said flatly. "You saved me about three minutes."

Wilson was not exaggerating much. The agency's ability to sort metadata and identify phones and where they were being used was startling.

"What do you want me to do with this number?" Bryce asked.

"The call to Potomac Power and Energy from Shamiri's phone."

"What about it?"

"It wasn't answered."

Wilson Bryce raised his left hand as a pause sign and paged through a document on his desk. It was the report he had sent to Admiral Brew and his team. "Right. Four rings, no answer. The caller ended the transmission before the answering machine came on."

"We want to know whether a call was made from this guy's cell after that. *Right* after that," Audrey said.

"Why?"

"It's possible the call from Shamiri's phone was a signal. Not even meant to be picked up. This guy, Harrison James, manages that office. He was there that day. If it was a signal to him, he might lead us somewhere."

"Interesting. You want to wait for it? It will take an hour or so."

"I thought you said I saved you *three* minutes?"

Wilson Bryce smiled. "Well, if he *did* make a call then, I assume you want a history of all his calls, and another one for the number he called, so you know who that guy called. That takes another fifty-seven minutes. Give or take."

37

A GRIM HISTORICAL FACT

In Brooklyn, Evan Reese was feeling almost left out. It was true that his communication duty had doubled; he was now making a daily morning call to the counterterrorism team led by Admiral Brew, in addition to his regular check-in to Hannah Harris in the FBI's financial crimes unit. But he was not having much to report on either one.

Life for the Kievs seemed routine, he advised. There were the usual cash collections from the bar owners and restauranteurs—which the Kiev members made personally with their own brand of diplomatic acumen—and then the laundering drops of the cash to the network of small businesses needed to clean the money before its ultimate access again to the Kievs. Evan observed that he was being selected for more and more of those laundry drops. His trust index with the Kievs was rising. He knew that the group closely monitored the progress of the cash as it moved from its first drop point to its final transfer into the account of the nonexistent Mirvatka Tea Company, from which the Kievs withdrew it, clean as a whistle. The arriving amounts were always exactly correct. Never a shortfall. And that could be true only if Evie Rezcepko was shepherding each drop with honor. Indeed, the young undercover agent was giving leader Yuri no cause to regret his assurance to the Middle Eastern caller just before the Pirates game at Nationals Park: "Evie is good boy and loyal."

But there had been no further contact, as far as Evan knew, from the Middle Eastern "customer" of the Kievs. No additional cash transfers had been arranged. He *did* know from another courier that before the large drop that Evan had made to Nationals Park, there had been others on behalf of the mystery customer to different drop points. A few had been for substantial sums but none as large as Evie's, and none had occurred since.

His yearning for involvement in the broader investigation of what was happening around the White House was soon satisfied. Admiral Brew had asked that every member of the inner circle be on the secure line for that morning's daily call. As Brew stood at his office credenza, Hannah Harris, L.T. Kitt, Evan, Jack Renfro, Audrey Sanderson, and Wilson Bryce beeped in successively.

There were no pleasantries; the admiral began immediately with business. He told the group that he'd received a detailed briefing from Bryce earlier in the morning, and a second from the CIA analyst team working leads on Balish Behzani in Tehran.

"Each of you know some of this already," the admiral said. "But none of you know all of it. I want you to. One of you might see something the rest of us don't. There's a lot that still isn't clear. But what *is* clear is that all of the murders were coordinated out of Tehran and that they're connected to the money laundering operation out of Brooklyn. That's bad. Because the only logical explanation of the tie to the money is that it's funding an attack of some kind. And not a simple one."

Brew did not have to tell most of them on the call that the *amount* of money known already to have been funneled through the Kievs suggested a major operation in the making. The work of the 9/11 Commission, painstaking in its reconstruction of that tragic attack, established that it had all been carried out—from first planning to the deadly flights—for merely $500,000. The drop carried by Evan Reese was fully half that amount, and who knew how much more had been laundered in before that—through the Kievs and probably other channels too. Everything about the plot sounded big to Brew.

"Wilson," the SEAL admiral said, "I'd like to start with you. Go through what you've found at the NSA."

Brew didn't have to ask the others to hold interruptions. They knew better. The NSA surveillance technology chief methodically recited all that he and his team had confirmed. The first victim found in the bed at the Willard, Mustafa Misham, had checked into the hotel the night before he was killed after traveling by train from New York. While in New York the previous day, he had taken the subway to Brooklyn and entered the Purity Diner in the Park Slope neighborhood on Seventh Avenue at Sterling Street.

Wilson Bryce shared a grim historical fact about the location. In December 1960, a United Air Lines DC-8 carrying eighty-three passengers had crashed at that very corner in Brooklyn after colliding in flight with a TWA commercial airliner carrying thirty-three passengers. At the time, it was the worst American aviation accident on record.

Bryce reported that cameras showed Yuri Kotva, the Kiev chief, entering the diner minutes before Misham and the two men emerging together thirty minutes later. A yellow taxi was awaiting Yuri, who stood next to it and made a phone call.

"He was calling one of his other taxi drivers," Bryce said, "as a ride for Misham to Grand Central. Complimentary."

Bryce went on. The next afternoon, Ranni Shamiri and Davoud Dafur walked into the Willard at two fifteen, he told them. The door to room 1205 was opened by the occupant. Shamiri and Dafur were in the room only nine minutes. They walked out of the hotel and directly to the Occidental Grill next door, he said.

"They were in the restaurant a long time," Bryce said. "After we saw nothing on the film for over two hours, we checked the cameras in the rear to see if maybe they had taken some other way out. But nothing. Eventually they left from the same front door they entered, at five forty-eight."

As L.T. Kitt would tell the group when Bryce finished, she had interviewed a waiter and a bartender at the Occidental who remembered the two Iranians. They'd spent almost two hours there after finishing their meal walking slowly around the whole restaurant, studying the photography, the employees said. It wasn't unusual, the workers said.

A lot of people treated the place like a museum. Not as unusual, they said, as paying in cash—an oddity anymore—as the older man had for both of them.

The NSA's Bryce then detailed the killings of Shamiri and Dafur in Lafayette Square just thirty minutes later and the immediate departure of their killer from the country. "He called Behzani in Tehran from Dulles Airport and flew out soon after. Eventually to Iran," he said. "We know he didn't get Shamiri's phone from his body in the square. Thank God. That phone is what ties everything—almost everything—together. It gives us Behzani, and it gives us Harrison James."

Kitt and Sanderson listened now with even keener interest. It was the first they'd heard of Wilson Bryce's findings on Harrison James's actions after the unanswered call to the transportation department of Potomac Power & Energy. "Before he was killed, Shamiri placed only one phone call from his phone," the NSA man reported. "He clicked a phone link on the website of Potomac Power & Energy. It was the general number of the company's transportation department, its truck yard. After four rings, he ended the call before anybody answered and before the recording machine kicked in. A shout-out here to Sanderson and Kitt. They learned that the department manager was on the premises when Shamiri's call came in. A guy named Harrison James. They got us his own cell phone number and asked us to see whether he made a call to anybody right after Shamiri's call. Turns out he did. To an *Andrew Barnwell.* At least that was the name used to buy the phone. There's nothing on that name anywhere so far, and he doesn't work for the power company, at least under that name. But we have his burnable cell number and its call history over the past eight weeks. We've plotted the cell towers he pinged on every call, which gives an idea of his movements. A few are close to the Potomac Power truckyard; the rest are scattered from the metro DC area all the way to central Pennsylvania." Wilson Bryce stopped.

"Anything more?" Tyler Brew asked.

"Yeah, there's no doubt that the launderer at the Washington Nationals, Chandler Bowes, was murdered by the same man who rode with Reese from New York with the money. Evan positively identified him from the film in the garage. We have a good facial of him. But we're coming up dry on matching him in any of the databases. Even Interpol has nothing on him. So he is still a mystery man."

"Anything else?"

"Well, that's the information. I can go into the geeky stuff on how we got it all, if you want."

"Spare us," the admiral said. "Jack, what have you got?"

Jack Renfro cleared his throat and paged through his notes. "Facts or theories?" he asked the admiral.

"Both," Brew said.

"Well, we know Chandler Bowes had help at the game that night. And he didn't live to tell us about it. But there is an old usher, Hiram Fowler, who was working near the aisle, and he's gone at least twice to the stadium concessions office asking about Bowes and whether he left something behind for him. I think he's involved."

"A bad guy?" Brew asked.

"I doubt it," said Renfro. "He's got no record of any kind. More likely doesn't know that he was being used. Or at least not in something horrible like this. Bowes liked him; he liked Bowes. Bowes gave him free tickets sometimes. If Bowes needed a favor, he'd be a natural choice. And Bowes knew there would be an undercover police officer at the game. He didn't know where—I never told him that when I arranged it with him; all he knew, and all *I* knew, was that it involved a murder investigation. But he might have wanted a safety valve if something happened down in row 2. He could have recruited old Hiram and told him, 'If there's a backpack lying around when I come down there, pick it up.' The money got to Bowes somehow. How else did it? I think it was Hiram Fowler. And I think it was Fowler who called Yuri after he did, because Bowes told him to. But if he did pick it up and get it to Bowes, there's one thing I can't understand."

Renfro went silent. No one else said anything. Fifteen seconds passed.

"What's that?" asked Tyler Brew. "*What* don't you understand?"

"Why's he still *alive*," the detective said, "when Bowes isn't? When every person involved who could lead us to what's happening has been terminated, and fast."

"But *they* didn't bring Hiram in," said Evan Reese. "If you're right, Jack, Chandler Bowes brought him in, not them. And maybe I have something in common with Hiram Fowler. *They* didn't bring *me* in either. Yuri did. And they know about me too. Their own man went with me to Washington. But they haven't come after me, like they haven't come after the usher. Or after Yuri. What does that mean?"

"It could mean they think you, Yuri, the usher, and this guy Harrison James don't know enough to hurt them," Jack Renfro said. "Which would be good for your and the others' safety." But he quickly added, "I doubt that it means that though."

"Then what?" asked Tyler Brew. "What else could it mean?"

"That they still need all of you or think they might."

"For what?"

"To pull this off." The veteran detective cleared his throat again. "To do something more."

38

MYSTERIES OF CAMP DAVID

"You weren't kidding, Henry," Stanley Bigelow said as the first father greeted him in front of Aspen Lodge, the presidential cabin near the front of the Camp David property. It was four thirty; the sun was splaying through the thick trees. "This place *is* really tucked away. No signs at all on the park roads."

"Tug sent you directions, didn't he?"

"Yes, but they weren't much help. I'm not good at reading odd markings on the bark of trees. If I didn't see the Secret Service agent he sent out to stand by the road, I don't know where the hell I'd be."

"Oh, c'mon," Henry Winters said. "Anyway, you're here. And I am happy you are, Stanley. And that you brought Augie." Sitting erect next to Stanley, head up and smiling broadly, the dog looked even happier than the old friends.

Nearly every American knew *of* Camp David, but few understood its significance in presidential security. In the beginning, the government had gone to great lengths to conceal its location, to the point of explicitly denying for a time its very existence. Now many decades later, surprising mystery still shrouded the presidential retreat built by Franklin Roosevelt shortly after Pearl Harbor for purely utilitarian reasons.

The truth was that the daily demands of managing the war made it impractical for President Roosevelt to travel often to his property in Hyde Park, New York, as he had in his earlier terms. He felt he needed to be closer to Washington and the military commanders. Doctors suggested finding a retreat in a higher elevation with prevailing humidity less than the capital. Such a refuge out of the public eye was important for the president's safety. Always a lover of boats and the sea, Roosevelt spent many weekends before the war on the presidential yacht, the USS *Potomac.* But after Pearl Harbor, the Secret Service convinced him to discontinue use of the craft, as too vulnerable to attack from the air, or even a German U-boat. Camp David was born, principally as a safe place for the American president to rest.

From the beginning, "Shangri-La," as Roosevelt originally named the encampment, had been used for presidential consultation as well as rejuvenation. In fact, Winston Churchill visited twice in the early years of the retreat to discuss war matters with FDR, including the D-Day invasion. And it was probably Churchill who did more than anyone else to expose the very existence of the compound and its general whereabouts. The colorful British prime minister occasioned the most public incident in the camp's early history when, to the consternation of the Secret Service and military guards, he persuaded Roosevelt to drive him to the nearest tavern in the rural mountain area, claiming he wanted to see what a jukebox looked like. To the enthralled locals who poured into the tavern when word got out of the pair's attendance, it wasn't clear whether it was the jukebox or the American beer that occupied the bulk of the orator's attention.

Renamed Camp David by Dwight Eisenhower, after his father and grandson, the government had ever since done its best to limit public knowledge about the property and severely limit access to it. Located just sixty miles north of Washington in the hilly forestland of Maryland, state and local maps do not mention it. To this day, the true size of the encampment is not officially published, though it is known that a tall fence completely wraps a parcel of at least 164 acres within the federally owned portion of Catoctin Mountain Park. The words *Camp David* appear on no road signs, as Stanley discovered, and there is no marked entrance. Invited guests, almost always delivered in government sedans or military security vehicles, enter via a small, unremarkable turnoff into the woods leading to a gatehouse compound manned by armed navy sailors and marines—because the camp is officially classified as Naval Support Facility (NSF) Thurmont, for the nearest Maryland town where Churchill had imbibed.

Henry Winters showed Stanley and Augie through Aspen Lodge, the largest quarters in the retreat. Stanley considered it more elegant and less rustic than he had expected; well-constructed with many excellent natural stone effects, tasteful.

"It gets cool enough at night to use the fireplace," the first father said. "We're up almost eighteen hundred feet out here. And how about this humidity? Beats Washington, eh?"

"*And* Pittsburgh this time of year," Stanley said. The dog looked up at them and nodded, as in agreement.

"You two can have your own cabin, if you prefer."

"Oh, we'll stay right here."

"It's really the nicest place."

"I had a feeling."

The retired general pointed to the oversized living room and the big-screen television. "For the ball games," he said. "If we can keep the damn thing working."

"Is there a problem?"

"There've been some with the buried electrical lines," Henry said. "They haven't been upgraded in an age. They looked at the conduit, and its breaking down all over the place. Letting the squirrels and chipmunks have a field day on the wire. So the lights and the TV flicker a lot. Tug says they're working on it. A crew will be out to re-lay the conduit and put in new wire. But it may be a couple days."

The three of them stepped out onto the expansive terrace at the rear of the lodge. "And we have a dinner guest tonight, who I think you will enjoy," the first father said. He did not make his friend ask who. "Tyler

Brew is coming up," he said. Augie raised his head at the name. Stanley was pleased too and showed it. "Wonderful!" he said. "But what for?"

"Tug Birmingham said Brew was thinking of coming up to meet with the security team here," Henry said. "When he heard you'd be here, it cinched it. There have been some things going on. You might have heard?"

"Well, I know you and Del have been shuttling back and forth from the White House. That's about all."

"There were incidents in Washington last week near the White House. Tyler and the FBI think they might be related. They rushed us out of there like the sky was falling. Brought us here. She went back first; then they let me go back too. Until they learned some new information that rattled them again. Said I had to come back."

Stanley looked concerned. "Then why isn't she here too?" he asked.

"My gut tells me she will be soon, which is probably why Tyler Brew wants to see Tug and the navy team here. But right now, she's got the Indian president and the British PM coming to town."

Stanley still looked concerned.

"But rest assured, Stanley. We couldn't be in a safer place. This is the number one so-called secure location. Did you know that on 9/11, *this* is where they brought the vice president when President Bush was still in the air? And once they returned Bush to Washington, they brought *him* here too."

"No, I didn't know that," Stanley said. "I mean, I knew they evacuated the White House because they thought another plane might be headed to it. But I didn't know where Cheney and Bush were taken."

"Well, it was right here. And the national security brass too. So let's both of us just sit down and relax." The general pulled two enameled Adirondack-style rocking chairs together. Augie didn't wait to see which one Stanley would occupy; he lay down prone in front of both of them.

Stanley was satisfied. "Well, in that case, Henry, how about a good cigar?" he said.

"*Just* a cigar?" the first father asked.

39

LIFE IS TOO LONG TO SUFFER SHODDY THINGS

If Tyler Brew was distracted by the events he was trying to cipher, he didn't show it when he walked into Aspen Lodge that evening. The African American SEAL looked as fit as he had ten years earlier and, on this evening, as relaxed as he might be on leave in New Zealand.

Brew's frame of mind did not surprise retired General Henry Winters. The first father knew how important it was that a military commander be able to steady his compass in times of great stress, to move from decision to decision in a calm mental state and imbue that serenity under pressure in those around him. He understood that to maintain that composure, a premier commander had to possess two rare but essential traits: a keen ability to compartmentalize stressful issues and events and deal with each on its own merits; and the ability to relax in between to nourish that resource. And he was as certain as night followed day that Admiral Tyler Brew was a premier military commander.

Henry Winters was qualified to make the assessment. He had lived his whole adult life in and around the armed forces. He came of age flying combat missions in Vietnam as a junior officer. As he rose through the ranks, even while raising the daughter who would become a president, he had led air force contingents in the expulsion of Saddam

Hussein's Republican Guard forces from Kuwait in the early nineties, and in the subsequent war to remove his regime in Iraq. After that, he'd been entrusted to directly command the nation's nuclear arsenal and, finally, as second in command of the entire air force, supervising the day-to-day operations of US air power around the world.

"Could I have one of those?" Brew motioned to the cigars Henry and Stanley had just lit before they sat down together in front of the fire newly burning in the fireplace.

"Of course," said the first father, "but I didn't know you enjoyed cigars." Without hesitation, he gestured to Stanley to retrieve one for the admiral, as if it were his own to give, as he might have signaled a junior officer to take something from his general's desk; his affinity to his old friend, though, made it seem natural, without offense. Stanley certainly took none.

"Eventually, every friend of Stanley Bigelow enjoys cigars," the SEAL said.

"Well, they *are* of high quality," Stanley said, handing him an expensive Davidoff.

"As you would say, Stanley, they are *the style to which you are accustomed*," Brew said.

"I *do* say that," the Pittsburgher replied. "Not because *life is too short*, as you hear everybody say. I've always thought that expression gets it wrong. I say life is *too long* to labor through it with shoddy things. If it were short, it might be more tolerable. But, of course, moderation is important." In a way, it summed up a fair bit of Stanley's approach to living. Sans baseball, bourbon, generosity, and a citizen's duty.

For an hour and a half, sitting before the fire and then at the dinner table in its view, the three men talked and laughed, mused and laughed, listened and laughed. *Was Brew still cooking often?* Stanley inquired. He recounted for Henry how the Navy SEAL's passionate hobby had inured to his benefit more than a few evenings in his first assignment under Brew and had helped in the forging of the two's friendship. *Oh, yes, hardly anything could take him away from that,* the Navy SEAL said. He'd thought even about cooking for the three of them this night, but he couldn't get away from the Pentagon early enough, he said. "Our loss," Stanley said, truthfully. The short ribs served by the navy chef at Camp David were serviceable, if a bit dry, but the mashed potatoes more or less tasteless. Henry, in particular, flailed the salt shaker at them.

"My word, Henry!" Brew remarked. "You're bombing the damn things!"

"They need it," the first father said.

"I'm with the general," said Tyler Brew.

"Moderation, my friends," Stanley said. "Moderation." It was as near judgment that Stanley ever went.

"The caution of a married man," Henry said, smiling. Brew felt self-conscious. He had not mentioned Helen Ames all evening.

"How *is* Helen?" he asked Stanley.

"Wonderful," Henry Winters answered for him.

"Wonderful," parroted Stanley, sending a forgiving glance to the first father. "I'd tell you she sends her regards, but I won't lie to you." Vintage Stanley. "I haven't talked to her since I got here. She doesn't know you're here."

"Well, give her mine," said Brew.

"Of course, I will, Tyler. By the way, I'm not sure I ever thanked you properly for all of that." The admiral looked at his plate and waved off the remark as unnecessary. "No," said Stanley, "I'd have never met her if you hadn't picked her and called her up from the reserves for that project. And we wouldn't be together if you hadn't talked to me."

He was referring to how the then captain Tyler Brew, overseeing the covert Eaglet's Nest project, had selected Helen Ames, then a fifty-seven-year-old unmarried colonel in the Reserve Army Corps of Engineers, as the most senior of the construction call-ups who would install Stanley's secret design to house—underground—the special drones for the fight against terrorism. Stanley and Helen and the dozen other call-ups working secretly under SEAL Brew's careful eye had spent a month together as Stanley trained the reserves on how to construct and assemble his unique and undetectable subterranean deployment base for the new drones. Then Helen had led the other reserves to Kuwait and overseen the final assembly. To this day, no adversary of the United States knew of its existence.

During the training, Brew had observed the mutual attraction between Stanley and Helen. He also sensed the reluctance of the senior citizen from Pittsburgh, owing to the age difference between them and Stanley's inexperience in romance since the death of his first wife, whose memory Stanley still cherished. Sharing Stanley's nonjudgmental nature, the SEAL captain had encouraged Stanley to move past his inhibitions, and even suggested their first off-base dinner together, in which he joined. It turned out that Stanley didn't need much help from there. The civilian's romance with the army reserve colonel flourished. They were married in Pittsburgh five months later, only Brew and L.T. Kitt attending.

"Are you staying overnight, Tyler?" Henry asked as they rose from dinner. "Stanley and I are staying up to watch the Nationals game on the West Coast." Game time was ten o'clock.

"No, I want to see Tug and the camp commander. I'm driving back down after that."

"Is there something new?" Henry asked. His eyes hinted a certain entitlement to know.

"We may be closing in."

"Will you bring Del here?"

"If it looks like the White House is the target, we will." Brew knew that even the possibility of an attack on his daughter was disquieting, to say the least, for her father. "But, Henry, we've got *everybody* covering her and everybody *else* chasing down the people doing this. We have leads. We're finding more. We'll thwart them."

"I would rather be with her."

"She won't have it, Henry. She wants you safe, out here."

Henry Winters became pensive. He stood before the SEAL admiral and looked down in thought. Respectfully, Brew waited at attention in case the first father had more questions. After a while, Henry looked at him, unsmiling.

"Well, don't cut it close, Admiral," he said to Brew. "At the first sign, get her out here."

"We will, Henry. We will. But try not to worry too much. You have a good team right here, and reinforcements too."

"Reinforcements?"

Augie rose from in front of the fire and walked to Tyler's side.

"This guy," Brew said, squatting to rub the German shepherd's tall ears. "This guy right here."

40

HOW IT CAME DOWN IN BROOKLYN

"Why the fuck didn't you call me? You were the senior-most agent on the ground."

The words flew like bullets from the mouth of FBI Director Jules Towne to the ears of Hannah Harris sitting with Tyler Brew across from her boss at bureau headquarters in Washington.

"I tried to," Hannah answered honestly. "Your machine picked up."

"And you never heard of texting?" He leaned forward and planted his hands on his desk.

"I was doing sixty in Brooklyn." Also, honestly.

Jules Towne had a point, even Brew agreed. It was never a good thing to blindside the FBI chief in an operation involving his agents, especially when it was predictable that he and the bureau would be picking up the media pieces if something went wrong.

"My God, Hannah, you basically deputized the Russian mob! And you didn't think you should talk about it upstairs?" The director was a large man, imposing in any mood. And he was seething in this one.

"Ukrainian, Jules," she said calmly.

"*What?*"

"*Ukrainian*, not Russian," she said.

Well, this woman has guts, thought Brew.

"And there was no time. There really wasn't," she said. "When I pulled up to the building, the tactical team and NYPD were already around it and beginning to move."

In the old days, it would be unusual in the extreme for a military commander to be on a first-name basis with the head of the FBI. Not anymore. The bureau's counterterrorism unit, growing every year, was increasingly interacting with special forces on missions, often in secrecy. And the SEAL admiral had cultivated working relationships with the leaders of all the law enforcement agencies, including Jules Towne. Brew had learned those relationships weren't important when operations went well, but they could make all the difference when they didn't. The admiral knew there were three things Jules Towne valued the most: toughness, trust, and turf.

"First, Jules, I need to say how impressed I've been with your agents," Brew said. "First rate, just first rate. Brave as my SEALs. We couldn't have hoped for more." Town looked at him and then at Hannah. He was attentive but unsmiling. "And the way you've let them act rapidly, trusted them to know their jobs. Outstanding, Jules. Really. It takes a well-managed organization to do that. You can be sure I'll tell that to the president," Brew said. Bull's-eye. Towne lifted his hands and leaned back in his swivel chair, drawing his big legs to one side, then lifting one over the other. He still wasn't smiling, but the frown had departed.

"Nobody hurt on our side, right?" he said.

"Not on ours," Hannah answered.

"Then walk me though what happened and how it all came down. The *New York Times* and the networks are going wild. I'll need to get it right."

"There's a lot you can't tell them," said Brew.

"I understand that. You wouldn't be here otherwise. Terrorists must be involved."

"Terrorists *at large*," Brew said. "Planning something big."

"In New York?"

"We think Washington, actually. But they're funding it from

Brooklyn with money laundered by these Ukrainians and maybe others."

"So that's how *you* got involved?" Towne looked at Hannah Harris.

She nodded, then looked to Brew. He gestured to her to go ahead. She told the bureau chief that her financial crimes unit had been running an undercover operation on the Kievs for months, how Agent Evan Reese had infiltrated the group, and about the large money drop he'd made for them at the Washington Nationals baseball game only ten days ago. She described the scare at the Willard, the mix-up at the game, and the other murders in Lafayette Square.

"What a clusterfuck," Towne said.

"All of the men killed near the White House were Middle Easterners," Brew said. "And all in our book. Since then, we've tied them to a wealthy Iranian in Tehran. We think he's behind it all, but we don't know what or where the end game is. It's clear he's concealing the plot by killing most of his own operatives once they've finished their part. We're piecing more together every day though."

"So why this take-out operation this morning in Brooklyn?"

"Overnight, the NSA picked up on two phone calls," Brew said. "One was from the leader of the Kievs to a person of interest who works as an usher at the ball park in Washington. A civilian named Hiram Fowler."

"A collaborator?"

"An unknowing one, we think. He knows he's in bed with money launderers but probably has no idea he's facilitating a terrorist attack. He was there when the big drop was made ten days ago. Last night, he was told a smaller amount was coming to him, to be ready for it by the end of the week. This time, he wouldn't be taking the cash to the concessions department at the stadium. He'd be told where to be to receive the money the night before and where to take it when the delivery was made to him."

"And the other phone call?"

"From Tehran to the Kiev boss. Just before the boss's call to the usher. Same subject. He was told a little more 'clean money' was needed in Washington. The Iranian told him there was no time to launder it through the usual channels. He asked if the Kievs could take some of its *own already laundered money* and 'get it to the usher' if they brought the Kievs three times the amount in dirty cash the Ukrainians could clean themselves and keep afterward."

"So the Kievs *are* in bed with the terrorists?" Towne asked.

"No, we don't think so, especially after this morning's raid," Brew said. "We'd always wondered if they were being duped. We wondered if they knew what this money was being used for; it could have been just another laundering account as far as they were concerned. They clean money for a lot of foreigners who aren't terrorists. And we've never linked this Ukrainian group to terrorism. We doubted they want to kill Americans. They even have a streak of patriotism in them—*American* patriotism. They believe this is a great country. We've thought they might help us if we could find a way to bring them in cooperatively. We were working on a plan to isolate their leader—Yuri Kotva—and talk to him. But when we learned this new information overnight, we knew time was running out. We decided to move on them the hard way."

"*Take* them first, *talk* later," Towne surmised.

"Sort of," said Brew. "This time, we had to do the taking and the talking at pretty much the same time."

It was not the usual order of things, but Tyler Brew and Hannah Harris both knew truly how it had gone down that morning at the building housing the diner above the Kiev cellar in Brighton Beach. Evan "Evie Rezcepko" Reese was still snapping on his FBI windbreaker when he ran down from his Queens walk-up and into the bureau's waiting tactical assault truck that sailed recklessly to Brooklyn. Three hours before—just after dawn—Brew and Hannah had coordinated with NYPD's antiterror command. The forces had waited three blocks away from the diner in unmarked vans until the FBI scout radioed, just before nine o'clock, that Yuri Kotva had entered the building. The NYPD team of thirty-five heavily armed, Kevlar-vested officers then surrounded the building. Four of them entered the diner and walked to the rear, past the kitchen and restrooms, to block the door to the cellar below. Two others raised fingers to their lips and methodically ushered the diner patrons and employees out the front door.

Evan Reese walked into the empty diner to the cellar door in the rear, holding a weapon more important at that moment than any the others burnished: his cell phone.

"Yuri?" he said when his call was answered.

"Yes, Evie!" the Kiev leader said. "You are early, my Evie!"

"There is a reason, Yuri. I must speak to you now. Alone. Are you away from the others?" Evan heard the Kiev walking and a sound, he surmised a coffee cup and saucer meeting a table top.

"I am away now. No one can hear. What is it, Evie?"

"You must listen to me carefully, Yuri. This is very important."

"Are you in trouble, Evie? Do you need me?"

"I am not in danger, Yuri. But I do need you."

"You confuse me, Evie."

"You have been good to me, Yuri. But I must tell you something. You must listen carefully to me. And you must not move from where you are or talk to *anyone* until you listen to me."

In the cellar, the rest of the Kievs were getting their strong morning coffee, mingling about. But a few, including Dirj the skeptic, observed their leader at the edge of the cellar. It was unlike him to walk away from them, no matter the phone call.

"I listen, Evie," Yuri said.

"You are not a bad man, Yuri. I know that," Evan said. "I want no harm to you."

"What are you talking about, Evie?"

"You must listen to me. I have deceived you, Yuri." The Kiev leader pulled the phone from his hear. He lowered his head. Seconds passed. The others noticed. Yuri turned away from them, facing the wall.

"Yuri," Evan called. "Yuri, listen to me."

"Evie," Yuri said softly. "What you mean, you deceived me?"

"I am FBI. I am FBI, Yuri … stay where you are. Stay where you are, Yuri. I must tell you much, right now. Right now, I must tell you much. There is no other way."

"What do you mean, there is no other way?"

"There is no other way for you and the Kievs to get out of the cellar. No way to stay free. Except to listen to me and what I say. The FBI and the NYPD have the building surrounded and the diner occupied. I am upstairs now with them. There is an army here, Yuri. They're even on the roof."

Some of the Kievs behind Yuri walked toward him, trying to hear him. He waved them back. "Evie, Evie," he said. "*What* do you want to say to me? *What* do I listen to?"

Brew at the Pentagon, and Hannah Harris standing behind the line of the NYPD tactical force outside the building, listened on the wiretapped line. Evan Reese spoke in an even tone, never interrupting the Kiev leader inside.

"They know all about the money, Yuri," Reese said. "They know more than you know, even."

"Evie, Evie, what do you mean?"

"The money to Washington, Yuri. The money for the Middle Eastern customer. Do you know what the customer is doing with it?"

"No, of course not. We get the cash to where they tell us; that is all we do."

"I know that, Yuri. I believe you. But the customer is a terrorist, Yuri. An attack is planned. They are using the money for the attack. To kill Americans."

"We do not kill Americans!" Yuri said. Some of the others in the cellar heard him and moved closer again. "Some of us *are* Americans. Or almost."

"I know that, Yuri. I believe you," Reese said again. "That is why I am speaking to you. We need you, Yuri. We need the Kievs. To help us stop them."

The line went silent.

"I am listening, Evie," Yuri finally said. "How do we help you? And if we help you, you will leave us alone?"

Brew and Hannah Harris listened intently. They knew the next words would be critical.

"*Alone* is not possible, Yuri. You know that laws have been broken. But if you come out now, unarmed, and then work with us when the customer comes again, things will go better for you. You will be helping America. You will be appreciated. And one thing I can promise. You will not be harmed here. You will not be fired upon. You will not now be arrested; you will only be detained. Stay on the phone now. Think about this, Yuri. I will say no more until you are finished thinking."

The young agent is smart, Brew thought as he listened to the exchange. *He is not threatening the Kiev, not making demands. Just requests, as if the Kiev has reasonable choices. Everyone wants choices. Choices mean a sense of control, at least some control.*

"I must talk with the others, Evie," Yuri said when he came back on the line. "Everyone is here. We do not hate Americans. We do not help terrorists to hurt Americans. But I must talk with the group. You say we will not be arrested *now.* But what about later?"

"If you will live without weapons and work with us with—cooperate with us in their next steps—maybe something can be arranged."

"I will talk with them about it, Evie."

"But you will do that *now,* Yuri. You will talk with them *now*, right? Because there is no time to wait, Yuri."

"I understand. Right now," Yuri said. "Call in ten minutes, Evie. No one will try to leave." He hung up.

Reese, Hannah Harris, and Brew quickly caucused on a three-way call. Brew was thinking like a SEAL. "How many men do you have in the diner above them?" he asked.

"Four, plus me," Reese said.

"Not enough," Brew said. "Fill the place. But keep them away from the cellar door."

"Done," said Hannah. A minute later, twenty additional FBI tactical shooters streamed in and took positions around the walls of the diner.

"And, Reese," said Brew, "are there any explosives down there?"

"None. At least I've never seen any."

"Windows?"

"Yeah, but they're all grilled. And we have NYPD people at each of them."

"I can tell you," Brew said, "if they decide to come up shooting, the first ones out *won't* be firing. They'll create the impression of surrender, trying to gain some element of surprise. Have two shooters zero on the first three that come up. Everybody else should zero on the men that follow them."

"Done," Hannah Harris said. She huddled the tactical team inside the diner and forwarded the instruction.

"Something tells me you've done this a few times, Admiral," Reese said.

"I have, but it was usually a little warmer."

Ten minutes had nearly passed, but before Reese could call him, Yuri rang on his own.

"We will do it," Yuri said. "We will do it."

Reese paused to see if the Ukrainian would add a *but,* adding conditions. But Yuri didn't.

"You must come up unarmed," Reese said.

"You said that already." It was the first irritation Yuri had shown.

"Single file, three steps apart from each other, hands as high as they can reach," Reese said. "Leave all of the guns on the tables. Put on all of the lights and leave them on. Open all of the closet and kitchen doors, the bathroom door too."

Good thinking, Reese, Brew thought as he listened. He hadn't even mentioned those things to the young agent. The most dangerous part of a raid was often the inspection after.

"Okay."

"Do those things now. I am going to open the door up here, Yuri, so that I can hear you. When you are ready to come up the stairs, call out from down there. No one starts up until you call out."

"Okay."

"And, Yuri. You come up last."

"Why?"

"Because I trust you to leave no one behind."

Above the cellar, the waiting assault team heard the men below gathering their guns and placing them on surfaces. More than a few were slammed down roughly. Light came up the stairwell and through the open door to the hallway of the diner floor. There was low talking. Then it became silent.

"We are ready!" Yuri shouted up the stairwell.

"All right then," Reese shouted back, edging nearer the cellar door to be sure he was heard. "One at a time, three steps apart."

And up they came, lumbering slowly, grim faced. A dozen NYPD antiterror policemen formed a human hallway, six to a side, across the diner floor to the front exit at the street. Reese stood in front of the officers, nearest the cellar door, acknowledging each Kiev as he came up. A few looked at him coldly; most made no eye contact, walking head down; none said a word. Eleven men, Reese counted as they proceeded up. Only two more: Dirj and Yuri.

There was a pause near the top step of the cellar stairs. "Get going. Up," Reese heard Yuri say in Russian. Dirj appeared in the doorway, rage in his eyes. His hands were raised until he pulled down his right arm fiercely and retrieved a Glock semiautomatic handgun from his waistband. By then, five of the surrendering Kievs had already made it outside to the sidewalk, where they were immediately handcuffed and encircled by officers. But six Kievs were still on the diner floor, flanked by the NYPD gauntlet. Dirj must have hoped his compatriots would react to his diversion and create a scrum. Maybe police guns could be wrested away? Perhaps an escape was still possible? He dove to the floor and managed to engage the Glock's ammunition clip. But he could not even raise the weapon before nine shots poured down on him like the stitches of a trained seamstress running from the back of his head and down his spine, all from the assault rifle of the NYPD sniper poised atop the coffee counter. Dirj's body partially blocked the cellar doorway. Yuri emerged, hands high and head shaking, as in disgust. He violently kicked the dead Dirj's legs out of the way, then looked directly at Reese.

"I told you, Evie," he said. "There is one in every fucking crowd."

PART THREE

41

IT BEAT GREENLAND, THEY SAID

It was officially summertime in Alaska—laughable as it seemed—as the C-130 Hercules transport, inbound from Thule Air Base in Greenland, touched down on the single airstrip at the secretive US Navy submarine testing base just north of Ketchikan. It was a late-June morning, but the seamen who jogged to the rear of the plane behind a diesel-powered cargo tug were all wearing gloves. And not for sanitary reasons.

It took a special sailor to enjoy duty at rocky-shored Ketchikan. About the most exciting attractions between it and Juneau—two hundred miles away—were the town's wooden totem poles, said to be the tallest in the world. But by Alaskan standards, Ketchikan was a hopping place. Its population of eight thousand made it the fifth largest city in the state. And most of the navy men and women stationed there were engineers and scientific types, less interested anyway in nights on the town than their work ensuring the acoustic health of the US Navy's entire Pacific submarine fleet.

To a submarine commander and his crew, two things above all others were mission critical: what the submarine could hear and what could be heard from *it*. For that reason, every submarine in the fleet came to Ketchikan on a regular schedule for two weeks of testing these vital capacities.

The sailors at Ketchikan were rightfully proud of their duty. Besides, they knew they were not "too, too far" from the Lower 48. You could not be in Alaska and be any closer to home soil and rational weather.

All in all, the sailors put it this way: it beat Greenland.

The commander on duty that morning had sent out a salt crew to season the runway when the navy plane was beginning its descent. Freezing rain had fallen intermittently since midnight, some less than an hour before. Overnight temperature had dipped to twenty-six Fahrenheit, the ceiling was low at a thousand feet, and the runway short. He knew it wasn't true that the best navy pilots were saved for combat readiness and the training exercises to keep them that way; in fact, some of the most experienced flew the transarctic routes like this one. But he thought it better to be safe than sorry. He sent out the salt.

"It's a real hodgepodge on this one," the petty officer driving the motor barge said as the plane's rear cargo hatch deployed. He studied his clipboard and removed one glove to flip the pages. "Pallets of linens for us and some foodstuffs. A lot of medical supplies that we move on to other stations. Some of the medicals are for the Red Cross. Those cartons are marked special. Keep them apart from the rest of the stuff. Stack them at the rear of the tug. They'll come off first at the transfer station."

"Why are we getting food from *Greenland*?" one seaman asked. It was a reasonable question. It received a predictable answer.

"Quit your bitching. Maybe we'll eat decent cod next week. Just get the stuff out of the plane. I'm freezing."

In the warmth of the ground transport terminal, the brown-suited UPS driver was waiting, watching for the petty officer to pull up with his wheeled barge. The officer was on friendly terms with the usual driver. But he didn't recognize the man waiting inside.

"A new man in uniform!" the petty officer said, entering the small terminal building. "Welcome to the navy's Southeast Alaska Acoustic

Measurement Facility. Or SEAFAC, as we call it." It was a mouthful, but the petty officer loved to treat visitors to the formal name of the specialized base. "What happened to Theo?"

"Change of pace, I guess," the man in the UPS garb said. "Another route for him today. Whatever the computer tells me, I drive it. Today, it says I pick up eight cartons from you guys. Is that what you've got for me?"

The petty officer looked at his paperwork. "Yeah. All medical supplies, nonperishable. Going to the Red Cross warehouse in Seattle. That's a hike."

Indeed, the drive down to Seattle through British Columbia and Vancouver was seven hundred miles and fifteen hours in good weather. Inconvenient, not to mention the nettlesome customs and inspection issues raised by bringing goods into the US overland. But it was just a two-hour flight from Ketchikan to Seattle, and it was classified as a domestic flight, unencumbered by DHS inspections.

"I'm just getting the stuff over to a company cargo plane over there," the driver said, pointing toward little Gravina Island, where even tinier Ketchikan International Airport was located. They stepped out into the cold air.

"There you go." The officer pointed to two stacks of four cartons at the rear edge of the lorry. "Just sign this for me." The driver whisked an illegible signature on the extended clipboard.

"Can you hold on for a minute?" the driver asked the navy man. "Before I leave, I want to check to see if I have anything to drop off to you."

He took the last of the cartons and disappeared into the back of the van. Inside, he quickly slit open two of them. He examined the cannisters of anesthesia but didn't find what he was looking for. The same with the third and fourth cartons. But in the fifth, his search ended. One of the cannisters, identical in every other detail, was marked on its aluminum bottom with a red circular sticker. He slipped the special container into the smaller box he had prepared in advance, sealed it, and applied the preprinted UPS address label:

Bethesda Naval Hospital
Bethesda, MD
Hold for: Dr. Andrew Barnwell

He had spent more time finding the cannister than he had hoped; he worried the officer outside might look into the van to see what was happening.

"Hey!" the officer called out. "You got anything for me?"

The driver came to the front of the van and leaned out the passenger side. "Sorry," he said. "I thought there might be, but there isn't. We're all set."

"Okay then. See you again, maybe," the petty officer said.

"Yeah, maybe," the driver said. He climbed into the driver's seat and drove off.

Yeah, maybe. Yeah, right.

42

THE FIRST RULE OF HOLES

This time, corporate headquarters of Potomac Power & Energy did *not* call ahead to let Harrison James know that L.T. Kitt and Audrey Sanderson were dropping by. The FBI agent and the DC detective hadn't told either about their return visit.

The truck yard manager was plainly surprised when the two roared up—with speed a little unnecessary—skidding to a stop directly in front of the entrance to his building. The disparity of the body language of the two officers striding briskly toward him did not assuage his anxiety about their unannounced arrival. Washington police detective Sanderson flashed her usual broad, friendly smile. An observer might have thought she was a pretty adult granddaughter approaching her beloved grandpa. But FBI special agent Kitt looked angry, intent, and all business. An observer might have thought she was a pretty wife about to strangle a malfeasant husband. Perhaps it was just serendipitous—simply the different personalities of two able lawwomen. More likely, they'd planned it on their way to re-interview Harrison James. Either way, it was good-cop-bad-cop from the neck up. And it made the subject of their interest uncomfortable in the extreme.

Harrison stood to greet them as the two women walked into his office. Sanderson extended her hand; Kitt did not.

"So tell us about Andrew Barnwell," Kitt said, without background or explanation. She stepped closer to him than Sanderson did.

"I don't know him," he said.

"You make a habit of calling people you don't know?" Kitt asked.

"All the time. There are a lot of people out there, Agent. We have two million customers."

"That would be plausible if you called him once. Maybe just returning the odd call to the department."

Harrison began to flush. He looked plaintively toward Audrey Sanderson. Her smile remained, but she said nothing. It was as if she was enjoying the scene.

"What are you getting at?" the manager asked.

"Oh, I think you know what I'm getting at, Mr. James. You didn't call Andrew Barnwell *once*. You called him *four* times. From your cell phone, alone. Who knows. Maybe you made more calls from other devices. And, by the way, *he never* called you or this department from the phone you reached him on."

"How do you know all this?" Very flushed.

"Harrison." Kitt stepped even closer. "What year *is* this, do you think?"

He stroked his cheek nervously. Kitt went on.

"And what is very curious to us is that your fourth call to this guy was made *immediately* after the call to the general number that we came here about the last time. The one that wasn't answered, the one the caller ended before the message machine came on."

"Immediately?" he asked. Kitt looked at her notepad.

"I'd call thirty-three seconds later pretty immediately, wouldn't you, Mr. James? Probably just enough time to fish his number out of your desk."

There comes a point in interviews like this, Kitt and Sanderson knew, when the tide of deception turns and truth begins to flow. Usually, it wasn't on account of the witness's sense of honor or desire to assist the pursuit of justice. It was because the witness understood the first rule of holes: when you're in one, stop digging.

"Okay, okay," Harrison James said. "I did call the guy. If you say four times, then four times. But it's true that I don't really *know* him. I met the guy once in my life. I don't even know if that's his real name. And he *did* call me—twice he called me." The two officers looked at each other, thinking the same thing. It was entirely possible Andrew Barnwell, whoever he was, had called the truck yard manager from a different number than that used by Harrison to call *him*. Barnwell may in fact have called him twice.

"So what is this all about, Harrison?" Audrey Sanderson asked. It was a wise time for the good cop to step in. They both believed the truck yard manager was ready now to tell the truth. "When did you meet him? Why'd you call him? Why'd he call you?" Her questions were direct, but her tone was even, almost kind-like.

"He came in here a few months ago. I had no idea who he was. He told them at the gate he wanted to apply for a job. There are always openings; they let him in. But he didn't ask anything about a job. He said he already had one for some contractor, that he had electrical training. He was doing a lot of side work from his regular job. If I could help him borrow a company truck with a trench digger and basic tools, he'd make it worth my while."

"How worth your while?"

"He offered five hundred."

"And you said?"

"Seven fifty, and he could keep the truck for a few days each time. I knew he'd need it that way because he said some of his jobs were out of state. Some of them were in Pennsylvania—pretty far in, I think. He said okay. I told him I didn't want to be seen with him again. I gave him a company uniform and a pass card for the gate. He said he'd call me when he needed a truck, and I'd give him the truck number and leave the keys in it. And that's what we did."

The officers asked for a description of the alleged Andrew Barnwell. *Foreign looking, dark features, good English with an accent Harrison didn't recognize. Polite. Thin, average height, work clothes and boots. A ball cap pulled low over his forehead. Never got a very good look at his face.*

"Do you know if he was alone?" Sanderson kept on, her even tone unchanged.

"I don't know. I didn't see anyone else."

"How many times did he get a truck?"

"Three times."

"You said he called you only twice."

"He did only call twice. When he arranged the first two trucks. But when he called for the second one, he said he'd need a third truck in a couple of weeks, but he'd need to keep that one a long time—two weeks, even; it was a big job. He could pay three thousand for it. He said he wasn't exactly sure when he'd pick it up. He was waiting for permits to go through. But he was pretty sure it'd be that same day you talked about before—the day the call came in to the general number. I said, 'So you'll call again then or whenever you need it?' and he says no, someone else will call in for him. That sounded screwy, but I figured, hell, he's on the take and—"

"*He's* on the take?" Kitt interrupted.

"Go on," Sanderson said. "Who was supposed to call you?"

"He didn't tell me. He just said a call would come in—he was pretty sure it would be that particular day—and it would ring four times and end. A message wouldn't be left. But when I heard that call, I was supposed to call him—this Andrew Barnwell—and give him the truck number that would be ready for him."

"How did he know you would be here to even hear the call?"

"He didn't. He said the guy would keep calling that way until I heard it and made the call to him—this Barnwell guy. But I guess I heard it on the first try. I *was* kind of waiting for it."

"And he came for the truck?"

"That night, I assume. It was gone when I came in the next day. That was ten days ago."

"Where is the truck now?"

"Still out."

"And you don't know where it is? There's no GPS element in it?"

"Not anymore. I took it out. Otherwise it would show up on the dispatcher's screens and …"

"You'd be found out," Sanderson filled in his thought. He nodded. An untrained eye might see remorse in his expression.

The three of them went out into the yard, and the manager showed them a truck like the one the alleged Andrew Barnwell had taken. The officers took thirty pictures from every angle, inside and out.

"For today, we're finished," Kitt said. "Don't leave town. Don't talk to anyone about this. Not even to your family. Understood?"

"I know I'm in trouble. How *much* trouble?" he asked.

"Like the truck, that's still out, too, Mr. James," L.T. Kitt said. "For right now, we need you to sit tight. Barnwell or someone else might contact you again."

"And I'm supposed to call you if he does?"

"We'll know."

"Oh. But if I help you, maybe this all goes away?"

"No promises," Sanderson said. "But you can help yourself by cooperating. Do what we ask you to do. And if you see anything out of the ordinary, call us."

"Well, he owes me three thousand bucks. He paid before; he might this time. Maybe he'll need a truck again. He may want to keep me."

Or kill him, the two lawwomen thought.

43

DEAD MAN WALKING

Jack Renfro and Tyler Brew were of one mind. As soon as they heard the report from Kitt and Sanderson of their second interview of Harrison James, their conclusions were simultaneous and identical.

"He's a dead man walking," the portly DC homicide detective said. The four sat together in Renfro's drab office, sans credenza. "We have to protect him. It's only a matter of time."

"Agreed," said Brew. "The record of Shamiri's call is a death sentence. What's surprising is that he's alive this long."

"That tells us a couple of things," Renfro said.

"I can think of one," the admiral said. "They don't know we have Shamiri's cell phone—don't know we're on to James's involvement; that we know they've used him."

"That's *one* thing," Renfro said. "The other is that even if they *do*, they still need him for more."

"Like they might need Hiram Fowler, Yuri Kotva, and Evan Reese," Brew said.

"Right," Renfro said. "But there's a difference."

"What difference?"

"Fowler, the Ukrainian, and the undercover agent are all part of the *money*," Renfro said. "But Harrison James has been used for *operations*. To execute on the plot itself. Providing equipment to the actors."

"So what kind of plot needs a power company truck?" Brew said it as if he was thinking aloud. "There are all kind of trucks easier to get, easier to load with explosives, or that can carry more men."

"You think it could be just a distraction?" asked Kitt. "A head fake?"

"No, I'm sure it isn't that," Brew said.

"How can you be sure?" Kitt asked.

"Because that would mean Shamiri's phone was left behind on purpose," the admiral said. "To fool us. To lead us to Harrison James and the power company as decoys. But that phone was *not* left on Shamiri's body intentionally. His killer wanted to go back for it. Remember Bryce's film? The citizen chased him off. And the phone is what gives us the Tehran connection. Behzani. They'd never want us to have *that*."

"You're right," Jack Renfro said. "The PP&E lead is real."

"Admiral?" Audrey Sanderson had been quiet until now. She was normally so polite and pleasant. But now she flipped onto Renfro's desktop three of the photographs she and Kitt had taken at the truck yard. "If you guys can track all these phone calls and reconstruct killings on video, how hard can it be to find a fucking power company truck?"

Sometimes the best questions are the hardest to answer.

44

UKRAINIAN HOSPITALITY

Evan Reese and Hannah Harris sat with Yuri in the NYPD's Sixtieth Precinct in Brooklyn. The rest of the Kievs were split into groups and waited in holding rooms down the hall. There was no rancor between the two agents and the Kiev boss as they talked. There *was* coffee and, at Yuri's request, tea; biscuits being unavailable, glazed doughnuts were on the table, compliments of the desk sergeant.

"I apologize again for Dirj," Yuri said. "Loyal but stupid. I was afraid he'd do something like that. That's why I made him go up after the others. So he wouldn't get us all killed behind him. Stupid, stupid man." He shook his head regretfully. "But, as I say, loyal."

It more or less summed up the Kiev leader's way of seeing things. Honest if brutal. Brutal if honest. Accepting of imperfection. Credit when credit was due. Loyalty first.

"I'm surprised you're not angry at me, Yuri," Reese said. "I was not loyal to you."

"Oh, Evie, Evie," the Ukrainian said. "You *were* loyal when you could be. And you were loyal to your country. This is as it should be, Evie. We feel terrible that we helped the terrorists. We didn't know this. We are not terrorists."

"We know that. We have always known that."

"It is not just me," Yuri said. "The others feel the same."

"That is important," Reese said. Hannah Harris studied the Kiev leader's eyes. Reese went on. "Because they must now be trusted, as you are trusted, Yuri. You must all act and speak in the right way now. To help us, everything must seem as normal. You must all go back and not let on."

"You know about the call for more money," Yuri said.

"Yes."

"And that is why you came for us today."

"Yes."

"You want us to take the man who comes to us."

"No. No," Reese said. "We want the exchange to happen as they've asked. We want you to give him the clean money and take what he offers you. They want your clean money so they can use it in their attack without it being traced back to them."

"Such a small sum? Not even ten thousand dollars? Why this, Evie?"

"It's actually not a good sign." It was the first thing Hannah Harris had said. Yuri looked at her, puzzled. "It probably means they don't *need* much more," Hannah said. "They are near the end. They are almost ready to do whatever they are planning."

"We want you to offer a taxi to their messenger to take him where he wants to go with the clean money," Reese said. "So we can follow him easily." Yuri nodded. "And we want you to wear a wire, and the driver too. We want his voice and anything he says. Even if he will not take your cab."

"Oh, he will accept the cab, Evie." Yuri looked offended. "I will be sure."

"How?"

"Ukrainian hospitality." The Kiev boss smiled. "It's a specialty."

45

GPS DOESN'T LIE. BUT YOU CAN LIE ABOUT GPS

Audrey Sanderson was not the only one who thought a power company truck ought to be findable. Tyler Brew ordered twenty-four-hour satellite surveillance over the entire DC metropolitan area, and beyond it for an additional hundred-mile radius. Then he revised the requisition to one hundred fifty miles. Every sixty minutes, a team of analysts under Wilson Bryce compared every vehicle sited by the satellites with the images on the central dispatch monitor at Potomac Power & Energy, looking for anything on wheels not accounted for on the monitor.

"Are you using company people for access to that live monitor?" Brew had asked Bryce.

"No need," the NSA technology guru said. "We went in with a worm. We see everything they see in real time. They won't pick it up for a month."

"Good. All we need is a leak and public panic."

"It shouldn't take long," Bryce said. "The images are clear from the satellites, and the GPS devices are current grade."

But it *was* taking long—much too long for Admiral Brew and his team in the field. Every time the images from the satellites were compared to the PP&E monitor, the same total number of vehicles appeared on each. No outlier truck was seen. At first, the premise was that the alleged Andrew Barnwell had either taken the truck out of the surveillance area or was hiding it under cover where the satellites could not record it. If either were true, it should only be a matter of time before he moved the vehicle within range or where it could be spotted by the constant search. But at the all-hands briefing call the next night, Jack Renfro raised another possibility. There were all looking at the PP&E monitor on the live feed Bryce had sent to each of their computers.

"What if he was lying?"

"Who?"

"Harrison James," said Renfro. "Lying about the GPS. He told Kitt and Audrey that he'd taken the GPS unit out of the truck. So the dispatchers wouldn't see it and wonder who sent it out."

"That's what he told us," said L.T. Kitt.

"Well, look at all those damn green dots on the screen!" the old detective said. "There must be three hundred of them, and half of them are moving! A great NFL quarterback can keep track of four or five pass catchers at a time. A Commanders quarterback, two or three. You really think one of these dispatchers is ever going to wonder, *Oh, look at that little truck over there. I didn't know we sent that one out*?"

"Jack could be right," Sanderson said. "It's probably more likely he'd be seen monkeying with the truck trying to pull the device out."

Brew asked Kitt and Sanderson if they could go to James's home and question him again. It was nine thirty.

"Of course," they answered, nearly in unison. "We'll go right now," Kitt said. "It's not that late."

"In the meantime, Wilson, keep your team on these pictures round the clock," Brew said. "We don't really know if he's lying."

"I'd suggest backup for L.T. and Audrey," Renfro said.

Brew seemed almost startled at the comment. No one had felt the slender, experienced truck yard manager might be dangerous. Corrupt, taking money on the side, yes. But violent? No one. But in his brain,

Brew was again glad he had solicited the veteran DC detective to his team. He sensed things.

"Who do you suggest?" Brew asked Renfro.

"Me."

46

WHEN EVIL SUCCEEDS

Who can know why evil sometimes succeeds or when it will? No one fully knows, but some have a better idea than others. Tyler Brew was one of them. He came to understand the ways, means, and patterns of terrorism not so much by choice as by duty. The Navy SEAL had spent twenty years and twelve hundred mission days finding and fighting that evil on the ground. At the tip of the spear, as they said. He had raided terrorist encampments on the verge of attack on innocents and thwarted the carnage; he had led missions that arrived too late and could only report it. He learned that, in the end, whether evil prevailed or failed came down almost always to two things: the relative diligence and attention to detail of the opposing forces; and timing. To defeat a terror plot, you had to pick up on the small things and the unexpected. And you couldn't be late.

Brew's gut told him it was getting late now. He agreed with Hannah Harris that the small size of the additional cash drop arranged with the Kievs was troubling. What could the terrorists do with just $7,500? Not much. Escape money probably. Needed soon.

The president was still in the White House, hosting the British PM and the Indian head of state. Brew had briefed her that morning and was scheduled to call her again in an hour. He wanted her to move to Camp David and join the first father, but he still lacked true proof that the White House was the target. Jack Watson at the CIA and Wilson

Bryce at the NSA each reported dramatically increased chatter on intercepted calls and social media—claims of a pending assault of major proportions—but none that tripped alarms for 1600 Pennsylvania Avenue or the safety of Del Winters. Brew didn't buy the last part. He tripled the Secret Service force at the presidential grounds. He ordered Blackhawk helicopters—three at a time—to circle a six-block radius of the White House continuously, night and day.

And he worried. The call from the home of Harrison James didn't ease his anxiety. At all.

47

TEAMWORK IN ROCKVILLE

Kitt and Sanderson rode together to Harrison James's house in Rockville, Maryland, in L.T.'s FBI Chevy Tahoe, Jack Renfro following in his unmarked sedan. It was a twenty-five-minute drive in the light night traffic. Kitt felt mischievous.

"How's the old guy behind the wheel?" she asked Sanderson, peeking in the rearview mirror at the sedan trailing them at a safe distance.

"Jack? Oh, he's frisky on the pedal. But he's a good driver. We've had a few chases. Jack's good at everything."

"Everything?"

"Well, I guess not marriage," Sanderson said. "He's had four of them. You're not going to try to lose him, are you?"

"I was thinking it might be fun."

"You're shitting me," Sanderson said. "They teach you that at Quantico?"

"*Evasion skills?* Sure."

"Well, show us some other time. Just get us to James's house."

"Debbie fricking Downer," Kitt said, kindly sarcastic.

Had he heard their exchange, Tyler Brew would have reassured Sanderson. He knew Kitt; he understood her use of humor and lightness under stress. He had seen her risk her life in the line of duty, first in her defense of Stanley Bigelow on the streets of Charleston and again a year later in the rescue of the same man when he was held captive by a deranged and heavily armed antigovernment militia in Michigan. L.T. Kitt might seem lighthearted, casual, and joke prone. But Brew would tell Sanderson to never doubt Kitt's interior of steel—her cool, unselfish discipline under fire.

The truth was Sanderson would never need anyone to describe for her the skills and traits of Agent L.T. Kitt. She was about to witness them herself and conclude she likely owed her own life to them.

As the two cars approached the residence of Harrison James on Foxden Drive, Renfro called his junior detective driving ahead of him.

"Park at the curb," he said. "I'll take the driveway."

"We don't expect trouble, Jack," Sanderson said. "He's no Rambo."

"I'll take the driveway," Renfro said again, flatly. To the veteran detective, it was just smart practice. You never left a means of egress unblocked. Over the years, he'd served hundreds of warrants and made thousands of unannounced knocks. More than a few times, a garage door glided up, and a suspect sailed out while he was standing at the front door. And all of this seemed foul to him. Even the neighborhood. How was a truck yard manager living in the Glen Hills section of Rockville anyway? The houses were large and interestingly designed, the wide lawns manicured. Renfro doubted even the DC chief of police could afford a home here.

Inside the one Harrison James owned, the PP&E middle manager was out of sorts. He was on edge, restless. He'd been so since the unexpected visit by the Washington detective and the FBI woman at the truck yard. He'd barely slept and told his wife he wasn't hungry. She'd made dinner for herself that evening and eaten alone while he moved anxiously from one room to another, to the basement and back, and even upstairs. He seemed to change the television channel every few minutes. "What is it?" his wife had asked him, more than once. "What's the matter?" He hadn't answered. But unseen by her, he *had* taken the semiautomatic pistol from its hiding place high in the bedroom closet, loaded an ammo magazine into it, and tucked it behind a couch pillow in the main room.

James was peering through a front curtain when Renfro pulled into the long driveway, cutting his lights as he turned, pulling to a stop just far enough up the drive as to not block the sidewalk behind the bumper. The homicide detective remained in his seat, lowering his window as Kitt and Sanderson strode past and toward the front door.

Inside, Harrison James ran to the couch and grabbed the handgun. His steps alarmed his wife, who leaned out from the kitchen archway. She saw the gun and was frightened. "What is *that*? Where did you get that? What's going on?" Rapid-fire questions from a fear-eyed face. They went unanswered. He raced past his wife and through the ample kitchen to a door leading down three steps to a short landing and another door to the backyard. "Let them in!" he called to his wife.

"Who?" she yelled, puzzled, until the front doorbell rang.

"Police!" Sanderson called out.

"FBI!" Kitt sounded after.

Susan Leslie James, the demure, caring woman and now terrified wife who would soon discover her husband's double life as an embezzler and traitor, stepped uneasily to the door and opened it. As soon as Renfro saw the woman standing alone in the doorway, he moved his eyes to the sides of the house and the rear. A tall stockade fence appeared to run across the rear property line. The driveway aligned with the right side of the house from the street; he could see dimly to the deepest edge on that side, all the way to the fence. But to the left, he could glimpse only the front corner of the house. If Harrison James was fleeing from the back of the house, Renfro knew the man would probably run to the left, away from the driveway, where Renfro would see him sooner. The stocky detective switched on the sedan's bright lights and climbed out. He saw the wife in the doorway point to the rear. He saw Sanderson push past the woman and hurry through the house in that direction. Kitt drew her service revolver and leaped down the front steps into the yard. She waved to Renfro, motioning him to cover the driveway side of the yard as she ran to the left front edge of the house. She slowed only slightly at the corner before running down the side of the house toward the backyard, out of Renfro's view.

Shots rang out in the near darkness. Unmistakably from an automatic weapon. Renfro's heart pounded. He ran in the direction of the gunfire, up the path Kitt had taken. There was no time, he adjudged, to go back to the car and call for more police. Besides, he hoped, the gunfire would prompt 911 calls from someone.

"Drop it!" he heard Kitt's voice. Later, in trying to remember every thought that had run through his mind, he believed he may have uttered Audrey's name as a prayer more than anything else. *Sanderson, say something!* If he had, his prayer was answered. "Drop it!" he heard again, this time hearing joyfully, because he knew it was Sanderson's command this time. She was not hit yet.

The three officers could not confer, plan, or consider. But they concluded independently the same thing in the seconds that followed. Harrison James needed to be taken alive. At almost any cost.

Renfro saw Kitt's position ahead, squatting at the left-rear edge of the house. Half her body extended beyond the cover of the building, her weapon trained on Harrison James somewhere in the backyard. He moved up quickly behind her.

"He's got Sanderson pinned in a window well against the foundation," Kitt told him, her stare around the corner unmoved.

"Is she hit?"

"I don't think so."

"You have a clear shot?"

"As a bell."

"Does Audrey?"

"Only if she brings her head up. He's ten, twelve feet from her and standing. Pointing right at her."

Still squatting, Kitt pawed at the ground, first her right foot, then the left.

"What are you doing?" Renfro asked.

"Making sure there's no mud on these fucking boots. I'm going to rush him. You step up to my place when I do. *Don't* take him down unless you're sure he's going to fire on Sanderson. If he turns away from her, *don't* take him down while I'm rushing him. Unless he fires."

"Bullshit." *How could he let the man fire on Audrey? Or on Kitt? How could he be 'sure' that the gunman was going to fire?* But Renfro understood. Brew and the country needed to know what Harrison James knew. And he also knew he'd get nowhere arguing with L.T. Kitt.

Kitt made more discussion a moot point. She lunged forward and streaked toward James. The measurements taken an hour later recorded the distance she sprinted until impact with the collaborator at thirty-one feet. From her improvised foxhole, Sanderson peeked up and saw the gunman turn at the sound of the charging FBI agent and redirect his weapon toward her. Sanderson raised her own gun and aimed. But the form of Agent Kitt racing full speed toward James entered her line of fire before she could squeeze the trigger. The impact of Kitt's body driving shoulders first into James's belt buckle was jarring. There was the clang of steel striking steel as their handguns clashed as they wrestled on the ground. Renfro raced from behind; Sanderson crawled up from the window well and started toward them too. A single additional shot from the gun of Harrison James pierced the night air. The medical examiner wrote that the bullet came from his own gun and traveled from below his chin through his brain. The body of Harrison James dropped dead weight—literally—onto Kitt's below him.

Ten minutes passed before Kitt said a word. It would have been longer if Sanderson had not spoken first.

"I thought I was going to die right there," Audrey said.

"I'm glad neither of us died," Kitt said. But she did not seem pleased or even relieved. "I just wish he hadn't either. We failed."

48

THE TAILOR WAS THANKED

The Tehran tailor had produced a masterpiece. And the slender man wearing the dress blue navy uniform who stepped into the small front space of the receiving department of Bethesda Naval Hospital was wearing it.

Balish Behzani had spared nothing in the uniform's making. He'd insisted that the tailor work only from authenticated photographs of recent vintage culled from footage of military funerals or news coverage of international diplomatic receptions. No images from commercial movies or unofficial, nongovernment websites, he'd ordered. Who knew what liberties a costume designer may have taken? No, *every* detail must be true and exact, he'd said, down to the embossments on the buttons, the thread count of the fabrics.

"I am Andrew Barnwell," the man said to the young navy seaman behind the counter. The place resembled a small-town post office. "I was told you have a package for me."

"Lieutenant," the seaman greeted him, noting immediately the two gold fabric straps on the customer's shoulders. "Is it *Dr.* Andrew Barnwell?"

"Yes." He smiled.

"You're new here?"

"Just arrived. From sea."

"Because we couldn't find your name on the personnel list."

"So you have my package."

"Yes, it came in with the UPS delivery this morning. I'm sorry we didn't get it to your office. We didn't know where to take it because your name isn't on the list."

"That's why I came down for it."

"I'll get it, Lieutenant. I have it close by." The seaman disappeared through swinging doors behind the counter. He returned seconds later with the parcel, about the size of a shoebox. He reached for a clipboard and raised a hinged section of the countertop, stepping out to Barnwell's side. After all, he was assisting an officer.

"Just sign for it right here, Lieutenant. I only need some ID."

"I've just gotten here," the imposter said. His expression was one of tolerant surprise. "They haven't given me my name badge yet."

"No problem. Any military ID will do."

"Sure, if you must." Barnwell smiled and lifted his leather bag to the counter, turned his back on the seaman, and unzipped a side pocket on the satchel. "Have a pen?" he asked, digging into the pocket out of view of the young navy man. Then he swung violently toward the seaman, grabbing his outstretched pen-grasping hand. He snapped his arm back and up, viscously. The startled seaman's chin dropped reflexively to meet the imposter's sharp knife blade, instantly driven deep into his throat and dragged to his left ear as he spun to the floor. There was no shout, no scream, only the briefest gagging.

Dr. Andrew Barnwell did not even consider moving the dead seaman behind the counter and out of sight. No point would be served. Blood was filling the small floor area and could not be concealed. He carefully stepped around it, placed the parcel under his arm, and left the room. He walked quickly—but not too quickly—to the first staircase down to the civilian parking area behind the building. He made eye contact with no one; he resisted the urge to look up or around to see if there were cameras. He was as professional a terrorist as there was, but his nerves were trembling. In a mission punctuated repeatedly by moments of danger, none was more precarious than this one. And none more binary to the whole effort. As Behzani had said to him, "Without the weapon, brother, all is lost. All will be for nothing."

It was six minutes before the dead seaman was discovered. By then, his killer was easing onto I-270 toward his hotel in Gaithersburg. He would change out of the officer's uniform and contact Harrison James, the collaborator from the power company. He was owed $3,000, and the truck was out eleven days already. It was important that James not become alarmed, he thought.

But first, he called Behzani in Tehran from a new burner phone, as he had been instructed.

"I have it, Balish," he reported. "I have the weapon."

"That is very good, Andruzal," Behzani said. "Very good."

"But there was a problem."

"Problem?"

"I had to kill a navy man to get the package out."

"Did the uniform not deceive him?" Behzani sounded incredulous.

"No, it was not that. The uniform worked perfectly. But it was not a substitute for a military ID. Even at the navy hospital."

There was a long silence. Behzani considered the implications of Andruzal's report.

"Did I do the right thing, Balish?" the operative asked.

"Yes, my brother, yes. If you did not get the package, everything would be over," Behzani said. "But it changes things. We must move more quickly now to the end. They will discover us soon. But there is a way for us. I will get you instructions. Do not be found until you hear from me."

"I understand. Tell the tailor he did well."

"I already have," Behzani said.

Perversely, it was the truth. Behzani *had* thanked him weeks ago, in the name of Allah. Just before he'd had him strangled and thrown down a sewer drain in south Tehran.

49

A PLAYPEN FOR EVIL

The dark web. Admiral Brew knew it was a playpen for terrorists and a preferred billboard for communications and signals between them. But when the FBI cybercrime specialist explained ten hours after the shoot-out in Rockville how it had facilitated the sick life and recruitment of ordinary Harrison James, Brew's skin crawled. The bureau specialist had worked through the night combing Harrison James's home computer. Brew came to FBI headquarters to hear and see his findings.

The dark web. A treasure trove of criminality, corruption, perversion, and persuasion. A black market for the movement of alternative currencies, like bitcoin, and the purchase, often with them, of every repugnant article of vile commerce imaginable. From kidnapped children for sex trafficking, to bomb-making devices for terrorists, to stolen credit card numbers.

The dark web. It was global. It was local. It was across the world in a Yemen hut. It was next door in your neighbor's basement. Especially if your neighbor was Harrison James.

It had started innocently enough for the truck yard manager. Headquarters had sent over a middle-aged techie to reconfigure the transportation department software. He was amiable and too talkative. He told James that he had worked previously in a government job. *Oh, really?* Intelligence work. *Oh, really? Interesting.* Spooky, though, the techie said; he couldn't believe what he saw, what went on in the dark web. *The dark web? Tell me about it.*

Harrison James would still be alive if the company computer genius had declined. But he hadn't; instead, he'd spent three hours with James, showing the manager how he could "jump" selected URL addresses, "crawl" others, and eventually find a window into the dark web and its treasures. He told him about so-called *block chain* encryption, the technology that protected the secrecy of dark web transactions.

In the weeks that followed, James practiced his new discovery, trolling the internet's dark underbelly, marveling at its offerings. Forensic psychiatrists say that of the many exposed to the opportunity of extreme criminality, only a few will choose it. Who are those few? The deeply ill, the depraved, the hateful, the radicalized. And as often as not, the greedy. Greedy like Harrison James. If the persistence of terrorism proved anything, it was that money was not, after all, the root of *all* evil. But it showed also that money was still a deadly—and often used—lure in its pursuit.

James started by buying hacked credit card numbers. Just a few at first to see if they would truly produce purchases. *Be certain to place merchant orders from burner phone under false name,* the dark web sellers cautioned. *Make only one purchase with each set of numbers. If you cannot pick up goods in person, arrange delivery to another address, such as apartment building or place of work, and meet delivery there, never at your own address.*

Wala! Harrison James was hooked.

But was there a way to find *cash* opportunities on the dark web? James searched. Some were too tawdry, even for a greedy man: *van driver needed to transport humans from port to warehouse.* Others seemed too dangerous: *person needed to store armaments.* But a few appeared less risky: *space needed to hold hijacked cigarettes for short time pending further transfer, $5,000 per day.* And one seemed to be right in Harrison's wheelhouse: *commercial/construction trucks, pickups and larger, needed for discreet rental mid-Atlantic region; payment negotiable. Click for encrypted reply.*

But all the dark web advertisers omitted one crucial instruction: never let the FBI get its hands on your web-searching device.

"Did he know he was working with terrorists?" Brew asked the bureau's cybercrimes agent who scoured the dead man's computer.

"There's nothing to show it on any of the transmissions or sites he visited. There are plenty of Jihadist websites, but he never visited any. No sign of radicalization or even political interest."

"So it was just for money?" Brew said.

"Afraid so, Admiral."

"And no further instructions? Nothing about what they were doing with the trucks?"

"No."

Another dead end. Dead ends were growing on trees, Brew thought. Though he didn't yet know about the murder of the seaman at Bethesda Naval, he sensed more was afoot. A big tree was about to fall. Where? Renfro urged patience. Reese was coordinating the Kievs for the cash handoff scheduled for the next morning. "We should have a Tehran operative in our hands, hopefully one still breathing," he said. But Brew's patience was nearly exhausted. He wondered now if he had erred in the decision to wait on the rendition of Behzani from Tehran. The CIA plan was risky, but even if unsuccessful, it may have disrupted the plot, at least bought time.

As he was driven back to the Pentagon, the Navy SEAL called Jack Watson at Langley.

"Do you have your rendition team in place?" Brew asked him.

"Of course. All we'd need is a couple hours to mobilize. We can go anytime on the president's order."

"You may have it soon, Jack. We're not getting very far on our end."

50

TAXIS, TAXIS, EVERYWHERE TAXIS

Never in his life did Yuri Kotva imagine he'd be wearing a wire taped to his burly chest in aid of the FBI, of all people. But as Evan Reese affixed the device and stepped out to Second Street in Brighton Beach to see if the Ukrainian's voice came through loud and clear, the Kiev felt oddly satisfied. *Maybe this is what redemption feels like,* the large man thought.

The terrorist's courier was due in an hour. The wiretap on Hiram Fowler's phone had revealed nothing of relevance since the call from Tehran earlier in the week. Surely, the stadium usher in Washington would be given instructions soon, Reese and his team surmised. Four bureau agents had joined Renfro and Sanderson surveilling Fowler's side-by-side duplex apartment on Ives Place in DC's southeast district. They'd tracked his movements, which were few, since six o'clock the night before. He'd walked to a nearby market to purchase a prepared dinner and stayed home for the rest of the evening. This morning, he'd visited the Starbucks three blocks from his apartment, staying inside for twenty minutes before returning with a newspaper and a breakfast sandwich.

Where would Hiram Fowler be told to meet the courier? Or maybe the money would be dropped cold and he would be instructed where to find it? Union Station was not far; Renfro knew it was a favored location for drug transactions. The teeming foot traffic and convenient wheeled luggage made it a veritable Where's Waldo? scene. Renfro knew you could get away with murder there; more than a few had.

Back in Brooklyn, Yuri's taxi driver stood ready at his cab outside the diner, wearing his own wire. Inside the US Postal Service van parked across the street, bureau technicians completed their sound checks. Five SWAT team officers crowded around them in the windowless truck. The phone rang in the Kievs' cellar. It was from the diner above.

"Your visitor is here, Yuri," the diner manager said.

"Ask him to wait by the taxi outside. I will be right up."

The big Ukrainian strode across the diner to the front door, smiling at the thin man awaiting him. Watching from the corner of the room, Reese was pleased. Yuri did not look around furtively or appear nervous in any way. He looked straight and amiably at the man outside. A leather case, like the ones European men sometimes carry, hung across his chest. He looked Persian, perhaps Syrian. He did not share Yuri's relaxed manner. He rocked from foot to foot and looked up and down the sidewalk, even as Yuri extended his hand to him in greeting.

"You found our little home," Yuri said.

"You have money for me?" the man said tersely, in struggling English.

"If you have mine for me."

The man opened his case and withdrew three large brown envelopes. "Three," he said to Yuri. "For your one." He handed the envelopes over.

"Correct," Yuri said, still smiling warmly. He handed the man his own envelope. "This is clean. This is washed," Yuri said. The man took the envelope and nodded.

"Perhaps you have traveled far," Yuri said. "Are you hungry? You can eat here."

The man shook his head no.

"Then take our taxi here. The driver will take you wherever you want to go. I pay him. Allow me this kindness." The man looked again in each direction, expressionless. "Besides, it is better in a taxi in case you are followed." Yuri spread his arms wide and turned slightly, nearly laughing. "Look! There are taxis all over the place!" The man's eyes flared, as in recognition. He nodded approvingly. Yuri stepped past him and opened the rear door of the taxi. Reese got into his unmarked sedan across the street and prepared to follow.

"Misha," Yuri called to the driver. "Take this friend wherever he asks. No charge. If he wants to stop for food, pay for it." Ukrainian hospitality. The man climbed in. The technicians in the postal van trailing the cab spoke to Reese on his earpiece.

"We only have nine words out of his mouth. Do you want us to relay it over to Bryce or wait for more?"

"Send it," Reese answered. Who knew if the passenger would utter *any* more words. And Wilson Bryce had queued up the voice recognition software awaiting anything the team picked up; he could match it in minutes to a year's worth of phone intercepts, he'd assured Brew and Reese. That was, of course, if there *were* any matches.

"So, where to?" the Kiev taxi driver asked. They had traveled only a block. The passenger looked out at the passing street signs and simply pointed straight ahead. He was texting. "You need to buckle the seat belt," the driver said. The passenger ignored him. "You need to do it," the driver said again. "The police stop us for that now. No shit." He saw the passenger grudgingly reach for the belt. Then he handed up to the driver an index card bearing only a typewritten address: 181 Third Avenue.

"This is where you want to go?" the driver asked. The man nodded.

Say the address! Reese said to himself. *Say the goddamned address!*

But the taxi driver didn't say it. It simply didn't occur to him. Reese and Yuri had instructed him to get the passenger talking if he could, but they'd said nothing about reciting addresses. He knew the Third Avenue neighborhood well. Known as Gowanus, after the canal there, it was an older light manufacturing and warehousing district in transformation. Retail had not arrived in force yet, but many of the buildings had been converted to art studios and lofts. A new hotel had opened, and modern high-end-looking apartment buildings were going up.

"Do you want to stop for food?" he asked. The man said nothing. "Yuri said you're his guest. He is paying." Still nothing. The passenger only pointed with urgency to the index card in the driver's hand.

The Brooklyn traffic was typical: terrible. Yuri's statement about the ubiquity of yellow taxis was true—too true to be good for the FBI team trailing the Kiev cab. The taxis in front of the agents cruised left and right, making seeming figure eights as they changed lanes back and forth. Reese could not slot his sedan in close to the Kiev cab—never within three car lengths—and soon was unsure which taxi in the sea of yellow before him carried the target. Reese called to the postal van behind him.

"Have you got eyes on our cab?"

"Shit no. They're sliding around like spaghetti noodles."

Two of the taxis ahead turned right, one of them using its turn signal, and another moved sharply to the left lane amid wailing horns. Reese followed the two to the right, thinking Yuri's driver had signaled to assist them; the post office van moved left and moved up close behind the third. Both bureau guesses were wrong. Yuri's driver proceeded straight for eight blocks, then took a serpentine route to the Third Avenue address, a modern, high-rise Fairfield Inn and Suites.

The passenger stepped out without a word. He hurried into the lobby, past the unoccupied registration desk, and down a hallway. A rear exit opened to a narrow parking area cramped by a low brick retaining wall and a construction site beyond it. Concrete pilons with protruding rebar shafts dotted the site. Workers were gathering around an earthmover, talking over coffee. The courier scaled the wall easily and walked briskly to the side of the site opposite them. He saw the open gate to Douglas Street ahead, just as he had been told. He turned to confirm he was not being followed, then slid between cars parked at the curb, raising and waving his hand. In twenty seconds, he was riding away.

Yes, in a yellow cab.

51

EIGHTEEN HOURS AND NOTHING TO SHOW FOR IT

There was not much that irritated the veteran Jack Renfro. His patience grew with his age. He'd come to learn that police work was filled with false starts and dead ends. And his own specialty—homicide—imbued in him a strange but undeniable sense of ever-present gratitude. He was always better off than his subject.

But what did irritate him was sitting watch for eighteen hours with nothing to show for it. When he heard from Evan Reese that the FBI had lost the trail of the terrorist courier in New York, especially *how* the evasion had occurred, he doubted that old Hiram Fowler was still in the terrorists' plan in any event.

"Maybe he's coming to Fowler now," Reese said when he called from Brooklyn.

"Not likely," Renfro replied. "The guy had a plan to avoid us. Something changed. Maybe they're in a hurry now. They don't want to spend time with middlemen like Fowler. I think they took his link out. I think they're taking the cash directly to where they need it, not using the old man."

"Well, you might be right," Reese said. "Bryce is monitoring every call coming in from outside the country, and we're listening to everything on Fowler's phone and seeing all his texts and emails. Not a damn thing to him. No instructions about the money."

"Well, there you are," Renfro said. "They've dropped Fowler."

Reese's phone dinged with an incoming call. It was Tyler Brew.

What the admiral told him changed everything. Not for the better.

52

CLUE FROM AN UNLIKELY SOURCE

A week earlier, Brew had put out a standing order to all of the agencies in the joint terrorism task force calling for the immediate report to him of any acts of violence in the New York or Washington regions, but the last one he expected to hear from was the NCIS at Bethesda Naval Hospital.

The NCIS commander did not wait to contact the admiral when the slashed body of seaman Will Bentley was found in the hospital's receiving room. Brew was appalled by the news that had come with the commander's first call yesterday, but the admiral SEAL had not then sensed a connection to his ongoing preoccupation. Nothing in the labyrinthian terrorist plan had so far been linked to the military or its facilities. More out of concern for the fellow navy man's family than anything else, Brew thanked the commander and asked him to keep him updated on his investigation at Bethesda. He reacted much differently when the commander called again this morning.

"We think seaman Bentley's killing is related to a missing package that arrived the morning he was murdered," the NCIS commander said. "We think the killer took the package. We have no idea what was in it."

He told brew the UPS manifest on the delivery to Bethesda listed an eight-pound parcel addressed to a navy doctor.

"What doctor?"

"That's just it. We don't have one by that name. *Dr. Andrew Barnwell.*"

The admiral froze. "Barnwell?" he asked.

"Yeah. And there is no Dr. Barnwell here or anywhere else in the navy."

The commander told Brew what was known thus far about the missing package. It had been included with a large shipment of medical supplies. The Red Cross in Malaysia had initiated the cargo in cooperation with the US military. It had flown with separate military supplies to a NATO air base in Greenland and from there on a navy C-130 transport to the Ketchikan submarine testing base in Alaska.

"UPS picked it up at Ketchikan and flew it into Seattle," the commander said. "It was supposed to all go to a Red Cross distribution center in Seattle. Nothing was marked for Bethesda," the commander said. "We haven't run down all the UPS slips once they took custody, but we've seen the manifest from the navy plane that brought in all of the cargo to Ketchikan and the list of what our sailors transferred to the UPS truck at the Alaska base. There weren't *any* eight-pound parcels on that plane, and nothing that light was put on the UPS truck. All were heavier. Somebody tampered with the boxes and diverted a smaller carton to Bethesda, to the attention of this *Dr. Barnwell*, but we don't know who or where. But it had to be after the navy plane reached our base in Ketchikan."

The commander said UPS was cooperating, and he hoped to know more in hours.

"What does all this mean, Admiral?" he asked.

"Nothing good," Brew said. "Just find that killer, if you can."

53

THE DOTS CONNECTED AT LAST

The NCIS commander in Maryland did not find the killer, but he did find his clothes.

In truth, it was the housekeeper at the Rockville Marriott who discovered the faux navy uniform in room 303 after the guest's early-morning departure. She didn't see it was a counterfeit; it looked to her exactly like her nephew's military dress garb. Her first thought was that the lieutenant had mistakenly left it in haste. Until she saw the maroon spatters on the jacket, near the right shoulder. She didn't take it to the lost and found room near the business office, as she usually would. Instead, she brought it right away to the manager on duty at the front desk.

"Is that blood?" she asked the manager.

"What room did this come from?" he asked.

With one hand, he reached to the desk computer and punched 303. With his other hand, he dialed 911. The screen listed the occupant as Antura Baranwili. He'd checked in with a Turkish passport.

It wasn't said enough. Anyone could be important in thwarting terror—even a maid, even a desk manager.

Not twenty minutes lapsed before Brew's Pentagon office phone rang and the NCIS commander advised him of the finding. The admiral's blood heated. It was coming together, he sensed. *Andrew Barnwell.* It was the alias used on the package sent to the Bethesda Naval Hospital. It was the alias used in the communications with Harrison James. Brew now believed it was really Antura Baranwili, or a man using that alias, who had taken the package, killed the seaman at the hospital, and was now at large with the missing utility truck. *But did anything connect him solidly to Balish Behzani, the wealthy Tehranian?*

Brew stepped to his credenza to confirm his recollection. He wanted to be sure before making the call. So much had happened in the last nine days. The table was covered in neat rows of documents, photos, and notes. He picked up Wilson Bryce's report on the contents of Ranni Shamiri's cell phone taken from his body in Lafayette Square. There it was on the third page; it was as he remembered. Shamiri had received seven calls on the phone, all from a blocked number in Tehran—determined to be the number of Balish Behzani. And Shamiri had made just one call *from* the phone—via website link—to the truck-yard at Potomac Power & Energy, the signal to Harrison James.

Behzani to Shamiri to James to Barnwell to Baranwili. Call them dots; call them leads. Whatever, they all connected. It was enough for Tyler Brew. He called the president.

54

AN IMMEDIATE DECISION

President Del Winters was lunching in the White House with the Indian president and his attaché when Brew's call came in. A navy captain entered the private dining room and silently held up a secure cell phone. The president exchanged nods with the other head of state and rose. She took the phone and stepped past the captain into the corridor. As she passed, the captain said quietly, "Admiral Brew." She nodded and closed the door.

"You have me, Tyler," she said. "What is it?"

"We should take Behzani in Tehran. We should take him now."

"Obviously, things have changed," she said. "You didn't want the rendition when we discussed it last week."

"I didn't think then that we had conclusive proof that he was directing a plot. Now I do."

The president knew in that moment that the admiral SEAL was about to explain his recommendation. He would provide her detailed information and answer fully all of her questions. But what she did next was the best evidence of her deep faith in Brew's judgment, though it couldn't have seemed that way to him in the moment. She put him on hold.

"Just a minute," she said to Brew. She dialed Jack Watson at the CIA. He answered instantly. "Jack," she said, "activate your rendition team for Behzani in Tehran. Get them moving. Assume it's a go, unless

I countermand it." The spymaster never got a word in; she returned to the waiting Brew.

"Okay, Tyler. Tell me."

She winced when Brew told her of the murdered sailor at the naval hospital and the connection to man who had corrupted the employee of Potomac Power & Energy; how the same man had taken a package from the sailor, a package that had been secreted into the country as alleged medical supplies; how there was one common thread between the Lafayette Square killings, the money funneled through the Kievs in Brooklyn, and even the murder of Chandler Bowes in the Washington Nationals parking garage: *Balish Behzani*, the grudge-holding Iranian living the high life in the Elahieh district of north Tehran.

"He's the mastermind," Brew said. "He's directing it all."

"How imminent is this attack?"

"Imminent."

"And we still don't have the target?"

"No. But almost for sure, greater Washington."

"If we take him, you think it will be stopped?"

"We can only hope they wouldn't go ahead without his order."

"If he hasn't already given it," the president said.

"Right. We know they needed some more money but not much. They have it now. Their courier got away from us. They may have nothing more to wait for. The package from Bethesda? I think it's their weapon. Maybe a detonating device."

"Go ahead and take Behzani," the president said.

"Should I call Jack Watson?" Brew asked.

"I already did. That's why I put you on hold. I told him to mobilize his team. I knew you wouldn't want this unless you were sure. And maybe five minutes will make a difference."

55

GOLF AT CAMP DAVID, ABBREVIATED

The weather at Camp David was splendid. Stanley Bigelow, Henry Winters, and Augie the German shepherd were making the most of it and the most of the retreat's amenities too.

Dwight Eisenhower had installed a golf green, complete with a sand trap and three tee boxes approaching it from different distances to comprise a three-hole course. Ike and John F. Kennedy used the abbreviated golf course often, and Gerald Ford, not as frequent a visitor to Camp David as most other presidents, adjudged it the retreat's best feature. The first father made it a point to play the circuit at least twice every day during his prolonged stay and persuaded Stanley to give the game a try. The senior from Pittsburgh had never swung a club.

"It's really all engineering and physics, Stanley," Henry Winters urged. "Swing planes, angles, and speed at impact. You could be a natural." To the relief of the Secret Service agent pulling their carts, Henry's assessment quickly changed after Stanley took fifty blows to play the first two holes. The third tee box was the farthest from the green.

"Do we go out to that one now?" Stanley pointed to the last, most distant tee, undeterred.

"You know, Stanley, I think it's bourbon time," the first father said kindly.

For his part, Augie best enjoyed the walking trails around the perimeter of the entire grounds. He couldn't seem to get enough of them or the smells they offered. But the dog never stooped to sniff an appealing scent before stopping first and looking up to Stanley for consent. Permission was liberally granted. L.T. Kitt had told Stanley that a canine's olfactory skill was a principal source of pleasure for the animal, and even more so as they grew older.

The first father marveled at Augie's behavior as they hiked, particularly his discipline around the plethora of squirrels. Sometimes they darted within feet of the paths. Augie never pursued them.

"He must be the only dog in the world that doesn't chase squirrels," Henry remarked as the three walked.

"He's trained to stay undistracted," Stanley said. "Quantico boot camp. Kitt says they even bring in small animals and let them run the grounds. They teach the dogs to ignore them. To stay focused."

As they walked, they noticed that Tug Birmingham and his security detail were not distracted either. But were they nervous? Every hundred yards along the perimeter fence, Henry and Stanley saw a navy rifleman standing guard. The sentries never turned to acknowledge them as they passed. And when they approached the end of the long loop near the entry gate, a personnel van pulled through, and twenty additional armed sailors disembarked.

"More of them?" Stanley asked Henry, concerned.

"Sometimes Brew overdoes it," Henry said. "Let's consider it a compliment."

About the only disappointment of the visit so far was the electrical problem. The squirrels that Augie wouldn't drive out had plainly had their fill of the wiring to Aspen Lodge. It was to the point that the circuit was so intermittent that viewing a televised baseball game was like eating soup with a fork. You never got much nourishment. Stanley asked Henry why there was no backup generator available.

"I thought the same thing," Henry said. "They say the noise rules it out, it disrupts the sound monitors. 'Security concerns!' They say they need to hear *everything* out there."

But help was on the way, Henry and Stanley were happy to hear from Tug when they returned with Augie from a long walk. The security detail chief greeted them as they entered the main lodge, handing the first father a cordless radio.

"This will get you through the game tonight," Tug said. "They come in the morning to put in new conduit and wiring to the lodge. And don't worry. The chef cooks with gas anyway."

56

THE BRAVE CITIZEN AND THE MISTAKE

As the CIA mobilized in the Middle East, Admiral Brew asked Hannah Harris at the FBI to send her agent Evan Reese back to him in Washington to join L.T. Kitt. Brew wanted the two agents as part of his first response squad whenever the attack began or a new lead surfaced. He was sure the attack would happen in the nation's capital or near it. Nothing else explained the recruitment of Harrison James and the PP&E equipment and the surreptitious transport of the mystery device to Bethesda.

It was late afternoon in Washington and after midnight in Tehran when the counterterrorism chief assembled his domestic team in the Pentagon conference room. He told them about the decision to take Balish Behzani from his residence in Tehran. The mission was underway.

"When?" asked Jack Renfro. "Tonight?"

"Probably tomorrow afternoon, our time; nighttime there, after dark," Brew said. "That is, if they can get everything they need in place. They have to bring in special operators from out of country and get a stealth helicopter ready in the mountains. They're moving now, but it could take another day." He explained Jack Watson's plan to short-circuit Behzani's air-conditioning and gain entry to his residence in the high-rise with infiltrators disguised as repairmen. "The weather is hot there right now, which is good."

Kitt reported on the forensics search and what she had learned at the Rockville Marriott. Hotel rooms were always a nightmare when it came to fingerprints. There were always a slew of them, especially where the room was frequently occupied by short-stay guests.

"We lifted index finger and thumb prints from nine different hands," Kitt said. "But only one overlaid a partial from buttons on the navy uniform. And there's no match on that one in any of our databases. We're still waiting for Interpol."

Brew asked about Baranwili's passport and witnesses.

"The maid never saw him. Neither did the manager. The desk clerk who checked him in didn't get a good look at him. Said he was wearing dark sunglasses and a ball cap pulled low. Good English. She didn't think anything about the Turkish passport; they have customers from the Middle East all the time. Foreign government staff and tourists stay up there because the hotels are so much cheaper than in the District."

"She didn't make a copy of the passport?" Brew asked.

"No, she just looked at it and handed it back to him. So we don't have a photo, assuming it was really his face in it anyway. She *did* enter the passport number on the reservation file. It's a phony. There is no Turkish passport under that number or that name."

"Real pro," Reese said. "That means he didn't use it to get into the country. It wouldn't work for that. Any passport inspector would reject it."

"What about other hotels?" Brew asked. "He must be staying someplace."

Had it been asked by a fellow bureau agent, Kitt might have been offended. *Of course*, she'd had a team check every hotel, motel, and bed-and-breakfast within seventy-five miles to see if any guest had checked in with that passport. When she didn't respond immediately, Brew sensed the answer to his question.

"I suppose you've already looked at that," he said.

Kitt nodded. "It hasn't been used again anywhere. No one has tried to check in under that name either. As far as we can tell, that alias and that passport was never used before he used it in Rockville. Evan's right; the guy's a pro. Every step is covered."

"Oh, it's well planned all right," the admiral said. "As carefully as any plot I've seen."

"But there was *one* mistake," Jack Renfro said. "And we did get *one* lucky break." Brew thought he knew what Renfro meant, but the others looked puzzled.

"The man sent to kill Shamiri and Dafur in Lafayette Square fucked up," Renfro said. "He left Shamiri's phone for us. That was the mistake. It was made because we got lucky. Lucky with that citizen who came running at him in the park. That brave citizen. Without him, we wouldn't have that phone. And without it, we wouldn't know about Behzani."

"You're right, Jack," Tyler Brew said. "We do have that. Let's just pray it's enough."

57

LUCK IS EARNED

It may be true that necessity is the mother of invention. It may be true that chance favors the prepared mind. But one thing Jack Watson knew from experience was that luck was earned. Through intelligence relationships developed over decades, through deep-seated alliances. When you came upon information you had no way of knowing through your own designs, you could call it a gift, you could call it good fortune. But to Watson, and to Tyler Brew, to whom he quickly conveyed what he'd been told by Israeli intelligence, you called it a game changer.

When Brew saw that the CIA's Watson was calling, he assumed it was an update on the rendition of Behzani in Tehran.

"No, it's not that." Watson stopped him. "Something else entirely. But it may be connected in some way."

Brew listened as Watson described the new information. His counterpart from Mossad had just called from Tel Aviv. Israeli intelligence had learned from a graduate student at Hebrew American University that a scientist at the Institute of Technology and Mechanics in Tehran was working on a device to propel nerve gas under pressure. The Israeli spymaster assumed the threat was intended for use against Israeli targets but wanted to share it with the US in case there were broader plans for it.

"How is an Israeli student doing research in an Iranian university?" Brew asked.

"He wasn't," Watson said. "He heard it from *another* graduate student who was. A Pakistani Muslim. They met at a conference in Dubai. The Pakistani student did a fellowship in Tehran for two years. He told the Israeli guy that in his second year there, he'd been asked to help with a program sponsored by an odd professor."

"Why odd?"

"He said the professor was brilliant but a terrible communicator. Always talked in weird, incomplete sentences. Distracted all the time."

"Sounds like a mad scientist."

"Well, the word was he was also a radical Islamist scientist. The Pakistani student needed the stipend, so he worked on the program. For a while. He quit because it gave him the jitters. He couldn't see any safe or legitimate use of the thing they were trying to build. *Who'd want to disperse aerosolized nerve gas under pressure?* he wondered. This young student is like 99.9 percent of Muslims. He doesn't want to hurt anybody."

"Aerosolized?" Brew asked.

"Yeah. Nerve gas packed into cannisters like spray paint."

"How far did they get with the design?"

"He doesn't know, but he knows prototypes were produced," Watson said. "He left the project eight months ago. He guesses they're finished. I have some more details, including a diagram the Israeli student made from his memory of what the other told him. It's on its way to you. Is this any help, you think?"

"I hope not. But thanks."

58

FRENZY AT CAMP DAVID

It began as a lovely, quiet morning at the presidential retreat. Stanley rose before Henry and took Augie out for an early walk. The old engineer knew he'd been eating more during his visit, especially enjoying the appetizers that the first father ordered at cocktail hour. He remembered that at home Helen gently suggested an extra walk or two when he'd stayed too long at the table.

He was missing Helen. It surprised him that he missed her so much. He'd been widowed and alone for a decade before meeting the reserves colonel when he was already past seventy years. In those earlier days, he'd grown used to his solitary life, he thought. He didn't feel odd, off, or lacking when away on his own, such as when he traveled—which was frequently—for baseball games or engineering assignments. But now he knew he felt differently. It wasn't that he felt anxious to leave Camp David, though his visit was now in its fourth day; he was pleased to be with his friend Henry Winters, and he never tired of talking with the retired general. It was just a sense that it would be better if Helen were there. Everything was better with Helen. Augie seemed to understand. When the dog and Stanley were alone, he often spoke to the canine about her. Augie always responded warmly with wagging tail and nuzzling snout whenever Helen's name was used, as Stanley had several times this morning on their walk.

As the two of them made the last bend on the trail approaching the front of the compound and Aspen Lodge, they saw the Potomac Power & Energy truck stopped outside the front guard gate. Six armed navy sentries took positions around it, and a seventh swept its underside with a long detection instrument. An eighth questioned the driver and the companion sitting on the passenger side. When Stanley stopped to observe, Augie sat down, relaxed and unimpressed.

The two men stepped out of the truck, presumably on command. A sentry patted them down, checking each pocket of their cargo pants. The questioning sentry made a call from his walkie-talkie. Stanley presumed it was to Tug Birmingham or someone in the Secret Service station. There was a pause of a minute or so. Then the sailors stepped away from the truck, and the motorized gate slid open. The truck ambled in, passing directly in front of Stanley and Augie. *A trench digger at the rear of the truck,* Stanley noted. *And lengths of aluminum electrical conduit. Hooray!* he thought. *Televised news and baseball tonight!*

The PP&E vehicle pulled near the right-front corner of the main building, then slowly backed up about fifty feet on the grassy lawn. Stanley saw the main junction box for the electrical supply lines mounted just above the foundation. He and Augie walked over as the workers climbed down from the truck. One moved immediately to the rear and hoisted himself up to the controls of the hydraulic ditch digger. The other nodded to Stanley.

"Is he friendly?" the man motioned to the dog.

"When he's supposed to be."

The man did not appear overly comforted. But Augie walked with Stanley toward him, his red tongue hung to the side of a wide grin. He sat in front of the man and looked up to receive his hand to the top of his broad head. The man relaxed and rubbed the dog's ears.

"He's well trained," Stanley said. "But he may be rusty on laying conduit. How much are you putting in?"

"At least fifty feet," the worker said. "If it's corroded beyond that, we'll go back farther. But the images we took last month show that should be enough."

"I see that's the main circuit," Stanley said, pointing to the junction box.

"Yeah. That's the only one. It's got a conduit manifold inside it that feeds lines of flexible conduit to every receptacle and switch box in the house. You an engineer?"

"After a fashion," Stanley said.

"Well, I wish I could let you inspect it all when we're done. But the company is sending a supervisor to do that tomorrow."

Stanley worried that might delay use of the new power. "But we can use it tonight, can't we?"

"Oh, sure. We'll have it up and running for you by this afternoon. But it has to be inspected just in case."

"Great," Stanley said. "We'll leave you to it then."

He and Augie had barely settled inside when the pandemonium arrived, courtesy of Wilson Bryce and Tyler Brew at the Pentagon.

Bryce had studied so many reports from the NSA analysts detailing the ongoing satellite surveillance of Potomac Power & Energy vehicles that his eyes blurred when they landed on his desk, or his shift replacement's, at precisely three minutes after the hour, every hour. But the one that arrived at 9:03 that morning sent a flush of adrenalin to his brain. He pounded the speed dial number with so much force his fingernail splintered.

"Tyler!" he shouted when Brew picked up his call. "There's a PP&E truck at Camp David! It was at the front gate a half hour ago!"

The admiral didn't take the time to even reply. He hung up and called the Secret Service station at the presidential retreat.

"We have a code one at Camp David," he told the agent who answered. It meant an active, armed threat had been detected. "Get Henry Winters covered and everybody else into safe rooms. There's a utility company truck on the premises. Disable it and whoever is with it."

"But it was cleared in," his agent said. "For maintenance work."

"I don't care. Tell Tug to lock it down and immobilize whoever came in with it. And then transfer me to the navy commander on site."

Tug Birmingham had personally reviewed the arrangements with

PP&E and just authorized the truck's passage at the gate. But the hair on his neck rose on the word from Tyler Brew and the admiral's order. Maybe the work was a charade. Maybe terrorists had gained entry right under his own nose. *Thank God the president is not here,* Tug thought. But the first father and everyone else at the compound was exposed. He drew his handgun with one hand, his walkie-talkie with the other, and raced full speed from the small Secret Service station house behind the main lodge.

"Code one!" he shouted into the walkie-talkie to the entire team. "Unit three. Meet me behind Aspen. All others, fan out. I'm going for Papa POTUS. Don't approach the truck until I'm ready."

Tug's short, strong legs pounded like tree trunks against the hardwood floors as he burst through Aspen Lodge. He guessed correctly that Henry Winters would be near the breakfast room. The first father stood in the archway of the nook, calling to Stanley across the living room. Both of the older gentlemen looked stunned. Augie jumped from the couch and stood rigidly at Stanley's side. But the dog was not growling.

Tug knew better than to manhandle Stanley. It might arouse the dog's anger. He knew that the civilian engineer could not have a better protector anyway; the dog would bring Stanley wherever Tug took Henry. The agent was right. He went directly to Henry, threw an arm around the tall general's midsection, and led him swiftly through the kitchen. Augie pushed Stanley's knees from behind, sending him close behind Tug and Henry.

"Where are we going?" Henry asked.

"To the cellar," Tug said. He opened the door to the stairwell. "All of you, get down there. Right now." Stanley peered down the steps. It wasn't completely dark; sunlight poked through at least one window. "*Do not* come up until I tell you. I'll send two agents to you as soon as I can. They'll announce themselves before they open the door." Henry and Stanley, Augie following, went down the steps carefully.

Before he closed the door above them, Tug called down.

"And, Stanley. When the agents come down, don't let Augie eat them." He *wasn't* kidding.

The door closed.

"My God, Henry," Stanley said as the three of them huddled below. "What's going on?"

"I don't know. But I'm glad Delores isn't here."

At the Pentagon, Brew stood before an open mic, listening to the communications between the teams in Maryland. He'd sent three navy snipers to the roof of Aspen Lodge and fifty of the navy troops to the woods around the entire perimeter. He was pleased that he had earlier increased the standing force at the compound from its customary size of one hundred. He still had fifty sailors to keep within the fence to cover Tug Birmingham and his Secret Service protection detail.

Tug led four of his men in a V formation from the rear of the lodge, all with weapons drawn. One of the workers was standing near the junction box, holding a small device with a flashing bulb at its end. The other was at the rear of the vehicle, unlatching the truck bed's dropping hatch. Tug ran toward the man nearest the building with the two agents in formation behind him on his right flank. The two on the left flank raced instinctively to the other worker at the back of the truck. "Don't move!" Tug screamed. The men looked at the charging agents with ashen stares. "Get down!" Tug shouted. The man at the truck hatch complied at once and dropped to the grass, face-first. But the other froze, perhaps in fear, perhaps in utter puzzlement. Tug drove his shoulder into the man's chest, pinning him harshly against the wall of the lodge. The instrument fell from his hand. He looked terrified. And nothing like a terrorist.

"What's that thing?" Tug asked, still pinning him, nodding toward the fallen device.

"It's a line tester. To make sure the juice is off. God damnit, what are you doing to us? Holy fuck! They told us you knew we were coming."

Tug stepped back. Without removing his eyes from the workman's, he called back to the other agents. "Has he got anything back there?"

"Nothing, Tug."

Brew listened as the officers in the woods each checked in. Nothing. Nothing. Nothing.

Tug holstered his gun and waved for a navy officer. "You've got Admiral Brew live, I'm sure. Tell him it's all clear here. False alarm." The message was conveyed.

But the pandemonium was only beginning.

59

THE SCIENTIST DIDN'T SUGARCOAT IT

Jack Watson called the Defense Department and asked them to send him their three best chemical weapons experts to meet with him at Langley. He sent the technical papers he'd received from Mossad so they could study them on their laptops on the way over. Watson was neither an engineer or a chemist, but he knew enough to see that the drawings of the cannister, pump, and chemical compounds were ominous. But not as ominous as what he learned when the scientists arrived and explained what they depicted.

"The kid that gave these to Mossad," the senior-most of the weapons experts said to Watson, "have they hired him in?"

"The grad student? Probably."

"I wish we'd have gotten him first," the DOD expert said. "These drawings are unbelievable from memory. And the chemical notations and structures. Precise as hell."

The engineer and the chemists gave Jack Watson a ten-minute primer on chemical nerve agents, the history of their development and production and known uses to kill. The first nerve agents were invented for legitimate purposes by German scientists in 1936 looking for chemical compounds to function as insecticides less expensive and easier to handle than the nicotine-based substances then in use. The so-called G-series of agents were born, including sarin, tabun, soman, and variants of them. All were based on phosphorus, an element common in nontoxic products. The first developers were shocked—and horrified—by the extreme toxicity of their new phosphorus compounds and immediately ruled them out for agricultural use. At least one of the German technical workers was killed instantly by accidental contact with one of the new agents, and scores of livestock perished in the early testing. But they weren't horrified enough to refrain from handing over their research to the Nazi military scientists for weapons development.

The Nazis soon began building a production and test facility in Poland; their intent was to make the agents and incorporate them into missiles and artillery shells. They never got the chance. Before the Polish site was fully operational, the Nazis fell to Stalin's westward march, and the site and the research files fell into Russian hands. Like many deadly means and minds, they incubated and grew throughout the Cold War in the custody of the Soviet Union. Stockpiles of the G-series agents accumulated, which the Soviets shared with aligned militaries, including Syria's.

But the G-series agents, like sarin gas, were hardly an ideal weapon. Apart from their inhumanity as a tool of war, they were temperamental in manufacture, dangerous to handle, and deployable only at great risk to the deploying. For use in targeted killing in spy craft—of keen interest to Moscow—a wholly different molecule was needed. Readily available poisons were standard tools of assassination in Cold War espionage, but they required the target to consume them in beverages or food. Spies wanted a weapon that required, well, less cooperation of the victim. The quest for Novichok began.

No, Novichok was not a person. It was the Russian-developed nerve agent far more potent than any made before it—at least five times deadlier than even VX, the killing agent first produced by British industrial scientists in 1952, itself more powerful than the earlier G-series compounds. The Novichok molecule was "a whole new ball game," as Henry Winters or Stanley Bigelow likely would have described it. Even its name, Russian for "newcomer" or "new boy," evoked its perverse innovative nature.

The CIA director listened intently. He'd known of the US inventory in past decades of the VX agent. Britain had shared it with NATO allies. Its extreme lethality was demonstrated in 1968 when a large volume of the agent somehow escaped from a US weapons storage facility in Utah, killing three thousand sheep grazing downwind in a field more than twenty miles away in the Skull Valley. But the details of the more recent killing agent, Novichok, were new to him.

"What makes Novichok so different is its capacity for binary compounding," the lead scientist explained. "Think of binary as in two pieces, two stages. The old stuff had to be combined in a production plant. You made a batch of the stuff, and you had to store it, handle it, get it into a device or munition, all while it was in a deadly dangerous form. But Novichok can be made—reacted—at the time of actual end use. Not in advance. You can make the lethal agent from two separate precursors that are, in and of themselves, nontoxic, legal substances."

"So you can transport them—these precursors—without detection by the sensors we use to find banned substances?" Watson surmised.

"Exactly. And you can transport them without killing yourself."

"How do you make them deadly and use them?"

"You place the precursors in a device where they are held apart until the moment you want to combine them—react them—to form the Novichok molecule," the chemist went on. "That's what these diagrams show. The Iranian scientist designed a cannister to separate the precursors and hold them under pressure until an explosive signal sent to the cannister joins them inside. The same small explosion, or maybe a second one, triggers a pump—it doesn't have to be big—to send the agent, now deadly, out of the cannister."

"Terrible."

"The grad student says the pump device was Russian design," the military engineer said. "Intentionally. The Iranian scientist didn't want to use Russian engineering, but he was told to use it anyway. That way, everything would point to Russia when it was ever used.

Russian-invented Novichok and a Russian propulsion device. Only the cannister and the aerosolization were his own original work."

"Does Mossad agree with you? I hear they're great at this shit."

"They do, Director."

"So what do you think is the endgame? What's the most likely way they'd deploy this thing?"

The experts looked at each other. The senior scientist answered.

"Smuggle this cannister, loaded with the components, into the country. Smuggle in the pumping device at the same time or separately. Find a way to get the unit into a building. Detonate the charges remotely and kill everybody in the place in thirty seconds."

Jack Watson looked grim.

"Well, you don't have to sugarcoat it," he said.

60

DEATH AT THIRTY-SECOND INTERVALS

The first bomb detonated in an open-topped waste bin near the entrance of Old Ebbitt Grill on Fifteenth Street, around the corner from the White House. The time was 10:16 in the morning. At precise thirty-second intervals, three more explosions followed at locations more or less ringing the presidential grounds.

By the time the last of the bombs exploded in Lafayette Square, President Del Winters was shrouded by a bevy of Secret Service agents and rushed to a caravan of six armored vehicles through a side exit of the White House, shielded by thirty marines that surrounded it and eight snipers perched on the roof. The president was put into the fifth van originally, but as soon as the caravan turned behind the building and view was more restricted, agents leapt from the vans like pit stop mechanics rushing to change a tire. They moved her hurriedly to the third vehicle before the caravan streamed off, flanked on both sides by police on motorcycles.

Tug Birmingham was notified at Camp David; the president was coming there. Tell her father she is safe. Tyler Brew was patched through to her in the caravan within minutes.

"Is it underway?" the president asked him. "The attack?"

"If it isn't, this is one hell of a coincidence."

"You don't believe in coincidences."

"No, I don't."

"Are their civilian casualties?"

"There have to be," Brew said. "At least it wasn't lunch hour when the sidewalks are jammed. But there have to be. The devices were powerful enough but crude. Something like the ones used by the Boston Marathon bombers. Which bothers me. All of the bomb squads are on it. The Capitol Police have sequestered the whole area. Only medical help is getting in or out."

"Could it be retaliation for taking Behzani?"

"Can't be," Brew said. "We haven't tried to take him yet. The rendition mission is tonight in Tehran. There's no sign that our team has been detected."

"Why are you bothered because the bombs were crudely made?"

"Because *nothing* in this plot has been crude. Not in the planning, not in the execution. Until this. And last night, we received intelligence about an Iranian scientist building a sophisticated nerve gas weapon in the last six months. Overnight, we confirmed contacts between him and Behzani."

"Who gave us the intelligence?"

"Israel."

"You think it's credible?"

"I've never seen them wrong."

"But if they have something worse, why the bombs today?"

"It's possible it was plan B for them. We screwed up their money supply. Or the murder of the sailor at Bethesda may have made them nervous, fouled their timing. So maybe this is what they went with. Maybe it's over. But I really don't think we're that lucky. I don't think it *was* plan B."

"What was it then?"

"I think it was probably *part I*. A distraction, a diversion. I think *part II* is still coming." Del Winters paused.

"Do you have any ideas on the real target?" she finally asked.

"Not a goddamned one." It was Brew's turn to pause. "You know one of the reasons I wanted to rendition Behzani was to disrupt the attack before he could start it," he said to her. "That reason is off the table now because he's already ordered it. Do you still want to go ahead with the rendition?" He knew the international repercussions could be uncontrollable. But the president did not hesitate.

"Hell yes," she said. "Take the sonofabitch."

61

ALL AS PLANNED

CNN International and the overseas news channels were covering nonstop the frenzy in Washington. Reporters stood filing their updates before a backdrop of flashing ambulances and SWAT team trucks. So many military helicopters circled above—without relent; it seemed like the soundtrack to a war movie.

Balish Behzani watched pleasingly, if uncomfortably, from his opulent residence in Tehran. Uncomfortably, because the building's air-conditioning had failed four hours ago in early afternoon—when the heat was its most searing. All of the exterior walls in the spacious high-rise apartments were made, impractically, of glass from floor to ceiling. Behzani felt like he was sitting in an incubator.

For the moment, though, the events in Washington outweighed the inconvenience of the quarters in which he watched them. Fourteen were confirmed dead; dozens seriously injured. The White House, US Capitol, and the Supreme Court Building were all on lockdown. Incoming traffic was blocked for a twelve-block perimeter. Motorists and pedestrians inside the perimeter were told to stay in place until they could be cleared to leave. Hundreds of officers from federal and local agencies went door to door through business establishments and apartment residences looking for evidence and suspects.

At the president's request, Admiral Tyler Brew made a statement from a Pentagon podium at noon, as soon as he knew the president had safely arrived at Camp David. Some Americans did not even know he commanded all federal antiterror efforts. He was not a publicity seeker and never gave interviews unless the president told him to. He was an inexperienced public speaker and knew it. But he was clearheaded and clear speaking. He might be called salty. No one would call him wordy. All would say they understood him the first time.

His statement to the country was brief. He said no further explosive devices had yet been found. But he said he considered the threat to be ongoing. Other destructive events were entirely possible, even likely, in coming hours and days. The president was safe in an undisclosed, secure location. The vice president was in Chicago at the time of the explosions and was now safe at an undisclosed military base. Citizens should follow the instructions of law enforcement as they received them. He would not take questions, he said.

"Why will you not take questions?" reporters shouted.

"Because I have terrorists to catch," he said and walked out.

In Tehran, Behzani watched Brew intently. *He is formidable man, this Navy SEAL,* the Tehranian thought. But he smiled at the admiral's reference to "undisclosed secure location." *We shall see how secure!* Behzani thought. *We shall see how undisclosed.* He called Jameel Daash at the institute to commend him on the synchronization of the primitive bombs.

"All is good, Daash," he told the scientist. "All is happening as planned."

"Yes, it will be so," said Daash.

The NSA operator listening in real-time made animated motions with her hands, as if playing charades. *More, more, say more!* she silently urged. *Say what is next!* But they did not say more.

Brew was told immediately of the telephone intercept. He called Jack Renfro, who was at police headquarters in Washington with bomb squad specialists. Renfro had asked them to bring all they knew about the explosion sites and how they had been inspected before the blasts. Brew told Renfro of his suspicion that the morning's bombings were a prelude to more and about the phone intercept of Behzani and the scientist in Tehran. He asked Renfro to find Audrey Sanderson, L.T. Kitt, and Evan Reese.

"And when I find them?" Jack asked.

"Bring them up to Camp David. We have to brief the president. I'm heading there now."

62

HE HAD TOLD HIRAM THE TRUTH. AFTER A FASHION

It was unpleasant killing a man you appreciated. Even for Andruzal. He knew the old citizen was not a corrupt man like Harrison James. No, Hiram Fowler was enticed not by greed but by need.

In his heart, Andruzal had doubted the old man would in the end even do what he was asked. It was one of the reasons he had not paid him in advance, as he had James. But when the bombs did explode that morning, he felt gratitude the old man would never appreciate. If he had failed, Andruzal knew he would have needed to create the diversion himself. The explosions were essential to getting the president out of the White House. Without them, the entire plan was fouled. Who could know if he and his truck could deposit the bombs and escape unnoticed? As unnoticed as a slender senior citizen in a Washington Nationals baseball cap.

It was just after noon when Andruzal parked at the curb on Ives Place. He looked up and down the block. There were no signs of police despite the mayhem just a few miles away. He walked up to the modest side-by-side residence, pulling on a poncho as he approached the porch. The front curtain of the adjoining apartment was pulled to the side. He looked in and saw an elderly woman seated with her back to him. The television she watched blared so loudly he could hear the newscasters clearly from the porch.

Hiram Fowler opened his front door even before Andruzal knocked; he'd been watching for his visitor's arrival. The old man looked beside himself.

"Why didn't you tell me they were bombs!" he said from inside the closed screen door. "Look what has happened! People are dead! You told me they were only decoys that would smoke and burn! Get away from me! I don't want the money!"

"I told you the truth," Andruzal said. In the terrorist's own skewed calculus, he had told the truth. The explosives *were* decoys. He pulled the screen door open, stepped inside, and closed both it and the main door. "You did your job," he said emotionlessly.

Hiram Fowler stood before him, frozen, disconsolate. He made no effort to run, resist, or scream. Andruzal unhurriedly withdrew an eight-inch knife from his belt and thrust it deeply into the old man's abdomen, extending his left arm under the old man's right shoulder to keep him from falling as he pulled viciously upward three times. When he was sure life was leaving Hiram's eyes, he lowered him, not roughly, to the floor.

He removed his poncho, bundled it into a ball, and left it in the kitchen wastebasket. He rinsed his knife blade thoroughly under the faucet and wiped it dry with a dishcloth lying on the counter. He returned to the body inside the front door. He bent over the lifeless man splayed across a throw rug, counted out ten one-hundred-dollar bills, and placed them neatly next to him. He stepped onto the front porch and closed the door quietly behind him. He examined the quiet street. The convenience store and the Starbucks farther down were dark; businesses had closed in the wake of the morning's attack. He walked casually to the truck and drove away.

63

COMEDIC RELIEF AT THE MOTEL 6

Andruzal spent the afternoon randomly moving the PP&E pickup truck through suburban neighborhoods around Washington. He knew he couldn't leave it parked for too long in any one place. Harrison James had told him that it was better to leave the GPS transponder in the truck so that it would look like any other of the hundreds of company vehicles swirling around on the broad dispatch monitor at the truckyard. It made sense to Andruzal. But James had cautioned him that if the truck remained stationary for a long time during normal repair hours, it might be noticed.

"What about overnight?" the terrorist had asked James. "Can I park it behind hotels?"

"That'll work," the corrupted manager said, "so long as they are near the outer ring of the service area. Drivers with assignments out there are allowed to take their trucks home if they live nearby, or to hotels if they need to go back to sites in the morning that are thirty miles from the truck yard. By the end of the day, there are always a lot of stationary GPS signals. It won't be obvious."

Andruzal's nomadic pattern had been effective so far. He never stayed in the same hotel twice and was careful to select ones with filled parking lots. In earlier weeks, he was able to check in with the same forged passport. But as the attack date grew near, he used a different one with a new alias each night. Luckily, he thought, he had never presented the *Baranwili* passport before using it the night before the visit to the Bethesda Naval Hospital, when he had slashed the sailor in the receiving room. After that, of course, he could not use it again without triggering immediate pursuit. But he wasn't alarmed. Behzani had provided him a thick sheaf of passports. The Tehran mastermind had marked those that carried authentic control numbers—suitable for air travel—from those that should be used only for lodging. Andruzal checked the sheaf. Two remained in each category.

At dusk, he pulled the truck into a one-story Motel 6 off Interstate 70 in Mt. Airy, Maryland. It was twenty miles from his morning destination. He knew this was probably the last night of his life, and he was nervous. More nervous than he had thought he would be. But he did not think he was afraid, and he wanted *not* to be afraid. The nervousness embarrassed him. Why was he nervous unless he *was* fearful? Was he weak? Weaker than he wanted to be? Weaker than Behzani expected him to be?

He pulled the truck to the rear of the motel so that it could not be seen from the road. He took his duffel of clothing and the square leather case from behind the bench seat and walked inside to the tiny registration area. An affable man at the desk greeted him.

"Do you have a reservation, sir?"

"No. Is that a problem?"

"Not at all," the man said. "Unless you require a room on a high floor." He laughed at his own joke. Andruzal laughed with him, grateful for the moment of humor. "I suppose this is not a good day to be joking though," the motel employee said. "What with the mess downtown this morning and all."

"But we can all use a little laugh, can't we?" Andruzal said, smiling and placing an Egyptian passport on the counter. "And I will settle for as high a floor as you have."

"You know, our motel company is very American that way," the desk clerk said, glancing perfunctorily at the passport. "We treat *everybody* the same."

"Oh?"

"Yes. Everybody gets the same floor and nobody gets breakfast." He laughed again. Andruzal smiled again.

In his tidy room, Andruzal turned on the television and placed the leather case on the bedspread. He opened it and removed the draw-stringed cloth sack. *Make sure the cloth sack is dry,* he recalled Daash's instruction. *Check for any condensation on the cylinder. Remember to look carefully at the bottom rim. It should not feel cold.* Andruzal ran his finger slowly around the bottom of the cylinder. He held it under the bed stand lamplight to examine it. No moisture. The cylinder felt cool to his touch, perhaps slightly below room temperature. Definitely not *cold.*

He knew he should feel satisfaction, even joy. The plan—in seemingly every aspect—was working flawlessly. The device was stable, had passed inspection, and Balish would be pleased. But he knew too that a man who knew the day of his likely death—*such a blessing!*—should not deny himself the truth. He should not pretend to ignore the feelings of his soul. And Andruzal did not ignore them. *Nothing can stop this now,* he understood. *And I am not joyful. I do not welcome death, and I will try to live. But the cannister is ready. There is no reason to stop. The rest is up to me, to my strength. It is down to my duty.*

The television coverage lifted his spirits. Washington was in chaos. The death count from the morning's bombings had risen to nineteen. The hospitals cautioned it would likely rise. Jihadist websites celebrated the attack, and one group from Afghanistan, according to plan, falsely claimed credit.

He counted the money brought from Brooklyn. He wasn't sure how much the courier had removed for his own escape. The pressure cookers had cost more than expected because more than one could not be purchased at the same store at the same time. Notice might be taken. The Walmart price was far lower, but it was too risky to take advantage of it. The same was true of the other components, which he had mixed and assembled carefully to Daash's instructions. To his relief, he hadn't been burdened with the more complicated detonation switches and connectors; they'd arrived in the Rockville post office box "snap-in ready," with an easy-to-read diagram. He'd chosen the Motel 6 to conserve cash.

After paying for his room on check-in, $4,300 dollars remained. It should be enough to hide for another night, if he managed to escape, and still buy a plane ticket.

Dinner? He wasn't hungry.

64

DON'T BE RUDE, BALISH

At moments like this, Balish Behzani missed the days of heavy telephone handsets and their sturdy bases. In those days, you could slam down the phone with force, sending an unambiguous message of disgust to the other end of the line, with or without the aid of profanity. For the frustrated, it provided at least a measure of satisfaction and, to Balish's mind, an underrated catharsis now lost to the stampede of technology. How could you slam down a cell phone?

Of course, technology had not eliminated profanity; it more likely promoted it. Certainly it did for Balish Behzani.

"What the fuck are you doing about this?" he screamed at the building superintendent as soon as the man answered. "It is sweltering in here! You can't replace a fucking fuse?"

"It is not a fuse, Balish," the superintendent said. "We checked that, of course. Do not be so rude to me. We are doing everything we can. Somehow the whole system is down. We are trying to find the circuit that has impaired all the others. It could be in an individual thermostat in one of the residences. Nowadays, everything is integrated. We are looking at all of them. Teams of electricians have started in the middle floors. They are working up and down from there. We will find it. But it may take a few hours."

Balish did all that today's technology permitted. He hit the end call button without saying goodbye. Not nearly as satisfying as a good slam.

But it *was* satisfying to the NSA operative listening in. He advised the team of three CIA black ops officers gathered in the CityNorth Electrical van a block from Behzani's high-rise.

"You've caught a break," the NSA listener told the team in the van. "They think the problem's in an integrated thermostat, and they're moving up and down from the middle of the building to inspect each one. Trust me, that won't help. We took the cooling down with a worm bot to the main circuit in the system compressors. But now you won't have to break into his residence; he'll be expecting you. So long as you get there before the building's team does."

"When will they?"

"You've got sixty minutes, at least."

"How do you know?"

"We tapped the superintendent too."

The officers in the van were pleased. One of them, the lone CIA field officer assigned to Iran in-country, knew the Elahieh district well. To support him, Jack Watson had moved two other Muslim agents, one man and one woman, across the border from Iraq that morning. They'd posed as husband and wife traveling to Tehran for a family wedding. All three were awaiting the arrival of the stealth helicopter due to land on the rooftop in three minutes. The local agent had scouted the roof the day before and taped a translucent X in the center of the spacious rooftop terrace. The clear tape was barely visible, even in daylight, but would illuminate to a lime-green marker for the sensors on the underside of the chopper.

Riding with the pilot was a Muslim Navy SEAL garbed in an electrician's uniform matching the others. He'd been handpicked by Admiral Brew to join the rendition team on account of his hand-to-hand abduction skills and fluency in Farsi. The SEAL was to meet them on Behzani's floor.

The female agent in the passenger seat of the van stared through night vision binoculars at the sky above the high-rise. "*Thar* she is," she said. "Descending on a straight vertical from four hundred feet. Can you believe that thing? I don't hear a goddamned thing." They pulled from the curb and drove to the entrance of the high-rise residences.

The security guard at the lobby desk didn't even bother to look at the identification lanyards the agents extended to him. He was too busy handling the nonstop calls to the front desk from angry residents. With the phone in one hand, he simply waved toward the elevators with the other. Up they went.

When the three agents reached Behzani's floor, the Navy SEAL who'd come by helicopter was already waiting at the end of the hall. He didn't have far to come from the rooftop; the terrorist lived only two floors below it.

The rendition planners had always been concerned about the second residence on Behzani's floor. They knew it could have been a much bigger risk. Many of the floors in the building housed four apartments, and a few even six. But the highest floors held the most massive residences—just two on each floor—each occupying the entire length of one side of the building, the center hallway dividing them. Had time not been of the essence, the rendition could have been made when it was known that the residence opposite Behzani's was unoccupied. But time *was* of the essence. It was one of the reasons Tyler Brew had sent the SEAL along. He knew the seasoned warrior could react instantly—and lethally—to any contemporaneous interference or complication.

The team had also anticipated that Behzani would have a personal security presence at his residence. On this, they were correct. But later they would say they had not expected him to be so accommodating. Just as the SEAL approached Behzani's double-door entrance, a tall man in a finely tailored dark suit and tie stepped out into the hallway. The door behind him remained open. He did not seem alarmed or skeptical.

"Greetings," the SEAL said in Farsi. "I see you are expecting us."

The female agent stepped in front of the guard and smiled; the other two officers slipped quickly behind him and stood back to back in the open doorway. One faced into the residence, the other faced the back of the guard. The SEAL stood to the side, closer to the entrance of the residence across the hall, in the event anyone emerged from it. The security man looked straight into the eyes of the woman in front of him. She took the canvas tool bag from her shoulder and dropped it to the floor, drawing the guard's gaze downward. Then she drove a furious fist to his breastbone. The officer behind him simultaneously covered the guard's mouth with one hand and slapped a hypodermic needle into his neck with his other. The man sagged and fell backward into the agent's clutch. The woman picked up her kit and stepped quickly around him and into the residence, in case she was needed to assist the officer already inside.

"Amir?" a raspy voice called from the main room, out of sight. All four of the operatives were now inside the foyer, the SEAL entering last and closing the door. They heard Behzani's steps as he moved through the main room toward them, and the CNN International broadcast from the television. "Amir?" he called again. "Are the workmen here, Amir?"

The SEAL moved quickly up the side wall of the foyer so that he would not be seen immediately when the terrorist reached the large entry space. The unconscious guard was pulled forward, then swiveled facedown, blocking the door from the inside. Balish Behzani stepped into sight and gasped. His face went white around his black beard. Each of the team members carried a folded photo of the terrorist leader; none needed to consult it. It was him.

He who hesitates doesn't get to scream. The Navy SEAL pounced from his side position and planted a gloved fist in Behzani's mouth. It was synchronized rendition. One of the CIA officers pulled the man's arms behind his back while another instantly zip-tied his wrists, perhaps more tightly than required. The woman agent plugged his thigh with a self-injecting syringe. Behzani's eyes rolled up, and he collapsed. Only then did the SEAL remove his fist from the terrorist's mouth, replacing it with three whirling wraps of black duct tape.

"How long will he be out?" the SEAL asked.

"Which one?" the woman asked.

"Behzani."

"Not as long as the guard. About an hour."

It was by design. The team was told not to incapacitate Behzani for too long. He needed to be able to talk. The female agent searched the living room and office. Behzani's cell phone lay on the coffee table, and a burner phone was found in a desk drawer. She was surprised, though, by the terrorist's computer. It was a bulky desktop—vintage—with a heavy drive unit the size of a large cigar box.

"A guy with a house like this can't afford a decent computer?" she said.

"You have room for it?" one of her CIA partners asked.

She put it with the phones into her canvas bag, bulging it to its limit.

The SEAL spoke into the walkie-talkie clipped to his shoulder.

"Data gathered. Target subdued. Coming up."

"I hear you," the chopper pilot answered. "I'll be ready." He'd been standing with a machine gun between the helicopter and the stairwell, in case hostiles came up to the roof.

Ninety-four seconds later, the team and their passenger rose silently, lightless, and unpursued into the dark sky above the mountains north of Tehran.

Moments after that, air-conditioning compressors whirred once more in the warm evening air.

65

ADMIRALS AND GENERALS SHOULD NOT BE OVERRULED

At Camp David, Del Winters was as anguished as her father had ever seen her. Only once before had he witnessed her this distraught. That was the night she learned the love of her life, Captain Scott Anderson, had been killed by sniper fire while leading a team extracting fellow Army Rangers surrounded in Somalia. He had died heroically, exposing himself for the protection of his men. Del and the ranger were both captains then, planning to marry. Fifteen years had passed, but the first father remembered the pain as if it were running through his chest right now.

She wanted to speak directly to the nation. The attack that morning was the deadliest act of terrorism on American soil since 9/11. The president needed to address it immediately, she thought. But Tyler Brew urged that her duty to the country was otherwise. He was convinced the attack was not over. It was at least possible that the president herself was still under threat. Wilson Bryce had already advised that it would be impossible to conceal the source of transmission of any broadcast. If she addressed the country from Camp David, her whereabouts could be detected. It was not so much the ability to defend her on the premises there. That could be managed, Brew thought. It was defending her *while getting her out* in the event of a penetration that worried him. There were hardly any roads out of the camp, and helicopters would be vulnerable to rocket launchers.

"What about a radio speech?" Brew had asked Bryce.

"Even easier," the NSA guru replied.

The admiral sat across from her in the main room of Aspen Lodge. Her father and Stanley flanked the SEAL in wingback chairs.

"You *cannot* do it, Madame President," Brew said. He was rarely so formal with her.

"Tell me, Tyler. What could be more important to the people than hearing from me in this situation?"

"Your life," he answered.

She looked somberly to the side, then back into Brew's eyes. She nodded. The discussion was over, for the moment. "Dad, why don't you take Stanley and Augie for a walk," she said. "I want to talk to Tyler privately about some things." Stanley took the cue immediately and rose, but Henry Winters didn't. He rustled in his chair and leaned toward his daughter. Put it down to a father's concern. He was eighty-three years old; she was nearly fifty and the president of the United States. He still felt protective.

"Please, Dad," she said, unsmiling.

"You're not going to overrule him, are you?" Henry looked at Brew. "He's right."

"I am not going to."

"Well then," the old general said. "Good. Admirals and generals should not be overruled. They get grumpy."

He joined Stanley and the dog. The three of them left the room.

66

RENDITION IN TEHRAN

The CIA helicopter flew at maximum speed—185 miles per hour—and at much lower altitude than the pilot would have preferred. But his orders were to deliver the target to the black site as soon as possible. The mountain ridges seemed so close below as the chopper sped north that the three CIA officers blanched, especially when the pilot ascended precipitously to clear a higher top approaching. A speeding car darting through city streets—their normal fare—was one thing, the agents thought. This was something else entirely. Only the Navy SEAL seemed at ease as he looked down.

"This is nothing," he said calmly to the others. "We're not even taking fire."

It was 0100 hours when the chopper's infrared strobes picked up the landing zone lights at the black site. The pilot slowed the craft and circled as he descended to the ground with a quiet thud. Conveniently, Behzani was just coming to.

CIA and FBI interrogators had learned over the years that there usually was one advantage in questioning rich terrorists. They weren't accustomed to discomfort and talked quickly to avoid it. Even Saddam Hussein had cooperated when he was finally captured in his desert dugout and, in the end, was found to have told his interrogators mostly the truth.

But Balish Behzani was an outlier. And a plain liar, period. He *didn't* cooperate, and what he did offer was nearly all calculated deception. His first lie came in his first answer: "I don't speak English." It was the interrogator's opening question, not because he hoped the terrorist could; the CIA professional was fluent in Farsi and expected to use it. It was asked as a test of attitude. Behzani failed it. The interrogator calmly entered a few keystrokes on the console between them. Balish's raspy tones—in near perfect English—floated from a small wireless speaker on the table. It was an NSA recording of his phone order from a British clothing merchant a week earlier.

"So, it's going to be *this* way, Balish? I don't recommend it. If we have you on tape ordering shirts, what else do you think we have?"

"How should I know? Why should I care? My work is finished. All is done." So much for not speaking English.

"What do you mean, all is finished?"

"What do you not understand? Should I say it in Farsi? And, anyway, you have taken me illegally from my country."

It was tempting to strike the terrorist, and it would have been lawful. It was not torture—not even a so-called extraordinary measure—to inflict pain during interrogation. But Tyler Brew had been clear. He wanted Behzani brought to the US to face justice "without a mark on him."

"That reminds me," the interrogator said. "This is for you."

He placed folded papers before Balish. It was an indictment handed up by a federal grand jury in Washington. He waited for Behzani to read it. It charged him with conspiracy against the United States and the murders of Ranni Shamiri and Davoud Dafur in Lafayette Square. Brew had worked with the US attorney to obtain it on an emergency basis. Rendition from a country with whom the US had no diplomatic relations was a gray area. The indictment did not resolve the legality or justification of the taking, but it sure didn't hurt.

"It gets worse, Balish," the agent said. "You'll be served with another one when you land in the US. For the killings yesterday in the Washington bombings."

"Impossible!" Balish shouted. "My country did not agree to send me to you!"

"You mean *extradition*? What has that got to do with it? There *is* no extradition treaty between our countries. Which is a good thing, Balish. No red tape, no hassles. Not even airport lines."

Every twenty minutes, the CIA specialist stepped out of the room to speak directly to Tyler Brew at Camp David. Jack Watson joined from his office for each update. Little information was forthcoming.

"He's still saying there is nothing more," the interrogator reported. "Keeps saying he's done his job."

"Do you believe him?" Brew asked.

"No. I played him his last call to the Kievs about more money. It made him nervous. I asked him where the man was with the power company truck. It made him even more nervous, like 'How do they know about the truck?' He's deceiving."

Watson suggested they put him on a plane to the US and continue the interrogation aboard. He was concerned Iran might send troops to find him across the border. "We don't think the government had anything to do with this. But we did take one of their citizens, and they can't be happy about it. If we have a firefight in those mountains, it will distract the world's attention from what happened here. Or what may be coming." The admiral agreed.

"Bring the bastard home," he said. "Our home."

67

SUMMONS TO CAMP DAVID

Jack Renfro had never been to Camp David, and, truth be told, he wondered if it was the best use of his time to go there now. The events of the day had been extraordinary and deadly. Since the explosions that morning, he'd been meeting nonstop with the Capitol Police bomb squad and surveillance experts from Wilson Bryce's team at the NSA. Tyler Brew wanted to hear firsthand how it could have happened when the area around the White House was on such high alert. President Winters did too. But they wanted also the smart detective's thinking on what was now an even more critical question: *was more coming*?

The DC homicide detective fetched L.T. Kitt and Evan Reese from FBI headquarters in his police sedan. Audrey Sanderson was already in the front passenger seat, so the two agents climbed into the rear. Kitt's earlier curiosity about the older lawman's tendencies with a gas pedal were quickly answered. Before he could even say, "Buckle up," he squealed from the curb and darted at high speed through the Washington streets, still lined with police vehicles from the morning's chaos.

"My God, Jack!" Kitt called out. "Be careful, will you?" She looked at Reese in disbelief.

"The president is waiting," Renfro said flatly, and hardly anything else as they sped to the Maryland retreat.

Henry Winters greeted them at the door to Aspen Lodge. He extended his hand first to the women, with a slim smile on his face, more solemnly then to Renfro and Reese. Stanley was standing near the fireplace. Augie sat next to him.

"I know L.T. is well acquainted with my friend Stanley Bigelow and his dog, August." Henry said, motioning to the Pittsburghers. "But have you three met Stanley and Augie?"

"Not until now," Audrey Sanderson said, walking toward the two of them with hand extended. Jack and Evan followed. Stanley looked each in the eye, then shook their hands. Audrey had heard Kitt's description of the old engineer—his oversized frame, huge hands, and friendly, thickly browed face. But she was still surprised by his largeness and gentle affect.

"A sad day," Stanley said. "A sad day for everyone."

"Del and Admiral Brew are in the library," Henry said to the officers. "They're waiting for you." He pointed toward a hallway off the living room.

As soon as they were seated in the pine-paneled library, Renfro spread out a satellite map on the coffee table and began to describe the location and time of the first blast. It was what Tyler Brew expected, but the president interrupted.

"The victims," she said. "Tell me about the victims first. Who were they? Were there children killed?"

Audrey Sanderson placed before her the police sheet. It was a simple list of names, known addresses, and ages. The legend read: "DOS." Dead on scene. The president ran her finger slowly down the list, reading aloud each name. For the adults, she said their ages. But there were four children on the list, each under eleven years old. She could not bring herself to recite their ages. There was silence in the library for several minutes. Finally, the president raised her head and straightened in her chair. She nodded, first to Brew, then to Renfro.

The DC detective reported all he had learned. Specialists from the Capitol Police had been sweeping all outside receptacles in a six-block radius of the White House three times daily since Tyler Brew's order the previous week. These were skilled experts, the same technicians who routinely swept the Capitol Building and the Senate and House office buildings. Their devices were the best available, their inspection records meticulous.

"They even made the inspections on an irregular schedule, randomly changing the order in which each receptacle was examined," Renfro said. "To be unpredictable."

He reported that each of the four waste bins had been checked and cleared just prior to the blasts.

"How close in time?" Brew asked.

"The last one to go off—the fourth—only eight minutes before," Renfro said. He looked at the inspection record in his folder. "The first one to explode at Old Ebbitt Grill was checked thirty-two minutes before."

"The bins were being watched," Brew said.

"Clearly," Renfro said. "It was planned and timed. As soon as the bomb team had cleared a bin this morning and moved out of sight, somebody dropped in a pressure cooker. They were hidden in black plastic bags to look like garbage."

The explosives themselves were not sophisticated, the detective said. Pretty much standard internet fare. But the detonation devices triggering them were high technology, he told the president. The modules on each were identical, the wiring leading to the explosive material unusual, the soldering of the circuits intricate. They were detonated wirelessly by a modified cell phone, remotely.

"How remotely?" Brew asked.

"Wilson Bryce thinks it could have been from a considerable distance—even a helluva long way—because the quality of the wireless circuits was so high."

"And what do *you* think, Jack?"

"I think the bomber was very near the fourth waste bin. All of the bombs were detonated by a single send command to the first bomb. The first sent the signal on to the second, the second to the third, the third to the last. I think he triggered the command right after he moved away from the last bomb, but to a place where he could still see it clearly. Arsonists and bombers are like that. They want to see their prize."

The most disappointing thing in Renfro's report was the surprising lack of helpfulness of the satellite imagery. Brew knew from Bryce that surveillance from above was far from foolproof. Variables came into play. Cloud cover. Building structures such as scaffolding. Reflections off windows or chrome. Even wind. As luck would have it—or *not* have it—those contingencies mightily impaired the sight lines to the waste bins at critical moments. A deep awning concealed view of the first receptacle near the wall outside Old Ebbitt Grill. All that could be seen were groups of pedestrians moving in both directions past it until the startling blast that felled three of them. Tree limbs and lush leaf cover obscured the view of the last receptacle in Lafayette Square. Neither of the other two locations provided a clear image either.

Importantly, there was no sign of a PP&E truck near any of the receptacles in the intervals between their inspections by the bomb squad and the subsequent explosions.

"I asked Bryce to go back and look again at every minute of footage," Renfro said. "He says, 'No truck.'" The detective seemed disturbed by that confirmation.

"Isn't that a good thing?" the president asked.

"I don't think so," Jack said.

"I don't either," said Brew.

"Why?" she asked.

"Because it suggests these four blasts were not *the* plan," Renfro said. "*Part* of the plan. But not *the* plan. We know they've been using a PP&E truck. If not for these bombs, then what for? Either they used it for something else we don't know about, or they intend to. For something else still coming."

Tug Birmingham entered the library. He told them that cabins were ready for each of the visitors. He asked if they had brought personal supplies. All said they had. Secret Service agents escorted them to their quarters for the night.

None of them got much sleep.

68

TWO PRESIDENTS SPEAK

Del Winters would have preferred to call the Iranian president immediately after the secret rendition of Balish Behzani, but by the time she received confirmation of the successful taking, it was the middle of the night in Tehran. The so-called *phone call at three in the morning* was true, and not that infrequent, within your own government. But in relations between heads of state, it was just poor manners. She made the call when she rose in the morning in Aspen Lodge, coffee in hand. Admiral Brew sat across from her; she'd asked him to be there.

"President Rahoud, thank you for taking my call," she said when she was transferred to him. "I appreciate that you didn't refer me to someone else."

"You have been the American president for, what is it, six years?" he said. "And yet we have never spoken directly."

"Which is something we should change," she said.

"Is that why you are calling now?"

She covered the mic of the handset and spoke quietly to Brew: "*He doesn't know.*"

"No, that isn't the reason for my call," she said to her counterpart. "But I hope that we can discuss our relationship whenever you would like to and as soon as you would like to. But we have an urgent issue right now. Of course, you know what happened yesterday in Washington."

"I do. But I know nothing of how it happened. Surely, you don't think I or my country does."

"I do *not* think that, Mr. President. I do not think the Islamic Republic of Iran did it or condoned it."

"Then why are you calling me?"

"Because just as we are certain that your *government* was not behind the bombings, we are certain that *citizens* of your country were, including the masterminds. And we fear that the attack may not be finished, that more may be coming."

She told Rahoud about Balish Behzani and the intercepted communications with the terrorist cell in the United States. He said he knew of Behzani, that he was among the wealthiest people in Iran. She told him about the scientist at the Institute of Technology and Mechanics and the nerve gas project. He had never heard of Daash.

"You still haven't said why you are calling me. Is there something you are asking me to do?"

"There is one thing I am asking you to do, and one thing I want to tell you that has happened already."

"*Already*? What has happened *already*?"

"We have taken Behzani from his residence in Elahieh. Forcibly."

"*What?* You have *kidnapped* him?"

"We have *apprehended* him. We have brought him to the United States to face justice. Without diplomatic relations or extradition arrangements, it was our only way." There was a long pause; the Iranian leader did not respond. "If citizens of *your* country were murdered in Tehran at the direction of an American *here*, I believe you would do the same." Another long pause.

"What about Daash, the scientist?" he asked. "Did you take him too?"

"No. I assumed *you* would."

"A correct assumption," Rahoud said. "The radicals at the institute are a threat. Nerve gas, for the sake of God!"

"Let us hope his work comes to nothing," Del Winters said.

"Yes, President Winters. Let us hope."

69

ANOTHER DAY, ANOTHER MURDER

At the Motel 6, Andruzal learned the desk clerk's quip about breakfast was true: there wasn't any. He had foregone dinner the evening before. The killing of Hiram Fowler left him without appetite, he reasoned. Or maybe the nerves were coming on. But he decided now he needed to eat. These months in the US had accustomed him to American cooking, and he was now enjoying some of it, especially the eggs and potatoes in the morning.

Nellie May's diner down the road served his purpose. It was in the same direction as his intended first stop outside Catoctin State Park, and the food, ordered to go, came quickly. He ate in the truck cab and checked the time. Ample.

Harrison James had said he could not promise that the inspector sent to examine the new wiring at Camp David would be Spiro Kanerka. He would schedule him for the inspection, James said, but the assignments were always subject to change by the operations manager from headquarters. Things came up. People called in sick. An emergency might divert an inspector. But Kanerka's deep Mediterranean complexion and dark features resembled Andruzal's, and certainly more than others who might be sent.

The terrorist waited at the base of the high hill near the entrance road into Catoctin State Park. He parked his Potomac Power & Energy truck on the shoulder facing the hill so that he could see the entire descending road. It was lightly traveled this time of morning. He would be able to see the other PP&E truck as soon as it emerged on the hilltop and started down. James had said the inspection would be scheduled for ten o'clock, but that too was subject to change; if it were, he would call him. But Andruzal had not heard from the collaborator. The inspector should appear soon, he thought. Camp David was fifteen minutes away, and it was already almost nine thirty.

Andruzal recognized the truck as soon as its nose showed atop the hill. He turned on his emergency flashers and reached for the orange danger cones he'd readied on the cab seat. He placed one at the driver-side front tire and another at the rear of the truck, about a foot onto the pavement. He moved to the front of the vehicle, his back to the other driver descending the slope toward him, as if he were unaware of his approach. *Better that he stop for me on his own, without my flagging him. Surely, he will,* the terrorist thought.

Of course, he was correct. Sadly. Spiro Kanerka sounded his horn, and Andruzal turned in feigned surprise, holding a tire iron—not unusual in the circumstance. The true PP&E engineer slowed, crossed the lane, and pulled to a stop, engine running, facing the front of the terrorist's truck. It was hard—and sorely insensitive—to call it good, but the only sympathetic thing that could be said of Spiro Kanerka's death was that it came less painfully than Hiram Fowler's the day before. The inspection supervisor had barely placed his second foot on the gravel shoulder when the tire iron crushed downward into his skull above the left ear. He was dead instantly.

Andruzal looked to the road. There was no one in sight. He pulled the body over his shoulders and put it quickly in the bed of his own truck. Spiro's name badge was snapped and—for extra measure—Velcroed to the shirt pocket of his uniform. The terrorist stripped it off and covered the corpse with a tarp, tucking it under the body to keep it secure. He picked up the orange cones and put them back in the cab. He removed the equipment he would need next from his own truck bed and put it in the rear of Spiro's, then returned to his own. His deceased cargo aboard, the terrorist drove into the woods, negotiating a shallow trench to reach them. He parked the truck about one hundred feet in, making sure it was perpendicular to the road; hardly any of the vehicle could be seen through the trees.

When he climbed into Spiro's truck at the road, he looked at the plastic identification badge closely. Spiro Kanerka could hardly have been more different than Andruzal in height, weight, or build. The small, slim immigrant from Crete may have weighed 130 pounds spread across a narrow, five-foot-three frame, Andruzal surmised. He himself towered above him at six foot two and 185 pounds, carried by an athletic build. But for his purpose today, it was the face that counted. Oh, there were differences, to be sure. But the similarities exceeded them. Same cheekbones, brows, and hairline with a widow's peak. Seeing only their faces, many might guess them brothers.

The terrorist took a Brillo pad from his shirt pocket and dipped it in his coffee cup. He dabbed the plasticized photo subtly with the edge of the pad, like a painter adding tone with small strokes. He obliterated one eye on the photo, smudged the jawline slightly, and finally dulled the card's entire surface with a few gentle passes of the abrasive. Serviceable, he concluded.

He snapped the badge to his breast pocket and drove into Catoctin State Park. He was four miles from the unobvious turn off to the Camp David entry gate when he stopped the truck. Balish Behzani had instructed that he must hide and set the timing of the detonation trigger before he reached the camp. Andruzal knew why. It was likely he would be apprehended at the site. The trigger could not be on his person where it would be found and diffused. Daash had said the wireless trigger signal surely would be sent so long as there was at least moderately strong cell reception where it was left. Andruzal checked his phone: four bars. He walked quickly into the woods. He could not know exactly how much time it would take to clear entry into the retreat and then install the propulsion equipment into the electrical conduit. But an hour should be sufficient, he judged. He added thirty minutes to allow for his escape before detonation. He set the timer on the device at ninety minutes and placed the device on a work rag to ensure it would not dampen from the earth or blowing leaves. He pressed the start button on the little device, the size of an old flip cell phone.

The small screen illuminated; the digits began to descend.

70

AN UNDETECTED ASSASSIN. MOSTLY

In their own ways, each of the detectives and FBI agents breakfasting at Camp David with Del Winters felt uncomfortable about the whole experience.

Audrey Sanderson wanted to enjoy the chance to be with the president of the United States but knew the circumstances forbade pleasure. Evan Reese felt such remorse over losing the trail of the terrorist money courier in Brooklyn that enjoyment was out of the question.

L.T. Kitt's awkward sentiments were more personal: it was odd sleeping without her husband, knowing he stayed a mere two hundred feet away in a different cabin. She knew Tug Birmingham had to stay close to another woman, the one in Aspen Lodge. It didn't mean she had to like it.

Jack Renfro may have seemed the least bothered—he'd asked for seconds on the hash browns—but in his heart, he may have been the saddest of anyone. He didn't resent being called "Mr. Homicide" at headquarters, but he was reeling inside from the fact of nineteen of them in a single hour in his beloved city.

The president had decided overnight to overrule Tyler Brew and speak to the people live from Camp David. She could not be dissuaded. The Navy SEAL told her that if she insisted on transmitting from the site, she would have to remain at the retreat until the threat was confirmed as over; it would be impossible to remove her safely—or her father—once her location was disclosed.

"But we are safe *here*, right?"

"Of course."

"Well, then, we need to tell the people what is going on and that we're going to keep *them* just as safe." She wanted to speak from a chair in the living room of Aspen Lodge and tell the country exactly where she was. She refused to consider a fabricated backdrop to conceal the location. "I am *not* going to look huddled up in some staged cubicle, afraid," she told the admiral. Tell the networks to be ready at noon, she said; she did not want any more discussion. There was none. And little at the breakfast table either. It was as if everyone was waiting, without knowing what for.

"L.T.," Stanley said as he rose from the long table, "how about a long walk with me and Augie? Like old times." The memories of their daily walks with the dog when L.T. had first been assigned to guard the Pittsburgher—*and* help bring his weight down and his fitness up—were fond for both Stanley and the FBI agent. Those walks, as much as anything, had bonded both her and the dog to the big senior citizen.

Kitt looked to Tyler Brew, sitting next to the president. He was stewing mightily. But he nodded assent. Then he looked to Tug Birmingham. "Send an ATV to follow them, Tug. In case we need her back in a hurry."

"Henry," Stanley called. "Would you like to come along?" He'd been walking the dog with the first father every day and did not want to slight him.

"No, you two take Augie by yourselves. You've got a lot to catch up on."

"Are you sure?" Stanley asked. He knew Henry relished the walks.

"Yes. Besides, maybe I will be consulted on a speech of national importance." He looked dubiously at his daughter.

"Don't count on it," the president said. But it was the first time she had smiled in a day and a half.

Stanley and L.T. *did* cover a lot of ground, literally and conversationally, as they circled the perimeter of Camp David twice. L.T. spoke a lot about Tug and their life together in Washington. Washington was more expensive than Pittsburgh, and she missed the hills. Stanley listened without interruption. She said their marriage wasn't everything she hoped for, but the good times were far more plentiful than the bad. Stanley listened without judgment. But he did comment that it was "pretty clear to me, he loves you very much."

The three of them had just passed the front side of Aspen Lodge after their second lap of the grounds when they heard the buzzing of the guard gate signaling entry. They looked back and saw the Potomac Power & Energy vehicle rolling in about two hundred feet from them. It turned toward the trench where the new conduit pipe had been laid the day before for the wiring into Aspen Lodge.

Neither Stanley nor Kitt thought anything of it; each knew of the mistake made when the workmen were accosted during the installation yesterday. They knew too that the work was scheduled for inspection this morning. But Augie reacted strangely, they thought. He moved in front of Stanley, though it was Kitt holding his leash, and stood rigidly, glaring at the truck. It was not like the dog to respond to the sight or sounds of any kind of truck or vehicle, or to random strangers.

They saw Tug come out the front door of Aspen Lodge and approach the worker as he climbed from the truck. Tug and the man talked. The Secret Service chief motioned to the man's shirt, and the worker removed his identification badge. They saw Tug look at it for a few seconds. Then he walked to the left rear fender to see the vehicle number. It matched the number on the scheduling order sent to the Secret Service the day before. The worker pointed toward the trench, still unfilled from the prior day's work. Tug handed back his name badge and waved to the guards at the gate.

Stanley and Kitt turned to resume their walk. The dog resisted.

"You take the leash, Stanley," Kitt said. "He's your dog now. Maybe he just needs your command."

It seemed to work, if incompletely. Stanley leaned toward the dog and gave the leash two moderate snaps. "Augie! Let's go, Augie! Let's go. One more lap."

The dog turned reluctantly, only halfway, and looked up at Stanley, then at Kitt, then back toward the workman. "Now, Augie!" Stanley said, not loudly but more sternly than either he or the dog was accustomed to. Kitt watched the canine intently. Finally, he turned in the commanded direction and started forward ahead of them.

"Funny," said Stanley. "He saw the same kind of truck with two workmen yesterday, and it didn't bother him a bit! Sat there next to me cool as a cucumber, even when Tug's people and the sailors were going crazy."

"That *is* odd," said Kitt.

The three of them continued ahead on the perimeter trail, but every ten paces or so, Augie would step to the side to see around them and look back at the workman. Eventually, the bend in the trail eliminated his line of sight, and he strode diligently forward.

"He's picked up his pace," Stanley said. It was noticeable.

"Also odd," Kitt said. "He doesn't like that guy for some reason. He wants to make it around and see him again."

"He'll probably be gone anyway by then," Stanley said. "And I'll probably be exhausted."

71

THIRTY-THREE MINUTES TO DETONATION

Andruzal knelt with a tool bag next to the trench just in front of the main electrical box mounted near the foundation of Aspen Lodge. He drove an eye hook into the ground and attached the end of a measuring tape. *At least twenty-five feet,* he remembered Daash's instruction. *Install the propulsion device behind the cannister at least twenty-five feet from the junction box. If it is closer, the aerosolized gas will not have time to expand and be compressed in the thin conduit to gain sufficient pressure. It must enter the receptacles and light switches inside the house under force.*

Luck was on his side. He pulled the tape down the trench and reached twenty-five feet with room to spare. The trench was long enough; he would not have to dig to expose additional conduit. He hammered another eye hook into the ground at a mark twenty-eight feet from the house. He saw Tug Birmingham walk to the gate and call for a marine. They spoke briefly. The marine stepped inside the gate and walked about halfway to the trench, then stood ramrod straight, watching him. Andruzal looked up and smiled courteously. Tug walked back to the small terrace in front of the door to Aspen Lodge and took up an observing position there.

Eerily, the terrorist thought, their observation did not cause him to be nervous or cloud his concentration. He calmly walked to the truck and gathered the propulsion device and the nerve gas cannister he had already attached to its forward end. He returned to his marker at the side of the trench.

Inside, Henry Winters came to the front door.

"What's this about?" he asked Tug.

"He's the electrical inspector, General. He's cleared. It's the supervisor they scheduled to come this morning. His ID checks out."

"Well, I hope he doesn't find anything wrong," Henry said. "The Nationals have a day game this afternoon. It hasn't been cancelled, at least yet. Stanley and I are counting on watching it after Del's speech."

With a wrench from his tool kit, the terrorist quickly mounted the propulsion device atop the piping, securing it tightly with an extra turn. He checked to see that the backup baffle was properly positioned at the rear of the pump, as the large, old engineer had showed him in the Pennsylvania field. He drilled the intrusion hole into the piping through which the gas would be propelled. The fitting on the cannister snapped into the hole snuggly, sealed with a self-seating hard rubber gasket. All that was needed now was the detonation signal to release the pressurized cylinder and send the deadly nerve agent in a rocket of air through the pipe and into the main box, where it would be directed to every receptacle and switch box in the presidential lodge.

He shoveled the piled earth next to the trench into it, covering the devices, and filled the trench all the way to the junction box at the foundation. He checked the time. Thirty-three minutes to detonation.

72

AUGIE IS AROUSED

"Sir!" Andruzal called out to Tug Birmingham. The terrorist didn't have to say goodbye, and there was risk in the gesture, but he couldn't resist the hubris evoked by his success. Tug stepped toward him.

"All finished. All is fine," he said, smiling. He didn't go so far as extending a hand, and neither did Tug. The protection detail chief simply waved to the still-watching marine, motioning for him to open the gate for the workman's exit. Soon after, the truck and its terrorist trundled through the opened booth and out of sight.

It was only a few minutes later that Augie pulled Stanley and Kitt around the last bend to Aspen House. As soon as the place of the inspector's work came into view, Augie came to a dead stop. He raised his head high and moved it left and right, searching. Saliva began dripping freely from his extended tongue. His long tail slung low and curled under his stomach.

"He's aroused," Kitt said.

Stanley was puzzled. He crinkled his brow and stooped to look under the dog's belly.

"Not *that kind* of aroused, Stanley!" said Kitt. "I mean he's upset. He doesn't like this." The old engineer seemed distracted, deep in some thought as if trying to remember something, bring something from the past into his focus. "Are you all right, Stanley?" L.T. asked.

"Is that truck still here?" he asked her. "Is it outside the gate?"

"I don't see it out there. It's gone, I think."

Stanley started walking briskly. The dog accepted his pace and added to it. Kitt was almost jogging to keep up. "What is it, Stanley?" she asked. "Where are you going?"

"I need to see that trench."

It all came back to him, rushing with fear and regret into his mind—the memories of the day in the field outside Altoona. *How could I not remember that truck? That Potomac Power & Energy truck and the piping in the field! My God, I showed him how to connect that device! For fracking, he'd said! A prototype to be scaled up. Yeah, right. That's why Augie was so alarmed in the field and so upset at home that night. Augie sensed danger. I should have told Brew!*

The dog pulled so hard as he charged toward the trench that the tension snap on his leash released. Kitt broke into a sprint to follow the dog, and Stanley did his best to run too. He called to Kitt, "Get Brew!" The FBI agent diverted to the front of Aspen Lodge, shouting for the admiral and Tug. Henry Winters was closest to the front door and heard her shouts. He stepped outside and saw his big friend chugging across the grass. He had never seen Stanley move like this, or Augie in action. The retired general, though considerably older than Stanley, was trim and fit. Immediately, he broke into a run to join him.

Stanley went first to the junction box mounted above the foundation and ripped it open. His engineer's eye raced over the circuits. Nothing was out of place; all of the wires and connections were secure. He clicked the main circuit breaker to "off" and turned to look down the trench line. "Stanley!" the first father called. "What are you doing, Stanley? What is going on?"

They saw Augie moving up and down the newly covered trench, thrusting his snout into the tossed earth, shaking his head fiercely to throw the soil from his nose before diving again at another place along the line. Less than a minute passed before the dog stopped at a spot and drove his head deeply, repeatedly into the trench. For the first time, he barked, energetically, piercingly loud.

And then the dog dug. Furiously he dug, his front paws firing clumps of earth to the side of the trench.

Stanley and Henry moved quickly to the dog and watched as the bronze-colored apparatus came into partial view as Kitt, Brew and Tug Birmingham arrived.

"I've seen this before," Stanley said as Augie continued to paw away the soil concealing it.

"Where?" Brew asked.

"Later," Stanley said. "There's not time to explain now. We need wrenches. Two monkey wrenches with at least two-inch jaws. And a razor blade knife. Have you got those things?"

Brew said they would have them in the maintenance shop. He hollered to the marines at the fence to send for them. "Is it a bomb, Stanley?"

"I don't think it's an explosive. But I think it's dangerous. I think there's gas in that cylinder. Get everybody out of the house."

Tug blurted instructions into his walkie-talkie, and agents streamed from cabins on all sides to evacuate Aspen Lodge and the president. Not since Lyndon Johnson famously roared his Cadillac convertible at sixty miles an hour around the perimeter had a vehicle sped so fast at Camp David as the marine jeep that skidded up to them with the tools Stanley had specified.

"Sergeant," Brew said. He saw that the marine driver was armed. "Take Kitt and another marine and go after that utility truck that just left. I'll send backup. Go!"

Stanley dropped to his hands and knees over the trench. Augie's digging had exposed it all. It was the same propulsion pump he'd seen in the Pennsylvania field, complete with its flowback baffle. But affixed to the pump now was a cylindrical cannister, mounted so that it sat atop the pipe leading to the house. That cylinder had *not* been attached to the so-called prototype he'd observed in Altoona. He leaned low and saw the injection port from the cannister into the conduit. He studied the heavy bronze fittings fore and aft of the entire assembly that secured it rigidly to the electrical conduit.

"Can I help?" asked Henry Winters, stooping over Stanley's shoulder.

"I was just going to ask," Stanley said. The first father knelt at once next to him. Stanley pointed to the fasteners holding the apparatus to the electrical pipe.

"These are heavy bronze fittings, Henry. And they've been turned onto that pipe under great torque. I can tell from the indentations made by the wrench. We have to remove them. Twist them off. But bronze is soft. We have to apply *even* torque at both ends or we'll strip the threads. If that happens, we'd have to forcibly knock the thing apart. And who knows what the hell is in that cannister? Destroying it right here isn't an option."

"I understand," Henry said.

Stanley took one wrench and affixed it to the back fitting; he attached the second wrench to the front fastener. He carefully drew the jaws of each wrench to what he judged the same pressure, with the wrench handles rising vertically from the pipe.

"I'm going to *push* on the front fitting to loosen it. At the same time, you *pull* on the back fitting. Not real hard, Henry. But enough to keep it from moving when I'm loosening the other one."

Even a general can follow orders. Henry Winters said simply, "Tell me when."

The first connector loosened but not easily. Stanley could feel the bronze giving before the threads moved beneath his wrench, but Henry's gentle counterpressure allowed him to push with enough force to finally start them moving.

"Wala," Stanley said. "It's coming off."

Before moving to the front connection, Stanley took the razor blade knife and pressed and pried the sharp edge around the rubber gasket holding the cannister outlet port snugly in the conduit.

"What's that for?" asked Henry.

"The gas in this cannister gets propelled through that injection nozzle and into the conduit."

"When does that happen?"

"Hopefully not while we're kneeling here."

"It gets detonated somehow?"

"Yes, probably by a small electrical charge sent remotely. The charge inside starts the high-pressure pump and punctures the cannister. The gas shoots down the conduit under high pressure. Right into the house through the electrical lines."

"My God," Henry said.

Stanley's knife work unsealed the nozzle on the cannister. He gently pressed down on the conduit at the injection point to confirm it would dis-attach when they were ready to lift it from the pipe. It was still necessary to loosen the front fastener.

"Same drill, Henry," Stanley said. "But this time, *you* push, and *I'll* pull." The general nodded; the fitting loosened.

"What now?" the first father asked. He and Stanley were both sweating and breathing heavily.

"I lift it out."

"The whole assembly? The pump and the cannister?"

"Yeah, the whole thing in one piece. I'm going to lift it off the line of pipe."

Henry was not familiar with weights and measures like his friend, but he knew the assembly must be weighty, especially the bronze propulsion pump and its thick flowback baffle.

"Stanley," he said. "Let *me* lift it out. Your back might give out."

Stanley looked at his friend displeasingly.

"Don't be offended, Stanley," the general said.

"I'm not offended."

"You look offended."

Augie stepped close to Stanley. The dog rubbed his muzzle against the thigh of the heavy engineer kneeling on the ground over the trench. He looked up into Stanley's eyes, as if discouraging stubbornness.

"Maybe that is a good idea," Stanley said. "All this kneeling and bending. My back *is* a little tight."

He showed the general where to reach under the assembly and how to disengage the injection port from the electrical conduit beneath the gas cannister. Then he got to his feet, with effort, and stood to the side with Augie as Henry scooted over—limberly, Stanley noticed—to where he had been kneeling. Tyler Brew and Evan Reese stood nearby, silent. The old general's strong arms disappeared into the trench and rose smoothly with the terrorist's assembly. The device weighed sixty pounds and measured thirty-six inches from end to end, but the first father rose from his kneeling position fluidly, without grunt or groan. He held the assembly in outstretched arms, like lengths of firewood.

"Now what?" It was the first time Brew had spoken since the extraction had begun.

"You need to get this thing out of here," Stanley told him. "It has a wireless detonation charge. It could go at any time."

Brew was convinced the cannister held the nerve gas Israeli intelligence had warned him about. He was turning to the young FBI agent when his question was rendered moot. Evan Reese spoke up. "I'll take it, Admiral," he said. "Let me take it into the woods." Brew extended his hand to Reese and clasped it firmly and nodded. "Put that windbreaker on." The agent was holding his deep blue throw-over with the large gold block letters front and back. "We don't want to kill you out there."

"Do I hold it like the general is?" Evan asked Stanley calmly, pointing to the bronze assembly.

"Yes, just like that," Stanley said. "Take it out there a thousand yards, if you can. But if you hear any noise coming from it, Reese—*any* noise—set it down softly and run into the wind—*into* the wind, if there is any. So that the gas blows away from you."

Reese ran through the gate and into the woods, surefooted and erect, the device close to his chest. The general, the admiral, and the old engineer from Pittsburgh stood in front of Aspen Lodge, watching and praying.

Praying for silence. Praying for wind.

73

THE RUN OF EVAN REESE

Inside the lodge a minute later, Tyler Brew gave three orders. First, he called the on-site commander at the navy barracks at the rear of the camp. He told him to send three marine platoons to the woods south, east, and west of the compound, in case the terrorist was hiding there. "But nobody should move north of Aspen Lodge," he ordered. "Not a foot north of it. Not a *foot.* There may be a nerve gas release north of Aspen. And there's a friendly out there. An FBI agent in his jacket."

The commander asked for rules of engagement.

"No fire unless fired upon," the admiral said. "And even then, *non*lethal force. We want him alive."

Second, Brew asked Jack Renfro to mobilize local and state police and track their positions. He didn't have to tell the veteran lawman how to do it if even he knew himself. Within minutes, a hundred police cruisers were encircling Catoctin State Park, setting up road blocks and communicating over a common frequency. Renfro and Audrey Sanderson fielded the flurry of check-ins, marking the positions of each on a map spread across the lodge's dining room table.

Lastly, Brew sounded the all clear for Aspen Lodge. The president could return, he radioed Tug Birmingham. "Bring her in the rear entrance," Brew said. "Tell her that her father is fine."

Stanley and Henry walked into the lodge like old friends relishing the end of an exciting ball game decided in their favor. They were smiling broadly. Their soiled hands didn't dissuade them from clapping each other's back. But Tyler Brew's serious face did. The old men looked at each other. Joviality departed. They understood the admiral's consternation and even felt momentary regret for their premature celebration. Brave Evan Reese was still in the woods with his deadly cargo. The terrorist remained at large.

"How long would it take him to run a thousand yards?" Stanley asked.

"That's better than half a mile," Henry said. "And it's too thick in there to run in anything like a straight line. He's probably zigzagging all over hell."

The first father was correct. Reese was running, the agent judged, at about half his capable speed through the forest. He wished he could race full-out; he certainly was not interested in holding the device any longer than absolutely necessary. But the forest floor was uneven, to say the least. There were especially low areas holding water and mud; he was careful to avoid them. Fallen limbs and even some large trees seemed to appear before him every fifty feet. More than a few times, he was forced to stop at a large trunk and swivel his legs over it, one at a time. At his pace through the woods, he calculated he would have to run for eight to nine minutes to cover a thousand yards of forest. He looked at his watch often—probably too often, he knew. The minutes were passing excruciatingly slowly.

He was relieved to feel a breeze to his back and tried not to alter his path so as to lose it. He worried that he might not be hearing sounds coming from the cannister. He held the assembly high in his outstretched arms, even as they tired, to keep it as close to his ears as he could. But every step of his own feet sent up sounds of trampled leaves and breaking twigs. *Was that the cannister? Was that the cannister? No, I don't think so,* he told himself. *God, I hope not,* he thought.

When his watch showed that he had moved for eight minutes, fatigue and reason intersected. He stopped and bent over. He was breathing heavily. He felt the wind moving through the trees, still at his back. He lowered the assembly gently, bringing each end to the ground as simultaneously as he could. He took one step back, looking at it for signs of movement, listening for any sound. There were none.

Until, he later recounted, about his fifth or sixth stride—he couldn't be sure—running back into the wind from where he had come. His blood pumped with adrenaline. His footspeed was so much higher, he thought, relieved of the cargo. His senses were strangely keen, sharp. He heard birdsong all around and thrashing leaves underfoot. And then a deep, prolonged thud followed by a metallic howl. His heart raced. His legs pounded forward. *Run, run, run, run.*

He emerged from the woods near the marine gate in front of Aspen Lodge and lunged, spent but safe, into the arms of a soldier.

74

SHE WANTED TO SAY ONE THING. SHE SAID ANOTHER

L.T. Kitt and the three marines screamed down the road in pursuit of the PP&E pickup truck. Kitt heard the squawk from the driver's walkie-talkie. "Don't shoot to kill."

"What the *fuck*?" she blurted. She was ready to kill.

"The admiral wants him alive," the driver said.

The agent wanted to say, "Fuck him." But she replied, "Roger."

The jeep was almost to the end of the small trail where it met the two-lane roadway running through Catoctin State Park. Kitt saw the back of the truck parked in the woods to her right. "Stop!" she yelled. The marine braked. Then she saw the second truck next to it. "Holy shit!" Kitt screamed. She and the two marines piled from the jeep and headed into the forest, the sergeant barking into his walkie-talkie.

"We have him!" he called. "At the parkway!"

Andruzal had already pulled the dead PP&E supervisor from the bed of his original truck and retrieved an automatic rifle from behind the cab seat. He crouched behind the truck and committed his first mistake of the day. He fired. It was a meaningless burst through the woods, nowhere near Kitt and the three marines. But not meaningless to Tyler Brew when the report came: "Hostile contact! Taking automatic fire."

Tyler Brew, the admiral who'd been overruled by the president earlier that morning, knew he must overrule himself now. He didn't hesitate.

"ROE rescinded," he called back. "Shoot to kill. Protect yourselves. Everyone."

There was no room or time for debate. "Drop the rifle and come out!" the marine sergeant called. Automatic fire raced past his helmet in response. Kitt rolled in the leaves to her right and readied her sidearm on her left forearm, waiting for the terrorist to show himself at the rear of the truck. To his eternal regret, he did.

Kitt poured four bullets into his chest.

75

TODAY IT WASN'T

Del Winters gathered Tyler Brew, Jack Renfro, and Audrey Sanderson in the pine library of Aspen Lodge. The small desk was cleared; there was a single sheet on the coffee table. It was the list of the dead from the morning before.

"Where is your speech?" asked Brew.

"I haven't prepared one," she said. "I am just going to speak to the people. I am going to recite the names and ages of those killed yesterday and what we know of how this happened. Yesterday and this morning. Is there more that I should know before I do?"

There was. Jack Renfro had sent a squad to pick up Hiram Fowler for questioning. The money from Brooklyn had not been delivered to him for handoff, but the old usher must have some information that was useful, they thought. "Fowler was found dead in his living room," the detective reported. "He'd been gutted. There was a box of garbage bags in his kitchen. Forensics says they're from the same manufacturing lot as fragments from the explosions. And Bryce says the refocused satellite tape shows part of a baseball cap at three of the bins yesterday. We think it was Hiram Fowler who left the bombs. Why? We may never know."

Brew told the president that the renditioned Iranian mastermind was told by his CIA interrogator that the terrorist with the PP&E truck had been found and killed, that the device at Camp David had been removed, that the president was unharmed.

"He dropped his head into his hands at the news," the admiral said. "Swore a blue streak. In both English and Farsi. He named the terrorist as Andruzal Barneri, his nephew. That's his real name, not Barnwell or Baranwili, or any of his other aliases. He named the courier who slipped us in Brooklyn too. Another nephew. The two nephews were the only ones in the plot ever intended to get out the country alive."

"Family," Renfro said.

"So," the president asked, "you believe it is over? *Really* over?"

"I do," Brew said.

"And you, Detectives Renfro and Sanderson?"

They each nodded affirmatively. Del Winters stood.

"For once, maybe I have some information for *you,*" she said. "The Iranian president just called me. Like my call to him this morning, it was a first. He told me his government has picked up Jameel Daash at the scientific institute. Other students have confirmed what you learned from the Israelis. The Iranian president condemns it all; they will help us bring Daash and Behzani to justice, and any other citizen of his country that was involved."

"That *is* surprising," Brew said.

"Not as surprising as what he said next," Del said. "He wants to start talking through direct channels—government to government. I accepted. It does nothing to make up for the loss of life here. I won't say that it does. But in the end, it may mean they didn't die in complete vain. Something good for the world may come of this. Just maybe."

No one said anything for an extended pause.

"Well, then," Del Winters said. "Let's get this country back to normal."

It was ten minutes to noon. She rose and walked into the main room of Aspen Lodge with Tug Birmingham and Tyler Brew, where her father was sitting with Stanley and Augie.

"So I'm told it was Augie and you boys to the rescue today," she said.

Her father beamed from the couch, but Stanley, plopped at the other end, looked concerned.

"You're not going to mention that in your speech, are you?" Stanley asked. "Not me, at least."

The president walked to the sofa and sat between the two old men. "Stanley, what is it about you and not taking credit?" she asked, but not unkindly. She smiled at the engineer. She knew his deep modesty and disinterest in calling attention to himself. "At least let me thank you now. Privately. Thank you, Stanley, for what you did."

"It was really Augie," Stanley said. "It really was. Ask L.T. He took us to it; he wouldn't take no for an answer."

Stanley told her and Henry all that had happened after the call to his office for help in the Pennsylvania field. How the two men there were working from a PP&E truck, claiming to be testing a system to send liquids and gases into the ground for oil fracking. He could see the equipment was far too small to use in commercial fracking; the piping was the size, he now recognized, of simple electrical conduit. But he'd been fooled. The man who spoke to him in the field said the small propulsion system was merely a prototype to be scaled up for actual use. He suspected nothing. But Augie did. Stanley told her and the first father how unfriendly and guarded the dog was in the Altoona field and how he was restless—in the extreme—all that night, even after they had returned home to Helen in Pittsburgh.

Stanley said he'd not given that day in the field another thought until Augie's behavior this morning. Augie lay in front of the couch near Stanley's feet, his head resting on his paws. He didn't raise his head at the mention of his name, but he did look up at the president with his huge, dark eyes. She saw the dirt still under his snout and on his legs.

"He sensed it that day in the field," Stanley said, lowering his big hand to the dog's upright ears. "And he sensed it today too."

"That's quite a story," Henry Winters said.

"The three of you are quite a story," the president said.

"But you *will* leave me out of what is said about all this?" Stanley asked.

"Of course, Stanley. If that is what you want." She rose. "I'll be talking to the country from this room in a few minutes. Maybe you two could go out on the back terrace with August?"

"Is it too early for bourbon?" Stanley asked. Henry looked at his daughter with an expectant brow.

"It is," the president said. "But today it isn't."

She told Tug Birmingham to send them out the best in the house.

AFTERWORD

I like to write about real places and what might happen at them. For me, there is something about the truth of a real place that triggers imagination and a story.

Like nearly everyone else, I have never been to Camp David and expect I never will have that good fortune. (Yes, that is a hint.) But I have always been intrigued by the place and its standing as a kind of *other* White House; private, out of the way, unseen. Few buildings in the world occupy status more iconic and familiar than the official home of the American people's president, the White House. In stark contrast, mystery shrouds the people's president's getaway.

Perhaps it was this contrast that made President Harry Truman so uncomfortable that he proposed to eliminate the retreat entirely. Congress disagreed. (Truman had no qualms with the concept of proper accommodations for the nation's leader; at the same time he urged disposing of Camp David altogether, he was shepherding a major reconstruction of the White House—so expansive that he was required to move to nearby Blair House during the work, where an attempt on his life was foiled.) And it may have influenced President Jimmy Carter's decision to make the camp a location of great public interest—if not view—by brokering there in 1978 the thirteen-day peace talks between Egyptian president Anwar Sadat and Palestinian leader Yasser Arafat, which culminated in the Camp David Accords. That treaty has held ever since. Maybe President Carter, who enjoyed the retreat for quiet fly-fishing and fly tying, felt that the place providing so much relief to first families should also serve a larger public purpose.

The reader of *Too True to Be Good* should know that I did my best to capture the truth of the place known as Camp David but do not claim my descriptions to be precisely accurate in all respects. The historical references to real presidents and others occurring there are, however, true.

Also, there really is a US Navy submarine testing base in Ketchikan, Alaska, though it's airstrip and tarmac are my invention. Similarly, my description of the wealthy district of the city of Tehran, Elahieh, is intended as materially accurate, but the Institute of Technology and Mechanics is fictional. The Purity Diner in Brooklyn is real. Its food and service are excellent, and, sadly, the commercial plane crash described at its location really happened. Readers sharing an interest in quality Minor League Baseball can actually see the Altoona Curve play in its lovely stadium, where fans look out on the hills of central Pennsylvania beyond the center field fence.

I wish to acknowledge and thank friends and advisors who supported me as I wrote *Too True to Be Good*, including Sandi Fein, Deena Ralph, Ed Leary, John Wilson, Caren Breen, and John Reock. The writing and publication process are difficult. Their encouragement and helpful comments sustained me. Special thanks to Captain CR (Richard) Ralph (USMC Ret.) for his knowledge and advice on military facts, and for his friendship.

Finally, while the underlying subjects of this book—terrorism and its funding—are serious world problems, my only intent is to tell an entertaining story without political agenda, neither left nor right, or with animus to any person, ethnic group, or nation. It is just a story.

JB

ABOUT THE AUTHOR

Joseph Bauer divides his time between homes in Charleston, South Carolina, and Cleveland, Ohio. He is the author of *The Accidental Patriot* and *The Patriot's Angels. Too True To Be Good* is the third book in the Stanley Bigelow, Augie and Del Winters series. Each book is a complete and independent story; they can be enjoyed in any order. Mr. Bauer's fourth novel, *Sailing for Grace*, will be published next year by Running Wild Press. For more about his writing visit www.josephbauerauthor.com

Made in the USA
Columbia, SC
24 May 2023